Ivor Watkins spent two years in Berlin in Army Intelligence before returning to England to become a newspaper reporter. He worked on the London *Evening News*, the *Standard* and the *Sunday Express*. While writing his first novel, THE BLOODSNARL, he acquired a boxer dog which now appears in DEMON.

Ivor Watkins

Demon

Futura

A *Futura* Book

First published in Great Britain in 1983
by Macdonald & Co (Publishers) Ltd
London & Sydney

First published in paperback by Futura Publications 1983
This edition published by Futura Publications 1994

ISBN 0 7088 2304 1

Printed in England by Clays Ltd, St Ives plc

Futura Publications
A Division of
Macdonald & Co (Publishers)
Brettenham House
Lancaster Place
London WC2E 7EN

Prelude

Storms drenched Europe that year as never before. Wrathful clouds, fetching and carrying from a dark and mountainous Atlantic, deluged the land for weeks on end. Unrepentant rain danced without pause on an exhausted countryside.

Among the worst affected areas were the lonely mountains of North Wales which became bloated and dangerous. In places sediment was washed away, leaving many rocks precariously balanced. Some were dislodged and, in turn, jarred others from their foundations. At the height of a gale they bounded in isolation down the slopes, snapping off the trunks of great trees; or sometimes in the uncanny stillness of the dawn they slid in a flurry of debris that tore the skin off the earth.

One rain-lashed night several boulders cascaded through an overgrown hollow in which man had, long ago, practised primitive religions. There he had carried out ancient rites and forgotten sacrifices, based on elements going back into the mists of pre-history.

The hollow was barely fifty metres wide, choked by a tangle of twisted undergrowth and ivy-knotted trees, which had remained undisturbed since Roman legions marched the breadth of Britannica; undisturbed since Druids carried out their final orgiastic ritual; untouched since the last human sacrifice. Unheeded until now.

Across the belly of the hollow ran a narrow schism: dark, glistening with green algae and apparently bottomless – a fault in the earth down which terrified victims had been ritualistically hurled. Now the evil that had emanated from man, sharpened on the pain of its victims and ingrained in the hillside itself, moved infinitesimally for the first time in centuries. Moved. An intangible shadow, an indistinct whisper. But it was enough.

The demon was abroad again.

PART I: The Deluge

One

Forked lightning zig-zagged across the night sky, lighting up the brooding black heights for no more than an instant but long enough for it to feel out the belly of lowering rainclouds and rip open the contents.

The lightning was no more than three inches wide and it existed for only a fraction of a second, yet it concentrated a hundred million volts of energy in savaging anything that stood in its way.

Torrential rain beat down on the slate-hearted land, rebounded several feet into the air and hissed with an intensity that drowned even the shattering thunder.

Surely no one in his right mind would choose to be out in the downpour on such a night?

Yet there was one such person: a grinning, gasping man whose mind had slipped. His feet squelched in cardboard-thin shoes and lank hair was plastered across his youthful, idiotic face. Staggering, half-blinded by the rain, he tipped back his head and allowed water to stream unhindered into his mouth. He loved the elements and they, in turn, seemed to respond to Dewi, without taking advantage.

Electrical impulses ticked around him. Little blue lights flickered on extremities of rock, indicating that more lightning was imminent. He giggled with anticipation and waited for the shock of electric force to jolt the air around him; this time striking a solid oak tree and severing it surgically down the middle from the massive spread of its branches down to its paralysed roots. He performed a little jig around the smouldering remains, with an odd lopsided smile on his face, for all the world as if what had happened was a direct result of his presence.

By morning the storm had abated and patches of clear sky jostled for attention behind the clouds.

Dewi dipped his head between his knees and sneezed violently, then shook his head. Spray flew in all directions. He was soaked through. Not that it bothered him particularly. His intent, imbecilic eyes returned to a dilapidated chapel halfway down the wooded valley to Blaenau Ffestiniog. Dull red oxide paint flaked from the corrugated-iron roof which had rattled loose from its bolts down one side. A notice board carried the faded print 'Deliver us from evil – 6 St Matthew. verse 13.'

He blinked reproachfully at a glint of sunshine and strove to remember why he had been sent. Sometimes details of things which previously seemed incredibly clear simply swam from his mind.

It was then that a rotund figure appeared in the doorway of a cottage adjoining the chapel and he remembered.

The Reverend Lionel Pryce-Jones bustled towards the road, brushing imagined dust from the lapel of his best black jacket. He was a self-important man in his mid-thirties who was minister in name only. His sister was the real force behind the chapel. She was a dominating spinster and he escaped to town whenever possible.

He became aware of a ragged figure sitting on a gravestone on the hill: an indistinct shape blurred by the sun directly behind it, but he had the feeling it was watching him.

'Good morning.' He shielded his eyes. 'Is someone up there?'

Dewi inspected his victim without haste and simply smiled.

Pryce-Jones waited for a moment, then shook his head and made his way to an antiquated car. He squeezed backwards into the little vehicle and settled himself with a good deal of wriggling and grunting. By chance he caught sight of Dewi from a clearer angle, and slowly wound down the window.

'Are you looking for somebody?' he called.

Dewi made his way down with a vacuous smile on his face. 'Not especially, minister,' he said in the measured sing-song voice of the true Welshman. But he thought: So you are the one who masquerades as a man of God.

The look of indulgence faded from Pryce-Jones's face as the unkempt figure peered into his car.

'What can I do for you then?' he asked sharply.

'Nothing.' Your doing days are over.

'Just passing through?'

'Yes, sir. Just passing.' That's why I've been sitting up there on my botty for two hours, half-paralysed, on one of your boney gravestones. I always look like a gargoyle at this time of the morning. He gave a little gurgle of amusement.

'Something funny?'

'No indeed, sir.'

Pryce-Jones gave him a discouraging, watery smile and turned the key in the ignition. The engine clack-clack-clacked a few times before dying away completely.

Dewi took advantage of the break to edge forward. 'Oh, excuse me. Do you live here alone, sir?'

The minister muttered something unchristian at the dashboard and waved him into silence. 'Do you mind standing back?' he said irritably. 'Well back! There's a good fellow.' He held the choke full out and tried again. The starter whirred asthmatically for some time before the engine rattled into life. A relieved smile crossed his face. 'Now, what was that?'

'Err . . . do you live here alone, sir?' I do hope not, because I'm going to move in shortly with the one who truly understands.

'No, I don't. Why?'

'Well, I heard that Miss Pryce-Jones lived here. She was my Sunday School teacher years ago, like.'

'Really?' said the minister in a flat voice. 'My goodness, is that the time? Look, I must go. My sister, Miss Pryce-

Jones, is not home at present. But if you want to wait, go around the back to the pump and tidy yourself up. But behave, mind.'

Dewi stood back respectfully. 'Thank you.' But he thought: as soon as you're gone, I'll move into my new home. Sick to death of uncomfortable beds, and you won't be needing yours any more.

A plump hand waved airily. 'Perhaps I'll see you later.'

'Yessir. And thank you indeed.' Where you're going, there's no coming back.

The car started with a jerk and Pryce-Jones settled into a more comfortable position as he directed it downhill. Lunch in town followed by an afternoon with a publican's wife of considerable understanding and discretion was the mouth-watering prospect. A day out from under his sister's strict sectarian gaze was a welcome relief. She had been growing increasingly dominating of late.

He glanced up at the rear mirror. Dewi was standing in the middle of the road. He shivered, and the skin started to crawl on the back of his neck. Odd. It was as if he'd had a narrow escape and hadn't realized it until now. He looked back again, but Dewi had disappeared behind a thin blue haze of exhaust fumes.

Dewi wandered towards the narrow house alongside the chapel. The front door creaked open at his touch. He leaned into the flagstoned hall, smiling enquiringly, and bending his head almost in a corkscrew circle to look up the stairs for any sign of occupation. There was none.

The hall gave way to a scrupulously clean kitchen with an open hearth and a capacious Welsh dresser which spread along one entire wall and was filled with plates, balanced on end, and rows of dangling cups. He ventured inside, running his finger along the crockery and enjoying the flustered chink-chink of china on china.

A plate rolled nervously off the far end and shattered. He barely gave it a glance as he stepped over the debris, his attention taken by some pork pie on a dish. His hand closed greedily over the jellied meat and he attempted to cram it all into his mouth.

Dewi gnawed hugely, letting what did not make it crumble unheeded to the scrubbed floor. The house was silent and disappointing.

He peered out through a small kitchen window at a line of tall elms, swaying at the end of the back garden, and nodded in the way one might acknowledge distant friends.

On a sideboard in the front room was a hazy brown photograph of the Rev. Pryce-Jones next to a tall, bony woman of the same age and similar features. Miss Elliyn Pryce-Jones had masked her emotion in a cold gaze, just as she imprisoned her elongated body in a black high-necked dress, though it did not completely disguise her modest curves.

Dewi contemplated the picture before roaming upstairs, humming tunelessly, carrying it with him. His feet thumped on the bare wooden stairs. Within a few minutes he had run himself a bath, peeled off his wet clothes and stepped in. He lay back in the luxurious warmth and soaped his gaunt legs.

After a while he reached for the picture, which was neatly framed. He prised up the bent nails in order to lift off the back and get at the photograph, but tore his fingernail in the process.

He sucked his fingertip and looked spitefully at the parson's countenance, then tore the photograph down the middle, crumpling and discarding the half bearing the Rev. Pryce-Jones's frugal smile. Now he could contemplate the minister's sister without being overlooked. He had her all to himself, however formidable her appearance. He set her carefully down on a cork-covered seat and stood brazenly in front of her image while he towelled his thin ribs and buttocks.

Later he opened the bathroom window so that he had the grim, grey sky in view. And spoke to it in Welsh. Painstakingly at first but with growing fluency.

The clouds moved on, apparently indifferent, even when his voice grew in intensity as he reached the main point of his conversation. When he finished he looked up questioningly. The barely interested sky seemed to hesitate. Then the clouds reversed their direction.

Ten minutes later he left the house as slyly as he had arrived. Better not rush her. Perhaps she wouldn't thank him; no sense in letting her connect her brother's imminent departure for the angels and his own arrival from the same direction. He helped himself to a suit of mothballed clothes, gazed with furtive pleasure at his reflection, and left.

Lionel Pryce-Jones's over-indulged face peered through the windscreen at the wooded slope which rose up abruptly from the edge of the road. Ahead of him was a sign which warned of falling boulders and which he had passed scores of times, but he always paid attention to it. Just as he did to thirty-miles-an-hour and Halt-Major-Road-Ahead signs. He was a conformist and prided himself on the fact. Not that he had ever seen more than a scattering of stones on that particular stretch of the lonely road, but you could never be too careful. The effects of the cantankerous weather were not confined to the valleys. Everywhere was waterlogged.

At that moment and for no apparent reason, his skin began to crawl again. Something was wrong. He stopped the car, shivering, then took off his glasses and polished them busily. His palms felt inexplicably clammy and he darted a glance over his shoulder. He even got hesitantly out of the car before telling himself: This is ridiculous! You're already late. The road's clear.

He looked at the hill alongside the road and into which it had been cut. Some eighty to a hundred feet above, trees were beginning to bend in the wind. Odd. There was hardly any breeze down at his level.

A slow stirring on the flank of the hill drew his nervous attention. It sounded as if pieces of slate and stone had fallen from the fractured rockface and were now sliding clumsily down under cover of irregular bushes.

Better get moving. Quickly, Lionel! He jerked the door

handle of his ten-year-old saloon but it obstinately refused to budge. Each tug was more alarmed than the last. Oh, my God! Then it relented and he bundled quickly inside. He banged his knee and hardly noticed the pain. By now a slither of medium-sized stones had intruded on to the road. He tugged the starter knob. Twice, three times it coughed and died away. High above he heard the rocks grumbling, and one much larger than before entered his vision, rolling halfway across the road and gently bumping his front tyre.

The engine spluttered into life and he put the car into reverse so quickly that the wheels panicked as they spun for a grip. The elderly vehicle jerked backwards with its engine straining at a high pitch.

Diagonally above them a boulder the size of the car rolled almost lazily down the slope, increasing speed with each jolt. Somehow Pryce-Jones avoided a collision by a few feet. He was starkly aware that the world had gone berserk. He blinked desperately up at a clump of pines high above the road which shuddered and tilted perilously forward as their roots were dislodged in a landslip.

A wave of earth and angry stones engulfed the road behind him. He closed his treacherously slippery palm over the gear stick, causing a metallic screech which set his teeth on edge. The car juddered forward again. Up and down he jerked; up and down, across lumps of rocks that incited the aging seat springs to cut into his bottom. He lost the glasses off the end of his nose and his vision glazed.

A fresh rumbling noise from behind made him glance hurriedly over his shoulder. His foot pressed hard on the limp accelerator and the car plunged forward: flattening itself into a huge slab of rock at nearly thirty miles an hour. And with it went the Rev. Pryce-Jones.

Trapped upside down and grotesquely concertinaed, he glimpsed the hilltop, on which the sudden wind had now abated. A distant bird flew into his line of vision. He struggled feebly to identify it. It suddenly seemed important. A razorbill? But he died without being sure.

Moments later the sun came out of hiding. It was going to be a beautiful day after all.

Elliyn was the sort of woman who turned heads. She was tall, with large hands, a masculine nose and a no-nonsense stare. Not the dandy's idea of an attractive woman, but striking looking for all that.

She appraised through narrowed eyes a pair of aunts – twins from Cardiff – who stood at the graveside, sniffing and dabbing their noses. If they were genuinely fond of her brother, Lionel, they had been remarkably secretive about it while he was alive.

Her own unwavering gaze was hidden behind a half-veil which descended from the edge of her worn, black velvet hat. It was the very hat her mother had purchased years before upon entering the state of widowhood. Elliyn had known precisely where to retrieve it in the loft, and saw no point now in spending money recklessly on funeral finery which might then be buried alive in an attic chest.

Her eyes moved on to the mourners. The turn-out neither pleased nor displeased her. Sixty souls was reasonable, but then you would have expected no fewer for the funeral of any minister in the Principality. Some twenty older men had taken a half-day off from the slate mines and now stood, black-tied and bare-headed, while a parson from a distant chapel intoned the funeral service in Welsh on the donkey-cropped grass of the hillside.

She glanced down at the polished wooden coffin which lay an uncomfortable distance below her feet where it had been lowered, squelching, into nine inches of standing water. It will rot within six months, she thought. It seemed a waste: paying more than fifty pounds for a pine coffin with brass handles.

What made her raise her head at that particular instant she could not later recall. One moment she was gazing remotely down; the next her eyes were drawn up and over the sea of inclined heads.

She focussed on a distant figure and even lifted her veil an inch or two the better to see. There was a young man standing in the shade of the distant beech trees, leaning back against a trunk. A gangling figure with a lopsided smile. And, far away as he was, she had the distinct impression that he was watching her.

She averted her eyes and joined in a rousing hymn. There was no such thing as a mournful Welsh hymn. But when the melodious voices died away he was still there: staring across the dip directly at her. Wild, compelling eyes.

Elliyn Pryce-Jones had never been one for half measures. She pushed the veil back completely over the brim of her hat, and one or two of the more observant mourners surreptitiously followed the line of her gaze. But all they saw in the tree-dappled shadows was an awkwardly dressed youth. There was nothing wrong with his black suit and crumpled white shirt, if you accepted that he had buttoned up the wrong holes and that his loose black hair looked as if it had not been combed for months.

The cortege filed past him on its way back to the cottage, and one or two men cast stony glances in his direction, indicating that he had better wipe the idiotic grin off his face.

Elliyn paused opposite him, causing the twin sisters to bump into each other behind. She stopped, not to acknowledge his presence in any way, but simply to stare in astonishment at the suit he wore: her brother's suit! She recognized a scorch mark on the threadbare knee and the way it rucked around the collar.

The odd stranger could only have obtained it from the house, she reasoned swiftly. Walked in and taken it! He had gone into her bedroom, where an ornate Edwardian wardrobe contained their mothballed clothes, and then walked boldly out again!

That would account for the tell-tale signs of entry she had found the afternoon her brother died: a broken plate, crumbs on the scrubbed stairs, a grubby tidemark around the bath. The shock of Lionel's death had driven it from her mind, until now.

The realization took her breath away; as if someone had

laid their unknown hand on her leg in the darkness of the Caernarfon cinema.

She confronted him wide-eyed, daring him to deny his impertinence. But he showed no embarrassment and simply grinned back, bold as the brass on her brother's coffin.

Fifteen minutes later, when the lettuce sandwiches and tea were being consumed with a relish that would not have been out of place in an Old Testament orgy, he knocked at the back door. She shouldered her way through the chattering guests and answered immediately. 'You wait there,' she said crisply, indicating a mangle on which he could sit. 'They'll be gone before long.'

He nodded, satisfied. It was as if he knew their coming together had been predestined.

Overhead the dark clouds swirled in a celebratory dance.

Two

The car was a particularly small automatic and John Casson had long, rangy legs, but they suited each other as opposites often do. He drove west from London, skirting north of Bath at a steady fifty-five miles an hour, with his right foot on the accelerator and his left resting casually in the far glove compartment.

There was widespread flooding and a lot of diversion signs were out. Casson was waved down by police as he approached the big suspension bridge over the Severn and had trouble getting his wedged foot free: so much so that a constable put his head in a window and asked if he was a disabled driver.

Hetty slept undisturbed on the back seat, snorting occasionally in her dreams as they swayed through roundabouts or drove without pause over hump-backed bridges. He glanced over his shoulder at her squashed face and black jowls: a two-year-old boxer bitch in prime condition.

It was getting dark when he pulled in to consult the map and noted ruefully that there were still a hundred miles to go.

He started to look out for somewhere to spend the night. It was curious, he was accustomed to being alone but a trace of sadness usually touched him in the early evening. He sang a little louder than was necessary to occupy his mind and Hetty stretched and yawned and stretched in the back. It was no good feigning sleep in an attempt to discourage him, and she knew it.

'We're a couple of swells,' he sang off-key. 'We stop at the best hotels. But we prefer the country, far away from the city smells.'

A small section of his mind was not concentrating on the words. He would have been married two years now if she hadn't run off. Jenny. It hurt even to shape her name in his throat, and it invariably ended in a gulp.

At first it had been very hard to take and, even now, in the depths of the night he longed for her.

Why she didn't wait, he never understood.

They had agreed when he went to the Shetland Islands for a year that it was the way to accelerate promotion and a chance to buy life's little extras that she seemed to need: like a high-performance car and a house by the Thames.

Only, she met an affluent older man while he was away; the owner of four superior shoeshops, who must have offered the things he could not. The experience had left him bruised and now he never quite knew when some irrelevant phrase or object would touch his memory and bring the hurt back.

He told himself he didn't really care that much about Jenny. But here he was two years later heading for Wales, still remembering.

'We're a couple of sports,' he said in a muted voice. 'The pride of the tennis courts. In June, July and August, we look cute when we're dressed in shorts.'

He was easy-going and didn't think twice when the Central Electricity Generating Board decided he was the senior area engineer they wanted in North Wales. 'Right away,' they said. 'It's urgent.' So, at a time when everybody else was leaving waterlogged Wales or the drenched Midlands and making for high-rise cities, he was going the other way.

He spent the night at a motel outside Brecon, where each of the almost identical cabins had a list of regulations hanging on the inside of the door. After running out of change to feed an avaricious coin-in-the-slot television set, he read the list idly. It contained the warning 'Absolutely No Dogs'.

In the morning, screwing up his face to get the best out of a shave, he caught sight of Hetty's permanently doleful face peering from under the covers.

'Get your head down,' he muttered, indicating the printed rules. 'Haven't you got any sense of discretion?'

The mirror reflected a lean, thoughtful face and grey eyes. The eyes were used to narrowing concentration over engineering problems – during which time he grimaced a lot and ploughed his fingers through tousled hair, before relaxing good-humouredly.

Some people found him too casual for their liking. It was not the way he dressed but rather that he sprawled. His long legs never seemed to tuck neatly away. Usually one hung over the side of a chair and the other jutted out ahead.

Casson ordered breakfast by phone. Having smuggled the dog in, it had to be breakfast for one. But Hetty listened anxiously as he placed the order.

'Egg and bacon. That is . . . two slices of bacon. Oh, and sausages. Two sausages. Two helpings of bread and butter. Tea. And a jug of cold water, please, and a bowl. That's right, a jug of drinking water and a . . . Yes, I get very thirsty.' He cleared his throat. 'Is it always this humid in Wales? No? Well it is compared with London, and that's a fact.'

Casson put the phone down and blew out his cheeks in exasperation. 'You see how dangerously we're living?' he said to Hetty. 'And what do you ever do in return? Apart from lick me?' He backed away. 'No, not now. Just keep out of sight.' As he let himself out of the front door in order to pay the bill, he looked back momentarily. 'Have you got that?'

He found the final twenty-five miles a struggle. There was hardly any other traffic, which was not surprising considering the weather. It rained intermittently until the last leg and then he ran into a *niwl*: a clammy mist, peculiar to Wales, which descended on Merionethshire like a moist blanket, reducing visibility to a few yards.

His singing also slowed noticeably. 'We would sail up the avenue, but we haven't got a yacht. We would drive up the avenue, but the horse we had was shot . . .'

He got out twice simply to peer up at obscured signposts and got soaked. Not that it was actually raining. The *niwl* was tattered lace which drifted slowly across the wooded hill country, drenching all before it.

By the time he reached Trawsfynned, mist swathed the area so tightly he could hardly be sure he was still on the road. He knew that the village, which in English means Across the Mountain, stood at the corner of a huge reservoir and that his destination was now just a few miles due north.

Casson found his way into a general store, a rambling place with bare floorboards which smelled of soap powder and sold everything from Wellington boots to lollipops.

A plump girl in a pinafore greeted him from behind the counter with a flow of Welsh which tripped entrancingly from her tongue but meant nothing to him. He spread his hands and shrugged.

'Oh,' she smiled, switching her language. 'There's no way through to the Ffestiniogs. They say the water is higher than a double-decker bus in places. Police are turning everybody back.'

Casson groaned. He had only a mile or two to go. Nevertheless, he set about buying tins of baked beans, several cooked chickens, bread, milk and tea on the basis that if he did get to the power station he would be hungry and – knowing his luck – it would probably be short of food.

Without power being fed into the grid from Ffestiniog pumped-storage power station, people in the area were going to be in an even worse plight than at present. On the other hand, it could be kept going for some time by one self-sufficient engineer.

Hetty welcomed him back into the car with the barely sustained opening of an eye before relapsing into sleep. He found forward gear and nosed off into the grey drizzle.

Half a mile farther on he was stopped by a triangular police sign with a flashing blue light. An inspector with his dark blue raincoat collar turned up to the edge of his peaked cap hurried across from a patrol car and sat heavily into Casson's car to avoid the rain.

'Don't mind if I come in out of the weather, do you?'

'Not at all.'

' 'Fraid you'll have to turn back.'

'Oh?'

'Road's awash.'

'It's important that I go on.'

The inspector, whose youthful face showed that he could only recently have been promoted, smiled sympathetically. 'I'm sure it is, but not for a day or two.'

Casson felt in his inside pocket. 'I have, somewhere in here, Electricity Board authority for priority access to all property and land in time of emergency.'

'Have you now.'

Casson proffered a bent plastic card. 'Here.'

The policeman raised his eyebrows as if humouring him. 'Doesn't make a thimbleful of difference.'

'Look, I've only got a couple of miles to go. To the power station at Ffestiniog. I'm the relief engineer, and they need me there as soon as possible.'

'Ffestiniog? Why didn't you say so? God, man, my old woman cooks by electricity and I can't get to sleep without my electric blanket. Hang on, I'll talk to control.'

He returned to the patrol car and talked into a mouthpiece for a while with the door half open. Eventually he squelched back.

'All right, we'll give it a try. You follow my tail lights. But don't get too close, and stop when I stop. Got it?'

The two vehicles processed down a murky slope and were soon throwing out bow waves as they chugged ahead. The road was fairly flat now although it twisted a good deal. Gradually the depth increased and Casson instinctively levered himself up on his seat. The windscreen wipers were going at panic speed and he could see that surrounding meadows had submerged to form one great lake. The weight of water held the car back and he thought that, any moment, his exhaust pipe would go under, in which case he would have to abandon it and start wading.

There was barely an inch to spare when they eventually nosed up an approach road towards the long low-slung power station built along the lip of Tan-y-grisiau reservoir.

Ahead of him the police car was dripping like a bedraggled dog after a swim, but his attention was taken up by the building which stood on a narrow shelf at the foot of the mountains with water lapping its hundred-metre façade. A shroud of mist masked its low, deceptive appearance, yet he was well aware of the enormous surges of power it was able to generate by harnessing the strength of water it could release from a dam waiting high in the rain-shrouded mountains. It generated power for Wales as well as feeding it into the grid to be devoured by great cuckoo towns to the east, in England.

The patrol car swung in a tight circle on a waterlogged cinder parking area and a window wound down. 'Anything else I can do?'

'No thanks.' Casson got out and immediately regretted it. Water rose over his shoes. 'I'll be all right.'

A door opened in the main building and Casson heard his name being called. The inspector saluted with one finger. 'Be seeing you.'

Casson pulled his suitcases from the boot and beckoned to Hetty. 'Come on, sponger. I'm not going to be the only one around here with wet feet.' An elderly senior-relief engineer, whom he knew vaguely from a conference in the

Midlands a year before, met him at the top of a flight of concrete steps.

They shook hands and Casson noticed he was dressed to the extent of buttoning up his raincoat, as if anxious to get on his way. There was an attache case by the door.

The relief man, McPherson, did not look well and said he wanted to start his journey back to Birmingham before it got dark. He showed Casson the glass-sided control room with its consoles and lines of metres and clocks and indicated some paperwork that needed updating daily.

'Why not stay overnight? You look a little tired,' Casson said.

'No, no. I want to get shot of the place. A week's as much as I can take of my own company.' McPherson smiled in nervous spasms and glanced repeatedly at his watch. 'Well, I'll leave you to it.'

Casson saw him off from the concrete steps and watched until the rear lights faded into the dusk, then walked briskly back inside to the control room. It was brightly lit and extremely functional: just like the rest of the building, most of which was below ground level and housed the machinery that now hummed gently all around.

Hetty rested her front paws on a ledge and peered out at the *niwl*. Casson leaned to massage her finely shaped lines and detected a shivering. He glanced over his shoulder out along the gleaming metallic paintwork of the operating floor and shared the boxer's sense of unease: there was something unwelcoming about the place.

It was as if something wanted to exclude them. Yet how could a building generate a feeling of hostility?

Early the next day, as dawn filtered across the land, slowly awakening all but the giant Snowdon some seven miles to the north-west, which would probably slumber with its head under a pillow of clouds all day long, floodwater crept over the last open road.

Blaenau Ffestiniog was cut off from the outside world. The only route left open led up into the inhospitable mountains.

A good many families had already headed for what they regarded as the safety of the cities and their going made rows of sightless white-washed windows a familiar sight in the old slate town. But the majority withdrew into themselves, hoarded whatever tinned food they could and prepared for the worst.

They kept off the wind-chapped streets and soon even the perpetually dripping eaves of tall, religiously thin buildings in Blaenau seemed to be nervously awaiting whatever fate had in mind for them.

Three

Casson awoke abruptly in the dead of night. He lay absolutely still for a while, listening intently. Then sat bolt upright. He was frightened without knowing why. There was nothing around him but a heavy silence.

He was alone apart from Hetty. Alone in a rambling power station set at the foot of the Moelwyn Mountains in the Snowdonia Massif, touching the edge of Tan-y-grisiau reservoir. Nearly a mile above and behind him in the dark impenetrable night was a second smaller reservoir, Llyn Stwlan, whose cold waters could be unleashed at the press of a button to gush down concrete and steel tunnels towards Tan-y-grisiau with shocking force: millions of gallons of water to operate turbines, excite powerful generators into action to produce a great surge of electricity through transformers and out to overhead power lines which would carry its harnessed strength away into the distance to countless unseen towns and cities. Each night vast quantities of water were pumped back up from Tan-y-grisiau into the lap of Stwlan until the natural mountain lake, formed in the Ice Age, was brimming, ready for the moment next day when it would be needed again.

For the moment the inky darkness lay oppressively around him. He leaned to one side and listened hard.

Nothing, and yet he shivered and his arms were covered in goose-pimples.

'Here, girl,' he whispered hoarsely to Hetty. The bulky dog crept up on to his bed and snuffled beside him, as if she too were listening.

Casson had a disturbed feeling that something was watching them. He dismissed it as ridiculous but the idea persisted in creeping chillingly back into his thoughts and kept him awake for a long time, so that he monitored the shadows in a way he had not done since he was a boy. He kept telling himself not to be a fool, but Hetty was unsettled too, and he knew well enough that dogs have some instincts far more acute than man's.

Eventually, they both fell asleep.

At eight o'clock the following morning Casson walked briskly through the big echoing turbine room. The clinically modern building was alive again. The hum of mechanical activity encompassed buzzes, clicks and the occasional ding of a bell to announce the completion of a routine function.

He had forgotten his apprehension of the previous night until a single unexpected moment, when Hetty pounced out at him from behind the central desk in the white and glass-walled control room, and it was all brought back with a rush. He jerked to a halt. It was an appreciable time before the moment passed and he could let his agonized breath slowly escape.

They were alone. Quite alone and it was broad daylight outside. And yet . . .

He checked a bank of manual controls without anticipating the need to use them, then ran his eyes over the slanting display panels registering automatic sequences.

He glanced down at Hetty, who wagged her stumpy tail and trotted so close that she leaned heavily into her master's legs. 'Strictly between the two of us,' Casson confided from the side of his mouth, 'this place gives me the creeps.' Each was comforted by the other's presence and, when

Casson's written checks were completed, they walked back to the living quarters without delay.

Casson had no way of knowing anything was waiting for him around a blind right-turn in the corridor. He walked straight into a motionless figure in the middle of the passage.

'Jesus Christ!'

Hetty flattened herself to the ground, growling.

A hand pushed back the hood of a dripping oilskin coat to reveal the calm assessing face of the police inspector.

'I'm afraid not. It's only me.'

Casson sunk down to a ledge and pulled a relieved face. 'This is getting to be a habit. God. Do you know, I almost jumped out of my skin? I thought I was alone. How did you get in?'

The young policeman had a deliberate manner which gave him an air of authority even though he was dressed in civilian clothes. 'I've got a set of spare keys which your people left at the station. It's normal practice.'

He bent to let Hetty sniff his fingers suspiciously. She stopped growling but did not completely accept him. 'My name's apJones, Mr Casson. Rhys apJones.'

Casson gave him a limp handshake.

'Just thought I'd look in to see if you were all right.'

'I'm fine. Come on, let's go and have a cup of tea.'

The two men walked back to his snug quarters in the middle of the complex with Hetty trotting on ahead. It was as he extracted the teabags from the cups that Casson said, 'What did you mean, if I was all right?'

The inspector had a deep voice and a strong Welsh accent. 'Nothing special,' he said matter-of-factly. 'It's just that your predecessor didn't much care for this part of the world. Said it put him on edge. He was forever twitching and biting his nails.'

'Oh?' Casson would have liked to hear more about McPherson's doubts, but the inspector was not forthcoming. The tall engineer slapped the dog resoundingly. 'Well, don't worry about us. We're used to being alone.'

Hetty suddenly bristled and listened intently along the corridor. A growl rumbled in the back of her throat.

apJones got silently to his feet, listened as carefully as the dog, then disappeared along the corridor. Casson was mystified and followed them to the back entrance carrying his cup of tea.

Outside he found the inspector shading his eyes and looking up the towering overhang of mountain while Hetty bounded round in circles, barking at the rocks.

apJones stood watching for some time, then grinned reassuringly. 'It's nothing. Just a falcon.' He pointed up to where a peregrine had broken clear of the clouds and drifted out across the silver-flecked surface of the reservoir. It circled effortlessly, observing them, before arcing away into the distance.

Casson knelt down and rubbed his appreciative dog's ears. 'You old fat-head. That was nothing to get excited about.' He was still petting her when he heard the rear door click shut behind him. The policeman was nowhere in sight and Casson was locked out.

Damn it, he thought. Presumably apJones had walked back inside and it had blown to after him, pushed by the wind. He hammered on the door, but got no response.

It took him several minutes to clamber around the outside of the long building, avoiding standing water, to reach the glass-fronted control room.

He got a jolt of surprise to see apJones inside, leaning over the main console. Casson's immediate reaction was anger. What the hell was the man doing? He had no right to be in there. He pummelled on the thick glass with the sides of his fists. 'What are you playing at?'

apJones turned without haste and cupped a hand to his ear.

Casson indicated the door with vigorous jabs of his finger. But to his amazement he was again ignored while apJones picked up the direct-line telephone to the north-west region controller's office in Manchester.

'What the bloody hell are you up to, man?' Casson yelled indignantly, banging on the heavy sheet glass and stumbling along the side of the building at the same time, lurching knee-deep into water. 'Oh Jesus!'

The young inspector seemed unperturbed when he at last unlocked the door.

'Come on in, Mr Casson.'

'What the dickens are you up to?' stormed Casson. 'No one goes into that room without my authority! It's out of bounds to most personnel at the best of times.'

'I understand why you're upset. I just wanted to check that you're who you say you are. We've had Wales-for-the-Welsh protesters around here before and other people who wanted to get in for their own peculiar reasons. It's too important a place for us to take lightly.'

His candour took much of the wind out of Casson's sails. 'All right,' he said grudgingly. 'But let's understand one another from now on. In here, I'm the man in charge. And if anything needs changing or putting right, I do it. No one else. Right?'

'Right.'

Hetty nosed between them, her doctored tail wagging. It helped break the ice. 'Come on, let's finish off the tea.'

Back in the lounge, Casson said, 'By the way, do you play chess?'

The inspector chewed it over for a while. 'A little.'

Casson was beginning to get the measure of the man. 'How much is a little?' he asked suspiciously.

'Oh, I haven't played seriously for years.'

'Good, I'll give you a game. We can pass the moves between us whenever we see one another.'

'Fine,' the policeman said casually. 'We could even have half a bottle of whisky on it.'

'You're on.' Casson got his chess wallet from a drawer and started to line up the pieces when another thought occurred to him. 'Wait a minute. I bet you're a bloody grand master.'

The smile died from Rhys apJones's face, and he nodded in partial admission. 'Well, I was youth champion of South Wales, but that was a long time ago, see.'

Casson exploded with laughter. 'I bloody well knew it. Nothing about this place is what it seems.'

They began the game and it did not take long for Casson to realize that his opponent was extremely good: an aggressive and threatening player and not at all as he seemed to be in real life. But Casson blocked and frustrated the early attacks, biding his time and waiting for the chance to strike back.

Eventually apJones put on his oilskins and carried the wallet off with him to ruminate on his next move. He set off along the reservoir road with long strides before hesitating as something occurred to him. He retraced his steps and shook Casson's hand firmly.

'I meant to say welcome to Ffestiniog. Look after yourself now, and ring me if anything odd happens.'

'Odd?'

apJones shrugged and turned away. When he looked back from twenty-five metres the wind was beginning to tug his clothes. 'You'll be fine. Don't worry.'

Casson nodded, and Hetty licked his hand as he absently rubbed the brown-black ears. 'Nice fellow,' he said quietly, as his eyes searched the mountainside. The sun shone weakly and nothing moved that was not stirred by the wind. But still he had a chilling feeling that something out there knew he was alone again, and was waiting only for the darkness to come back.

He grunted at Hetty, 'Come on, there nothing to worry about. Let's go inside and eat.'

Four

Rain fell persistently for most of the day, easing off in the late afternoon. The clouds withdrew in dark silence to contemplate the effect they had had on the saturated countryside and the long, damp mountains.

Casson pulled on his heavy Wellington boots and

whistled Hetty into motion before squelching along the track towards the village of Tan-y-grisiau. The straggling little community was situated midway between the power station and Blaenau Ffestiniog, and to reach it he kept doggedly to a rough, flintstone path and avoided tempting shortcuts across the boggy ground on either side.

Rivulets of water streamed down the slopes as the mountains wrung themselves out. Here and there brilliant patches of bluebells glistened as they swayed; and a herd of wild ponies with dishevelled manes stood in the nearby gorse to watch him pass.

A meandering river at the foot of the valley had turned into a brawling torrent, barely able to squeeze under an arched stone bridge. He crossed it, dodging through gusts of spray.

In the village itself, although water still chased helter-skelter along gutters and swirled impatiently around choked drains, there was a fragrance in the air and, for the first time, he sensed Wales as a place of beauty as well as discomfort.

Now the road wound upwards, just as Rhys apJones had described, between houses squeezed shoulder to shoulder with their neighbours. But the only people he saw – apart from an occasional face behind a twitching curtain – were a young couple walking slowly along the other side of the street entwined in each other's arms.

His mind reached back. You never get used to being lonely. Not completely. It isn't so much the being alone, he thought, as he trudged up the hill scuffing his toecaps. The difficult moments came, as now, when he saw others wrapped in mutual bliss while he was no more than a forlorn spectator. A longing for Jenny lodged in his chest; an undigested ache that would not go away. Jenny, or someone like her.

The chapel and its minister's house stood alone on the far side of the village. It was a rectangular building, hardly large enough to contain a resonant Welsh hymn, and yet cold and unwelcoming. Privacy was its only apparent attribute.

As Casson ventured inside, the squeak of his shoes on dusty floorboards was picked up and magnified around the drab plaster walls and plain windows. Rows of simple wooden chairs faced an over-elaborate black pulpit, bearing a huge copy of the Bible open at Genesis. Wild flowers loosely arranged in a vase had died of thirst days before.

Casson glanced around the empty chapel and then backed out, partly in deference to the worship that normally took place there and partly for another reason which he could not quite define and yet which made him feel unwelcome.

The chapel house was not much more rewarding. He crossed a flagstoned hall and called into the unpretentious kitchen. 'Hello. Anybody about?'

The front room was equally unresponsive and that left only the stairs. He leaned upwards. 'Miss Pryce-Jones. Are you there?'

Eventually a woman's voice intercepted his own. 'Come up, if you wish. Top of the stairs and straight ahead.'

He ducked his head to avoid being stunned by a low ceiling extension halfway up, and pushed through the facing door, half expecting to find a cluttered little office: a place for writing sermons and counting the silver collection money.

Instead he was in a bathroom, three-quarters of which was occupied by a Victorian lion-clawed bath. A long raw-boned woman was leaning across its few inches of steaming water in which sat the huddled rib-thin figure of a man. She was steadily ladling jugsful of hot water over his head, while he pressed a flannel to his eyes and wriggled about in an agony of anticipation before each drenching.

'Aaaaah!' he gasped, pulling himself several inches out of the cast-iron bath before sinking down again relieved that, for the moment, the worst was past.

The woman was extraordinarily plain: a horsey face with large teeth, untidy hair and a long, straight nose. She had masculine arms and one or two coarse hairs growing from her nostrils.

In order not to agitate the figure in the bath further she

put a finger to her pale lips. Casson took the hint and settled in a wicker chair as directed.

He himself winced as another saucepan of steaming water cascaded over the young man's sodden black hair and streamed down his under-nourished arms.

'Right, Dewi boy,' she said briskly in a strong Welsh accent, 'that'll do.' She pushed the man's head away and straightened up, stretching.

Casson became aware of her penetrating brown eyes for the first time. Fine, bold eyes. Considering the rest of her ungainly appearance, she should have been the one to feel ill at ease; yet it was Casson who felt uncomfortable under her searching gaze.

He had no need to ask her name. It was easy to imagine why she had succeeded her brother as chapel leader. There was an air of authority and purpose about her.

'You're wet,' she said.

'It's raining again.'

'Perhaps you'd like a bath?' She stepped back fractionally, indicating the few inches of used water, as if it was only common-sense. 'No point in wasting God's good rainwater when it's just been heated and carried up from below.'

'Pardon?'

'A bath. Why not follow Dewi and get in? I'll scrub your back, man.'

He gave a small incredulous laugh. 'You don't even know me.'

She folded her arms solemnly and raised her eyebrows. 'I dare say you're very much like any other man. With similar things in the same sort of places. I expect I could manage to soap you down without damaging anything permanently.'

'No thanks.'

She seemed surprised. 'It's good hot water.'

'I'm sure it is.'

Dewi splashed his way sullenly out of the bath and scrambled for a threadbare towel. As he rubbed and shivered, he stared at Casson with understandable outrage at having been observed naked by a complete stranger.

'Pwy yw hwn? Bant a thi! Ffwrdd a thi!'

Elliyn Pryce-Jones shushed him, and glanced at Casson to see if he understood.

Casson did not but he stood up, embarrassed. 'I gather he's upset.'

'He wants you to get out.' She seemed amused at Dewi's indignant outburst.

'Of course. Tell him I'm sorry and . . .'

'He can speak English as well as me. But he won't. He sees you as an outsider intruding first into his land and then his privacy.'

Dewi hopped about rubbing his sopping hair and giving forth a stream of Welsh abuse. Elliyn Pryce-Jones, who was almost as tall as the long-limbed engineer, pushed Casson back down into the wicker chair.

The humiliated Welshman snatched up his discarded clothes from a heap on the floor, glared at them both and thundered downstairs.

She calmly wiped the bath around with a flannel and pulled the plug on the swirling grey water.

'First good rinse he's had this month. You'd never credit the struggle I have before he'll take a bath.'

Casson shook his head in sympathy, then got back to his feet and extended a hand. 'I'm John Casson, the new man at Blaenau Power Station.'

'I know.'

'I've only been here a day or two.'

'Yes.' She continued expunging all traces of grime from the worn bath. 'I know that too.'

'Do you know *why* I've come here to see you?'

She straightened to her full height, just over six feet, and held him with her disconcertingly steady gaze. With eyes like that she could conquer the world, he thought.

'You're here,' she said patiently, 'because you need friends.'

He shuffled his feet awkwardly. 'I suppose that's true.'

'You're also here because you know that the single most

important person in the Principality is a part of this chapel.'

He nodded whole-heartedly, assuming she meant herself.

She cupped his hand in her own, with room to spare. 'Bless you. I'll take you to see him.'

Casson tugged his hand free. 'Him?'

'The Son of God.'

'Oh, him.' He swallowed hard, rubbed his chin briskly and wondered how to get their conversation on to a different tack. 'Actually, it's your help I need, Miss Pryce-Jones. The people of Tan-y-grisiau are fine. That is, what's left of them; there can't be more than a couple of dozen families left in the entire area. But Inspector apJones tells me they all look to you before reacting to anything new. It seems to me you're more than just their spiritual leader.'

She smiled indulgently. 'It's understandable. Chapel has always been the centre of their lives. And more especially in times of hardship, like now.'

'That's it exactly. From what I'm told, you stick together, and I understand that. But I'm here to do a single-handed job which will quickly become impossible if I'm not accepted like any other villager in terms of buying food and provisions. I know supplies are short, the police have told me that. But, believe me, you all need me just as much as I need you.'

'Of course.'

'Then I can count on you?'

He again found his hand enclosed in a powerful grip. 'That depends on whether or not I can count on you.' She trespassed deep into his eyes. 'But I have a hosanna feeling about you . . . a feeling I can trust you.' She pressed his hand. Casson gulped and tried, in vain, to retrieve it.

'Come back here tonight, after evening service, and I'll instruct you personally in the way of the chapel. We'll bare our thoughts to one another.'

'Well, I don't know about tonight,' he began apologetically.

'Let's say ten o'clock.' She was not used to anybody questioning her directions. 'Straight after the last service.'

He finally got his hand back and kneaded it surreptitiously to restore the circulation. 'I really have to check all the readings in the power station at ten.'

'Do it earlier this evening,' she advised, then turned away and began unbuttoning the cuffs of her long black dress. 'Well, if that's all, I must get on. Time to cleanse myself.'

As Casson turned away, he glanced at the two galvanized buckets in a corner. They were empty. There was only one tap on the bath. 'I think you're out of hot water.'

She looked scornful. 'I never bath in anything but mountain water, straight from the tap. It stimulates me. On really frosty days it cuts into you like a frozen lash and I sing at the top of my voice to help me bear it.'

She calmly unfastened the neck buttons down to her waist and he was stunned to realize that, to her, nudity was natural as warm rain from a summer sky or the shedding of bark from a silver birch in the autumn. She had full, round breasts: objects of beauty magnified by contrast with the plainness of her face.

He stammered and backed out of the bathroom, colliding with the door on the way. 'It was nice to meet you and see . . . everything.' He missed a step halfway down the stairs.

Her resonant voice followed him. 'See you at ten. Don't be late. As you said, we need you at the Blaenau just as much as you need us. We'll talk in earnest, you and I. And I'll show you something special.'

Casson almost ran down the hill. He tried a short cut and the soggy ground sucked at his boots. But his adrenalin was flowing and nothing could prevent him putting as much distance between himself and that extraordinary woman as possible.

It would have taken dynamite to dislodge Casson and the dog from Blaenau power station that evening. He ambled about checking readings on the murmuring, smoothly efficient machinery, intent on not leaving the building again until next morning. There was no question of him returning to the Bethesda Temperance Chapel by ten o'clock. He'd made his point and would leave it at that. Even so, he felt apprehensive as ten o'clock passed and the clock ticked remorselessly on. He heard a hollow roll of distant thunder and he glanced swiftly at the main door, half-expecting her to appear and demand to know where he'd been.

She would be staring out of the chapel porch now, towards the chain of blue-grey giants that formed the mountainous backbone of Wales. He wiped a film of perspiration from his forehead and told himself not to be ridiculous. Forget her; forget the whole thing.

He bundled Hetty around in a game, and the dog growled with pleasure as its great soft jaws encased his hand. Sloppy jowls and a snuffling muzzle. 'You great, daft bundle of dogsmeat,' he chided, rolling the brindle over and massaging her powerful chest.

He went to bed and read until midnight, yet he was still uneasy. It wasn't the incessant hum of the machinery: that had long since merged into the background of his consciousness. Only if it stopped during the night would he become aware that anything was wrong.

The book slid from his hand and he slept fitfully.

When the telephone rang he awoke abruptly. One minute he was asleep. The next wide awake. It echoed around the distant control room, across the turbine hall and into the air compressor house. Again and again it rang. Insisting on an answer.

Damn it! He knew who it was without even answering. Couldn't she leave him alone? He set his feet down on the cold floor and touched Hetty, his hand halting in her warm, receptive fur, waiting for the phone to give up.

But it continued to summon him until, eventually, he stood up. For all he knew, it might be London on the line with some vital information about the functioning of the station. And yet, deep down, he knew it wasn't.

His finger brushed the cold and impersonal concrete

wall, switching on banks of lights, only to find when he arrived at the desk that the phone had finally stopped ringing. Relieved, he returned to bed.

The telephone rang again a few hours later when the grey dawn was giving way to morning. Outside a new day was stretching out along the sharply defined line of the horizon, preparing to face the rigours of the day.

Casson picked up the receiver quickly, to get it over with, and was surprised to hear apJones's voice. There was an urgent edge to his tone.

'I need your help. In fact I need every able-bodied man I can find. Over here at the police station right away. It's an emergency.' Casson tried to rub the sleep out of his eyes.

'Yes, bring the dog,' the inspector was saying. 'I'm sure that power station of yours can look after itself for a while. And wear your stoutest boots, man.'

'Why?'

'I'll tell you when you get here.' He gave hurried directions to the police station and rang off.

Five

Incessant rain flowing off the broad flanks of Snowdon overwhelmed the elongated lakes of Dinas and Gwynant. Their enormously increased weight burst natural barriers and millions of gallons of water cascaded eastwards. The farther it went the stronger the flood became, catapulting over waterfalls and roaring down gullies.

Ahead of it was a rock-strewn wilderness. If a flood had to occur anywhere in Britain, God could hardly have chosen a less populated spot: apart, that is, from H.M. Prison Gwynfa.

The squat prison building in the path of the torrent was unashamedly ugly and the only attractive thing about it was its name, which in English means Place of Bliss. But Gwynfa was anything but blissful. Its grim granite façade had no windows and was relieved only by a massive steel gate which occasionally slid aside to admit vehicles and then revealed a high wire-mesh fence some twenty-five metres inside.

Visitors were discouraged, and relatives of the eighty inmates were assured they had all they would ever need. What the authorities did not say was that there was one special-restraint cell for every prisoner.

The men all had mental problems, which was apparent on the few occasions they met, such as the regular Saturday afternoon film show. Most turned their backs on one another while waiting for the bland film to begin, or simply stared at their feet. Some were sullen and withdrawn, others constantly fidgeting with themselves. They were all lifers and, almost without exception, they were men the country wanted to forget.

Nothing ever happens here, a yawning warder had thought as he made his way off duty that night through the teeming rain. But what he couldn't have known was that a battering ram of floodwater was heading directly for the prison. There was no saving Gwynfa.

Casson bumped into the back of the inspector, who came to a sudden halt with the rescue party on a bedraggled rise overlooking the prison. 'Jesus,' he whispered, peering over the policeman's shoulder. 'I thought you said no one could get out of there.'

'So I was told.'

A deluge of water had smashed through the unlovely valley the night before. The prison was still there but its huge steel gate had been lifted off its runners and buckled. There was no movement of any kind.

Chilling grey water formed a placid lake in and around the building, and it was not difficult to imagine the destructive shock of its arrival in the middle of the night.

Casson stood pale-faced, contemplating the fear of men sitting bolt upright in locked cells, trapped and alone in the night; aware that death was reaching out for them but physically unable even to scream.

There was an awful silence as the group of about a dozen men arranged themselves, with apJones, raggedly along the ridge. One focussed a pair of Service binoculars. It was mid-morning, but there was considerable mist about and he had to polish the lenses.

'There are some people on the far side!'

'How many? Are they all right?'

'About thirty or forty, I'd say.'

The inspector reached for the glasses. 'Let me see.'

Within half an hour the rescuers had picked their way carefully down through the rocks to the foot of the valley. They splashed on past grotesquely scattered chairs and tables from inside Gwynfa and some sodden curtains floating in a random pool. A senior prison officer clambered to meet them. He had no jacket and no collar to his shirt, but a silver-tipped cane tucked tightly under his arm was the mark of his authority. He was a bristling former regimental sergeant-major from the Welsh Guards who had somehow found time in the numbed aftermath of disaster to polish the toecaps of his boots.

He straightened his shoulders and brought his heels together audibly. 'Morning, sah. Are we glad to see you!'

Inspector apJones nodded acknowledgement. 'Anybody killed?'

'Eight so far, I'm afraid. Three of my best officers, and five of *them*.'

'So far?' The young inspector raised his head questioningly to survey the dishevelled group sprawled out in the shelter of rocks ahead. Some had blankets around their shoulders; others were huddled around a wireless set.

The senior prison officer escorted apJones and Casson forward. 'All my people are accounted for, although some of them are pretty dazed. Governor's over there with a broken leg. And we've got one or two nasty head wounds from the fighting.'

'What fighting?'

'There was a lot of panic. I don't mind telling you I was

doing things in my trousers, too. One or two of the prisoners tried to make a break for it; we had to lay into them.'

apJones ran his fingers through his hair as he contemplated the precipitous skyline. 'How many missing?'

'Can't say for sure. Six, I think. We've poked about as best we could since first light and there's no sign of any other bodies. But they could have been washed on half a mile or more. On the other hand . . .' He left the sentence unfinished and indicated the rock-strewn hills hopelessly.

apJones patted the man's arm understandingly and threaded his way through the survivors to a bespectacled man lying stretched out, his head on a flat stone and his face the colour of cold porridge. A frail hand emerged from under the blanket and they exchanged words.

Casson hung back for a further word with the senior prison officer. 'On the other hand, what?' he asked.

Shrewd eyes regarded Casson and it seemed for a while as if he did not intend to answer. Then the eyes glanced up towards the *anialwych* of wilderness. 'On the other hand the buggers could be up there. Perhaps watching us at this very moment.'

The engineer followed the direction of the man's gaze. Rocks, shadows and a tangle of trees. It would be difficult to spot anybody more than a few hundred metres away in that landscape unless they deliberately moved.

'I doubt it. If it was me, I'd be across that mountain by now and heading for home.'

'It's not that simple, Mr . . .'

'Casson.'

'We had a roll-call twenty minutes ago. There seem to be half a dozen men missing, Mr Casson. Normally we would hardly need to look for them. In this sort of country and particularly in this weather, they won't get far before they realize they are a lot better off back here. Once they've missed a few meals and the cold gets to their nerve-ends they'll come shuffling back. With one exception.'

'Oh?'

The ex-RSM nodded. 'With one exception. A man

named Webb.' He glanced momentarily over his shoulder to ensure they were not overheard by any whose discipline he needed to rely upon. 'He worries me a little.'

'Why?'

'He's unpredictable and strong as a bull, so he could stay up there for a week or two. And, of course, you know his other problem.'

'No, what's that?'

'He's a double murderer.'

Casson looked at him in horror. 'Christ, I wish someone had told me this last night. I would have stayed in bed.'

A look of doubt crossed the other man's face. 'Aren't you a policeman?'

'No, I was press-ganged from the power station.'

'Oh, I see.' The prison officer coughed discreetly into the funnel of his fist and turned away. 'In that case, forget what I told you. No use civilians fretting about things that don't concern them.'

Casson later passed the stocky officer, bending over the limp figure of the governor. 'Everything all right, chief?' asked a thin voice.

'Yessir. Absolutely A-one. You just relax now.'

But Casson noticed the former sergeant-major frown as he turned to scan the tangled hillside. He was a worried man.

That afternoon Dewi was pitched out of the mine office so forcefully that he fell to his knees. But, once he got his breath back, the lopsided smile returned to his face. It had an uncanny, almost eerie way of finding its way back: rather like the bubble in a spirit level which no amount of shaking can dislodge.

Probert stood filling the doorway behind him. A vain man, who was said by the ladies to cut a fine strapping figure in his brown Derby hat and Sunday-best waistcoat. Even at work he made a point of wearing shirts a size too small in order to show off his biceps.

But there was nothing artificial about the solid impact

made by the heel of his palm thudding into Dewi's ear. It left the thin Welshman with his head dizzy and spinning.

'Tell her, if she wants me she knows where to find me! But I'm not going down on my knees for her or anybody! I want nothing more to do with her! Now sod off, you undernourished church mouse, before I do you a real bloody mischief.'

Dewi scuttled to a safe distance and doffed an incongruous bowler which he had acquired from the late parson's wardrobe. 'I take off my hat to you, Mr Probert.'

'What?' The mine manager had trouble hearing. It was a legacy from a lifetime of standing too close to blasts.

Dewi extended his bowler. 'I raise my hat to any sinner who does not fear the retribution.'

'You making fun of me, boyoh?' growled Probert, advancing.

Dewi backed off hurriedly and indicated the nearby Moelwyn mountain range with sly defiance. 'I've given you their message. *Their* message, mind. You'd best get down on your knees and ask forgiveness.'

'Sod off!' roared the slate mine manager. 'Or I'll kick your scraggy arse from here to Bangor and back.'

Dewi glanced quickly up at the black hanging clouds: some heavy with rain, others as yet shapeless and uncommitted. 'And very painful it would be, I'm sure. But I don't think you'll get the chance.'

The wind died away and for a weird moment or two there were no birds to occupy the silence. Dewi seemed to understand the awful stillness. He watched the sky like an accomplice. It was the moment before a storm when the elements paused to gather their strength.

Probert quickly picked up a heavy piece of discarded slate to disguise a cold feeling of dread that enveloped him. It narrowly missed the youthful head and skimmed over the edge of the chasm.

'I don't want to see you again!' Probert shouted threateningly.

Dewi turned away with an imbecilic smile. You won't, he said to himself.

Sydney Probert used the old, elongated upright telephone in his office to ring home and tell his wife he'd be late for tea. Had to walk up the gorge from Tan-y-grisiau into the high Cwmorthin Valley, he said.

Mrs Probert made some dissatisfied noises. 'But I've got you some kippers in butter.'

'Can't help it. I've got to check a couple of disused mine entrances. It'll take me until after six.'

'It'll be dark then,' she protested.

'I know that, woman. But the last time I tried to take the Landrover up that bloody gorge it took me half the next day to dig it out of the silt and slate debris. Treacherous isn't the bloody word for it. I'll have to walk.'

'Well it's up to you,' she said uppishly. 'But don't go stopping off drinking on the way home. I'll not have you coming in late, waking me. Not with my migraine.'

'I won't,' he groaned.

'Mind you don't.'

He still had a sour look on his face when he strode up the narrow pathway from straggling Tan-y-grisiau. Thunder rolled overhead, like barrels across an empty room. Falling away to his left was a deep cut in the rocks which contained racing spume-white water. Beyond it rose the great grey flanks of Moel-yr-Hydd and, to his right, masses of discarded slate sandwiched into a continuous bank a hundred feet high. But his eyes were fixed on the path ahead without taking in the splendid surroundings.

He cursed Megan Probert under his breath. His own hectoring manner made miners jump, but his wife would have none of his moodiness. Indeed she could make him wince with a single barbed sentence. Like many Welsh women she was as hard and impervious as the land of grey-green slate in which she was born.

He kicked a piece of slate with the solid toecap of his pit boot and saw it arc into the frothing water that leapt and bounded down narrow, six foot stairs in the rock.

Soon he passed between rows of roofless homes, built entirely of slate more than a century before, when the mines around Llyn Cwmorthin had prospered and countries throughout the world sought fine Welsh slate to roof their houses. Now the creaking company homes were inhabited only by the sighing wind. Gaps for windows stared sightlessly up the valley ahead.

Probert felt curiously uncomfortable. Silly really, but it felt as if the valley was waiting for him with hushed anticipation.

He was no more than a speck crossing the slab-of-slate bridge over an outlet at the lower end of the three-quarter-mile Llyn Cwmorthin, enclosed by mountains and a brooding sky that rested on their great broad shoulders.

Not a bird or animal stirred in the lonely valley.

But deep in the icy waters of Cwmorthin itself, a thin, bony specimen of Arctic char twitched and turned its head. It was as if the fish was aware of a minute current of energy. A danger signal: something from the past which was recognized now only by an ancient species surviving in Britain's handful of land-locked glacial lakes left by the retreat of the last Ice Age.

A tremor of low-energy fear had passed through the valley and none above ground had recognized it.

Sydney Probert strode on, cursorily checking the water level and condition of the ruins, then squelching across slagheaps on the foreshore and climbing to the shadowy entrance of an abandoned mine.

Six

Probert certainly did not get home at six. Nor at ten p.m. when his wife bitterly swept two plump kipper carcasses into her refuse bin and stumped off to bed. By God, she'd make him smart, especially if he woke her smelling of drink.

His body might not have been found for several days had not a Blaenau estate agent taken his pony out for a canter the next day around the edge of the lake, partly for exercise and partly to see if there was anything in his partner's suggestion that one or two of the old ruins might be restored as holiday cottages for affluent Englishmen.

The pony exhausted itself sucking its hooves from the waterlogged ground, and he pulled its head towards higher ground. There they found Probert lying face down, about twenty-five metres from the disused pit. The entire side of the mine entrance had collapsed, apparently catching him a crushing blow on the side of the head which now resembled a boiled egg cracked by a spoon.

The estate agent stared at the sight, horrified, then spurred his pony frantically back down the path to Tan-y-grisiau. He had neither the courage, nor the inclination, to dismount and check that the burly Welshman was actually dead. Not that it mattered. When Inspector apJones arrived on the scene with a doctor, he saw for himself that death must have been instantaneous. An odd thing was that one of the victim's feet was bare.

The wry little doctor, who had seen a variety of gruesome pit accidents in his time, hummed good-naturedly as he rolled back his sleeves and set to work.

'At least it was quick. Must have been all over in a second or two. Look at that, will you?' he said, as if drawing attention to a rarely observed butterfly. 'His ear's been squashed right into the cranial cavity. Crunched through two layers of bone. Hardly credit it, would you? Must have caught him an awful whack.'

apJones grimaced and turned away, peering into the blocked mine along the blind slate tunnel that stretched into the mountain. He called tentatively, 'Hello.' Then again, louder, so that his voice echoed inside, 'Anybody there?'

The doctor glanced over his shoulder cynically. 'If anybody answered you'd poop yourself, man.'

As apJones turned he almost stepped on a discarded pitboot. It had Probert's name indelibly marked inside the neck. He considered it from several angles as it lay twisted and half-buried in the mud. Then examined it, suspended from its back-tab on the end of his finger, before letting it drop back to the ground. He had the curious impression it had been wrenched off.

His eyes narrowed as he traced the route Probert probably took along the side of the lake on his way to the tunnel entrance. It was a routine visit he would be expected to make three or four times a year, to check that no unexpected danger awaited the inexperienced visitor: such as crumbling workings or black waterfilled voids.

But why would he take off a boot? Unless perhaps to tip out some intrusive water the moment before he was hit from behind by the collapsing pit entrance. Then he had staggered twenty-five metres and collapsed.

It didn't seem very likely, and apJones reconsidered. Perhaps Probert was in a hurry, running so hard that the boot was simply sucked off in the ankle-deep marshland. But what was there to run away from at lonely Cwmorthin?

Rhys apJones lifted his gaze slowly around the isolated valley. At the best of times it possessed a beautiful solitude. At others, Cwmorthin was a remote and forbidding place, long forsaken by man.

It would take more than a runaway prisoner to panic a big, domineering man like Probert. apJones returned to the doctor who was kneeling astride the blood-soaked body. 'Could it have been murder?'

The doctor looked over his glasses, and sighed as if to say 'don't be ridiculous'.

'There are men missing from Gwynfa, you know,' said the young policeman. 'And one of them's a killer.'

The doctor still did not respond, other than to take off his glasses and massage his eyes tiredly.

'There'll have to be an inquest, anyway.'

The doctor jotted down some notes and signalled to a nearby constable, who shook out a six foot plastic container ready to seal up the corpse. He winced in some discomfort as he straightened up.

The younger man persisted. 'I suppose the verdict will be misadventure?'

'I imagine so. Seems straightforward enough to me.'

apJones scratched his head. He had enough on his plate

without writing another maybe, maybe-not report for the coroner, yet he was not happy. 'I don't know. He was awfully unlucky.'

'How do you mean?'

'Well, he came all the way up here, to this . . .' the inspector glanced about questioningly before finding an appropriate adjective '. . . godforsaken spot. And then just happened to be standing at a mine entrance that has stood rock-solid for more than a hundred years, only for it to come down on top of him. I'd say that was bloody unlucky, wouldn't you?'

The doctor stuffed his pipe full of foul-looking tobacco and sucked at it once or twice with great relish. 'At least it was quick.'

apJones shook his head. 'I don't know. I've got an odd feeling about this one. I mean, look at the debris. It's almost as if it exploded outwards and yet there's no trace of gunpowder, or any sort of explosive.'

The doctor cast a pained look at the sky and packed up his belongings. 'God save us from policemen with odd feelings. Look, I'll do my best to get you my report by tomorrow evening.' He left apJones to it.

Constable Henry Jarvis was close enough to overhear, and took the opportunity to cough into his hand and disturb the inspector's thoughts as he looked down the valley and into the misty distance of the Vale of Ffestiniog.

'Are you thinking what I'm thinking, sir?'

apJones spread his hands. 'I don't know. What are you thinking?'

The PC's brow furrowed and he lowered his voice. 'I'm thinking that, perhaps, it was suicide.'

apJones retained a bland expression with difficulty. 'You mean, he came all the way up here – trudging miles through the mud and rain – in order to stand under that slate entrance there, and then jumped up and down in a frenzy until he'd butted himself to death?'

The constable hunched his shoulders in embarrassment. 'Well not exactly, sir . . .'

'Look, man. You just do your job. Shove that body in

the bag and let's get it down to Tan-y-grisiau. I'll worry about what to tell the coroner. I'm not so imaginative as you.'

The following day apJones rapped on the huge double-glazed window outside the control room at Ffestiniog power station to attract the attention of the lanky engineer, whose back was turned. The sound was muffled but Casson caught his visitor's reflection in each of a dozen dials on the control panel. He swivelled his high-backed chair, waved acknowledgement and pressed a button. He could operate most of the station doors and machinery by remote control.

apJones took off his sodden topcoat and accepted a cup of stewed coffee with relish. 'Just what I needed, boyoh.'

'Like a biscuit to go with it?'

'A biscuit?' enthused the policeman. 'I'll say.'

Casson produced a round tin of chocolate selections, and apJones dipped in appreciatively. 'You English are so polite, it's bloody painful at times. And to think that, just a few years ago, we used to hang any of you we caught west of Offa's Dyke.'

'Don't let it worry you. We sliced the ears off any Welshman found on our side.'

Casson swivelled his seat in order to adjust one of the controls, glancing up at the clocks registering depth of water, rate of increase and power demand from the grid.

The inspector sipped noisily as he watched, then withdrew the chess wallet from his breast pocket. 'By the way, I've got something for you.' He tossed it on the desk.

'You didn't squelch all the way up here just to drop that in?'

'Ah well, I wanted the pure, undiluted pleasure of saying "check".'

'Check?' Casson reached quickly for the wallet to inspect the latest position of the game. It did not take long, and he sighed.

'What's the matter?' apJones asked innocently as he foraged for another biscuit.

'I can't move.'

'Surely you can?'

'Not without sacrificing my knight.'

'Really?'

Casson gave the policeman an old-fashioned look, snatched back the biscuit tin and closed the lid with an air of permanence.

apJones gave a little laugh. 'Never mind, boyoh, I didn't come here to watch you suffer.' He collected his thoughts for a moment or two and became suddenly quite serious. 'There's something else.'

Casson's calm grey eyes assessed the furrows on the Welshman's forehead. 'Sit down.'

apJones gave a quick, worried smile. 'Actually, I'm a little embarrassed. You see, there's something curious going on and I just can't put my finger on it. Something's wrong. I can sense it right here.' He prodded himself in the pit of the stomach.

'Something to do with the missing prisoners?'

'Could be. See, we've got a body on our hands. A man died violently about a mile or two from here when some old workings apparently collapsed on top of him outside a disused slate mine. The doctor is content about the cause of death. But I'm not so sure. Seems odd that an experienced mine superintendent should get caught like that. It's too soft. Doesn't seem feasible to me. And there's something else. A strange, stealthy sort of atmosphere about the place itself that keeps nagging at me: and saying there's more to it than just an accident.'

'I see.' Casson saw only too well. He crossed to the plate-glass window and looked out at the choppy surface of the lake and the desolate slopes beyond. The ancient land stood gnarled as an old man, unable to move out of the drip-drip-drip of the rain, waiting for night and the chance to rest again. The whole place gave him the shivers. 'Do you have anything more substantial to go on?'

apJones rubbed his face. 'Not really. It's just an inexplicable feeling that something is dreadfully wrong. But I don't know what.'

He stared at Casson hopelessly.

The engineer felt sorry for the young policeman, who would have no senior officer on hand while the area remained cut off; he seemed burdened beyond his years.

'If I can help, just let me know.'

apJones poured himself another coffee and grimaced as he swallowed. 'Actually, I did want to ask if you were out on the mountain yesterday?'

'Yes, I took Hetty out for a run. We were gone about an hour.'

'Ah, well you wouldn't have heard yet about Probert. He was the man we found dead yesterday up past Tan-y-grisiau. In the valley of the Cwmorthin.'

Casson's mouth sagged open in astonishment. 'You mean, near those ruins by the old lake?'

'Yes, hard by the disused slate workings.'

'Good Lord, I was there!'

apJones sat down and gazed at Casson, absorbed. He held the moment together with his hands extended. 'All right, now take it slowly. Did you see anything of him?'

'Well, I'm not sure. I walked the dog around the lower side of the lake at midday, then turned around and jogged back. Mind, there was someone way ahead of me. I saw him climbing the hill about a mile off. Not much more than a blur on the edge of the mist.'

'Probert?'

'I don't know. I couldn't see all that clearly, and it was only for a moment or two.'

apJones grimaced frustratedly and let his attention slip back to a no-man's-land just beyond the rim of his cup. 'Pity.'

Casson glanced up at the megawatt clocks and checked that the four generator shafts were still on spinning reserve. The big oiled shafts hummed in the background, pulsating gently while there was no call for their full power. He swivelled back to face the other man. 'I can't swear to it,' he said slowly and with great concentration, 'but it looked to me like that bloke who hangs about the chapel at Tan-y-grisiau dressed like a ragbag.'

'Dewi?' The policeman got up, as if mesmerized.

Casson nodded. 'He's got a peculiar way of ambling along. Also, I'm pretty sure that whoever it was had on a bowler hat, and there aren't too many of those in the mountains.'

'Look, think carefully. Did you see anything of a woman? Elliyn Pryce-Jones. Any sign of her?'

Casson considered the idea. 'No, just the one rather indistinct man. Why?'

'Oh, nothing. I just wondered, seeing as her and Probert used to walk out together. I know she never really forgave Probert for using her, then marrying someone else.'

'But she's minister of a chapel now.'

'That may be, but chapel people can be as intolerant and hypocritical as all the rest of them put together. It's a harsh life here, see, and it doesn't always do to be too forgiving.'

'She seemed nice enough to me.'

'Oh she's nice enough when it suits. But take my tip, don't antagonize her and turn your back. Probert did and he had scratch marks for years from his shoulders to his arse. Look, all I'm saying is, you watch out for her.'

'Okay.'

Casson accompanied him to the main door and shook his strong, thin hand. 'And just one other thing,' said the inspector. 'Make sure you lock up tight here from now on. If any of those prisoners got through the flood and are still about, they'll be half starved by now. In their state of mind they could do something silly.'

'Thanks a lot,' said Casson derisively. 'You certainly know how to put the wind up me.' He waved apJones off. 'See you soon.'

He liked the Welsh detective. Perhaps it was because they were alike in some ways: both solitary people, content to live within themselves. Rhys apJones went on his way, a narrow figure leaning into the drizzle which had set in with the return of dusk. Darkness enveloped him greedily.

Casson remembered, too late, that he had meant to ask about Webb, the double-killer. How did he kill? It suddenly seemed important to know; especially as Casson was all alone.

A whisper. Like a voice, hoarse with laryngitis, trying painfully to express itself but, in the end, being reduced to a strangled inhalation of breath.

It came from one of the dark creases of a mountain cloaked by night.

No one paid any heed. How could they? There were no human beings for miles in any direction to stop nervously and listen, before hurrying on pale-faced and telling themselves it was simply imagination.

Except that there it was again. A whisper that reached hoarsely down the long slopes to the shadows of gigantic boulders, strewn by time across the mountainside with casual insolence.

These were the Moelwyns: one of the oldest and hardest of the world's rock formations, which dominated a lonely area of north-west Wales. Mountains whose sullen visage had remained unaltered since before man walked the land and would, no doubt, be there long after he vanished.

Night after night there were sounds, until eventually it moved. A great black shadow feeling its way grotesquely through numbed gullies.

When daylight returned and, with it, the passage of birds and the mournful sawing of wind across the waterlogged rust-coloured grass, the movement ceased. But each night brought a reawakening: until in time it became artful enough to move back and forth across the majestic wilderness at will.

Sometimes it signalled its presence with a rasping drawing-in of breath. But always it moved at night. Unseen and, as yet, without direction.

Seven

The peregrine falcon is a deceptive bird. Hunched high on a mountain ledge it can easily be mistaken for a pigeon. That is, if you don't notice its piercing eyes. A natural hood of black feathers covers its head but, otherwise, its colouring is an unobtrusive blue-grey. It sits motionless for long spells, simply watching for any untoward movement. Perhaps a rabbit. Then, with a fierce stretch of its neck and a flap of powerful wings, the peregrine becomes a killer.

Now the compact falcon shows its unrivalled ability: nosing into a dive that will increase its speed to close on one hundred miles an hour, it judges the moment and place of impact with incredible precision. The sight of a peregrine with its wings tucked back in streamlined symmetry is as thrilling as any spectacle of Nature. Hurtling down, it flexes a powerful hind claw which snatches its shocked prey off the ground and lifts it away to oblivion.

Elliyn stood at the bedroom window, luxuriating in the sight, a hairbrush momentarily frozen in her hand. Then smiling in approval she briskly brushed out her long black hair, ignoring the inevitable painful snags caused by her ardent and tangled movements during the night.

'What a beautiful, evil creature you are,' she murmured, caressing the distant predator with words. Behind her, Dewi lay stretched out in the enormous double bed which Elliyn and her late lamented brother had inherited from their parents. They had lived hard and unyielding lives, dedicating their days to the chapel and with nothing to look forward to except the nights.

The bed had a prosperous Edwardian look about it. The walnut headboard was elaborately carved. It gleamed with

French polish and was tautly sprung. She loved it: partly for its vulgar looks but mainly for what it turned her into.

Dewi opened his eyes, assuming that her words were intended for him, and gloated. He enjoyed being thought evil. Those of a nervous disposition were usually either frightened or confused by him. It gave him a feeling of power which in turn made him strut with pleasure, clench his hands until they ached with pain, and yearn for more.

As for his beauty, he gave a crooked smile. There was no doubt that his tumbling hair was blacker than any in the county and his long hands had a sensitive touch that excited her. But the real strength he possessed was as a harbinger of retribution.

'You're attractive too, my leviathan,' he conceded, before being overtaken by an enormous yawn.

Elliyn glanced irritably over her shoulder. 'Shut up.'

'Ummm?' He raised himself on one elbow, stretching his thin legs under the crisp white sheets in which he had come to luxuriate during the last few weeks. Previously he had slept wherever he found shelter when night fell: shivering on the rigid mossy ledge of a cave, or deep in the prickling, itchy hay of an isolated barn. Much more of it and he would have developed permanent rheumatism and shoulders that would never unhunch.

As it was, he had found a haven in her bed just in time.

The peregrine skimmed low across the valley, the furry victim hanging beneath its talons like a limp sack.

'You cruel bastard,' she whispered with subdued pleasure. 'I'd love to fondle your ferocious little body and draw your strength in through the tips of my fingers. And smooth your back. And perhaps even learn your dark secrets.'

Dewi's eyes opened wide behind her. She had been unusually physical the night before and he still ached from the vigour of her responses. At times he had been overwhelmed by her ardour. But now he was rested and ready to be roused once again. After all, it was rare for her to reveal such fervour in the morning. Usually she brushed him brusquely aside, as if the night before had never existed.

He flung back the top sheet to reveal all his rib-thin body. 'Come over here, my beautiful Elliyn. I'll close my eyes and you can stroke away.'

Elliyn wrinkled her large nose in disgust at the ringlets of grime encircling his ankles. She hurled the brush at his unprotected crutch, missing by a hairsbreadth but causing considerable incidental pain.

'Aaah!' he whimpered and scrambled back against the bedhead. 'What did you do that for?'.

'Get up, you hedgehog! Get up and make the bed. And, for pity's sake, give yourself a good brisk scrub.'

'But you said . . .'

'I said get up!' she snapped.

He slid into his bedraggled clothes, resentful and bewildered. No wonder he was beginning to twitch. He didn't know where he stood from one moment to the next. Sometimes in the dark of night she whispered such velvet passionate things into his ear that he barely comprehended. Licking and exploring his sensitive body until he writhed with an ardour that matched even her demands. But it was a passion that she switched off abruptly with the return of daylight. Her growing contempt during the waking hours confused him. She treated him increasingly like a dogsbody.

It was difficult enough trying to cope with the hidden power within him, but she compounded the problem. All he could do was to comply with her demands, whether he understood the reason for them or not.

Few people turned out for chapel that morning. Some were deterred by the weather. Others showed less than a proper respect because a woman had assumed the minister's gown. But most were afraid of the dishevelled man who followed her at a distance and of the curious powers he was said to possess.

There were no more than a dozen on their knees between the pews. The closest of them, a tight-lipped spinster with her hair in a bun, adjusted her short-sighted glasses and waited expectantly. May Thomas never missed a sermon. She lived on a farm with her three cart-horse brothers, cooking badly and mending haphazardly for them ever since their parents had died six years earlier. She dreamed vaguely of better days, based on silver promises from the pulpit.

To one side sat Mr and Mrs Efor Gwyn-Davis, in their nineties and almost blind, helpless without one another. They came shuffling slowly and painfully in and sat in a bemused mole-like state, grateful for the companionship.

One or two others drifted in near the back, sitting well away from Dewi, who was rocking slowly backwards and forwards on his pew, with his hands squeezed together between his legs, ready for the service to begin. Elliyn seemed not at all disturbed by the threadbare congregation. She knew well enough that nine tenths of the straggling community were acutely aware of her presence, and would heed her judgements.

Men in donkey jackets tiptoed in, in steel-rimmed pit boots, shuffling along the rows, and a youth headed towards the harmonium at the front, holding a sheaf of creased music in his hands. The latter settled himself and nodded to Elliyn that he was ready.

There was a prayer which Elliyn spoke resonantly. Then a hymn, 'Rock of Ages', in which she led the mixed voices in her rich contralto, which was deep enough almost to be masculine. She stood wide-legged in the high unadorned pulpit, singing to the rafters. Another hymn and then the announcements. They were chillingly matter-of-fact.

'Last week we talked of Dai-the-lorry who turned his back on our chapel. A man who worked so fervently to better himself . . .' she gave the word a bitter emphasis '. . . that he had no time for worship. No time to spare for the likes of you or me. Too occupied making money out of misfortune.' Her mocking voice rang out across the plain, high-raftered building. 'Too busy also to heed our warning.'

She dropped her eyes. 'Well, for those of you who don't already know, he passed away three days ago.'

'Oh dear, oh dear,' came the little voice of Mrs Gwyn-Davies. 'I do hope it wasn't too painful.'

May Thomas turned with the eagerness of a ferret. 'Can't say, can we? He fell down a gully and broke his back. An awful, dreadful way to die. All alone in an echoing chasm.'

Elliyn glanced maternally down at the two women who seemed absorbed in their own conversation. 'Remember where you are, ladies.'

May Thomas looked up quickly, confiding a final spiteful secret. 'Flung himself down, I heard.'

The elderly woman at the back gave a little whimper, but Elliyn's eyes shone like an avenging angel. 'If any man wilfully turns his back on God, he likewise will find God's back turned on him in the hour of need. Stands to reason, isn't it?'

'Amen!' came the response.

'Let us pray for his soul and that others may learn from his errors. For make no mistake, my friends, many others have erred and need soon to repent if they too are not to be irrevocably chastised.'

The dozen in the congregation bowed their heads and mumbled along behind Elliyn's boldly spoken prayer. All closed their eyes but Dewi. He lolled back, tilting his head and smiling contentedly at the surly clouds through one of the grubby windows. He was not called upon to pray. He had other attributes which would be summoned soon enough.

He was akin to the peregrine falcon: content to sit back in apparent innocence and, for the moment, show no sign of the dangerous hunting creature that he was.

There was still a slipshod grin on Dewi's face as he trudged into Blaenau Ffestiniog that evening, even though he was leaning into a wet wind. His arms were crossed over his thin chest: partly to shield himself from the weather and partly to cover a placard secreted under his jacket.

'Hey!'

He glanced quickly across the narrow high street to where the black-caped figure of Police Constable Henry Jarvis stood, just out of the drizzle, clearly illuminated in the doorway of a carpet shop. 'Hey, you there!'

Dewi looked around. He was the only other figure in sight, but the prospect of facing the flushed, overbearing constable did not appeal to him. He pointed to himself questioningly.

Constable Jarvis moved out to the kerb and waited for one of the last lorries still on the move in Blaenau to swish between them. 'Yes, you. What have you got there, man?'

Dewi feigned bewilderment and stared back along the meagre pavement.

'Under your coat, you dopey bugger,' called the policeman. 'You wait there a minute, I'm coming over.'

The lorry passed between them, sending out a fine spray which forced Henry Jarvis to step swiftly backwards. In its wake a strong gust of wind tugged at his short County Constabulary cape, and swirled a newspaper across the road. The rain seemed to intensify for a few seconds, hissing down into the sloping street and racing impetuously for the drains.

The policeman wiped the water from his face. He had heard whispers that the slovenly youth had a curious power over the weather. Of course, it was absolute rubbish but, on this occasion, it certainly seemed to be on his side!

Dewi's shapeless figure was no longer in sight. Jarvis stared intently both ways along the road, then stood in the middle of the street with his fists on his hips and snorted.

He peered into shop doorways and tried one or two door handles, but it was 6.30 in the evening and all were firmly shut.

Jarvis resented anything odd, just as he frowned on youngsters who wore outlandish clothes and acted in unconventional ways. They were potential trouble-makers. A threat to his orderly mind. He dressed punctiliously each morning, trimmed his toothbrush moustache scrupulously and polished his boots with the brisk fervour of a martinet. He understood discipline and lived by it. Bedraggled youths with impertinent ways made him tug his fingers in frustration until they cracked compliantly.

'You having a game with me?' he asked himself incredulously, looking along the darkened street. 'Because if you are, boyoh, I promise I won't forget you in a hurry.'

Dewi slowed down, breathing hard. He glanced over his shoulder to check for any sign of pursuit, but there was none and he crooned to himself. The night and the sullen weather belonged to him.

He was coming into his own echoing, unseen world like the grey prince he knew himself to be.

None knew what he knew. How could they possibly sense the frightening power that lurked just beyond the edge of reason? Something only his mind could reach out to in the claustrophobic mountains that hemmed in the town?

He trudged along the winding road that led northward from Blaenau, as far as the Winklepicker Club. Its small floodlit car park was well beyond the last row of houses, but it was so alien to the strict-chapel streets and tight-lipped traditions of the area that it might have been a hundred miles away.

It was a seedy place, its entrance outlined by coloured light bulbs. Inside was a long clubroom and bar, with an entrance hall at the front and a few changing rooms tacked on the back. The clubroom was lined with mirrors, edged with strips of glittering chromium. Twenty tables were clustered around a central dance floor.

The owner was a small-time impresario and ex-wrestler named Randy Williams, who ran it as a private club: that is, for anyone who cared to sign in at the door on payment of £1 for life membership.

Wednesdays and Saturdays were gala nights, which meant a cabaret of half a dozen hefty strippers who came over from Harlech. It was far enough away for them to adopt continental names like Zizi and Paris Lil, and not to be recognized as housewives who simply wanted a bit more in their purses.

But on Thursdays Williams held 'special' performances. Top of the bill was Randy himself, described as 'the outstanding male stripper of North Wales'. Before the floods came he had been running a winkle show every week for coachloads of office girls, hairdressers, shop assistants and packers. It was extremely popular and, for the money it attracted, he hired two other local artistes: a couple of butchers from Maentwrog who, after some initial embarrassment, turned out to be naturals.

But since the flooding, business had almost petered out. A turn-out like tonight, with twenty-four bussed in from factories outside Blaenau and most of them on gin-and-It, was a boon and he was as boisterous and full of banter as he could manage.

Williams was getting ready for his first act in a small, brightly lit dressing room when a woman with a cigarette gummed to her lower lip stuck her phlegmatic head around the door. She didn't bother to knock; she ran the till and knew all about Randy's ups and downs.

'You'd better come out front. There's an oddball walking about with a placard. He might put some of the customers off.'

'Eeh?' Williams slipped his arms into a sleeveless scarlet jacket. The buttons of a white silk shirt were open halfway down his hairy chest and a large golden crucifix swung in the gap. 'Tell him to sod off.'

'I did, but he paid no heed. Tell you the truth, I was a bit frightened. He's got a deranged look about him. And when I said it was private property he jabbed the bloody board in my face. Could have knocked my eye out.'

Williams sucked in his stomach and attempted to zip up the front of his impossibly tight, white satin trousers. Hurrying simply caused him to zip his pubic hairs in the process.

'Aaaah!' He gasped in pain and kept his mouth half open until he managed delicately to manoeuvre his flies open again. 'Jesus!' he breathed. 'All right, hang on, girl. I'll see to it. Here, it's nothing to do with that bloody chapel woman pestering me the other day, is it?'

His cashier, who was dimmer than the twenty-watt bulb in her kiosk, shrugged apathetically. 'I don't know. Perhaps.'

Williams disliked showing himself to an audience before the start of his show proper. Not with his gear on. It took the edge off the effect. He preferred to appear first in a dazzling spotlight to a clash of cymbals for maximum impact.

He draped a dressing gown around his shoulders and walked quickly across the clubroom, where a dozen customers had just arrived and were talking in little groups or fidgeting about in handbags before ordering the first drinks.

A wobbly blonde of about thirty-five, on her second visit, spotted him immediately. 'Hello, Randy luv,' she called. 'I'm back like I promised. All the girls wanted a bit when I told them what you were up to.'

Williams reached out and kissed her fingers before examining them momentarily. 'I told you to get those nails cut if you wanted to sit in the front row again,' he said playfully. She squeezed his arm, feeling its fleshy width with an exaggerated smile.

He turned away, bumping into two giggling women and making a meal of hugging them. Then he sucked his breath in noisily. 'I bet you two are a handful together. Do your old men know what you're up to tonight?' he asked. 'No? Well keep your eyes on me, girls, and I'll show you something they never come up with!'

He joked his way to the foyer where the smile faded as the doors swung to behind him. 'Right, where's the joker, Shirley?'

Outside Dewi was standing in his wrinkled jacket, holding up a placard which read, 'Forsake sin! Or HE will surely forsake you!' The club owner was just in time to see the effect Dewi had on a group of four girls, squealing as they scurried in from the rain.

'It's that mad chap from the chapel: the one who plays

about with the weather. Oh, dear God. Do you think he recognized me?'

Williams shepherded them inside. 'It's all right, ladies. Forget that dandelion. You just come in. I've got something better than that to wave in front of you.' He kissed a damp girl in a cardigan and pleated skirt. 'Take your glasses off, luv, if you're going to sit in front. You don't want them knocked off, do you?'

She blushed hotly and was bundled inside by her giggling friends.

Williams scowled out into the drizzle. 'Oi! Come over here, you scruffy object!'

Dewi was watching the road for further arrivals, but turned quickly. His face was masked by shadows. 'You've been warned already,' he called reproachfully in his sing-song voice.

Williams was reluctant to get his satin half-jacket wet. 'Come over here, where I can see you.'

But Dewi was not to be intimidated. 'Elliyn warned you yesterday.'

'Who's she, your wife? Been to one of my shows, has she? And now she wants to know why you kept her on half-rations? That it?'

Dewi seemed not to realize he was being taunted. 'Elliyn is from the chapel, you see. Elliyn Pryce-Jones. She came yesterday, and now she's sent me.'

'Oh yes?' responded the club owner, moving his head to make out Dewi the better. 'And what are you going to do about it? Wag your limp finger at me?'

Dewi stood still and glanced up at the sky, and for a moment the rain eased. Even the perpetually swaying, rustling trees seemed to pause into silence. 'Oh no. I've simply come to tell you that retribution is on the way. Evil begets evil. Sin begets retribution.'

There was something about the eerie, echoing voice that made Williams feel uneasy. Behind him, Shirley the cashier made a nervous half-noise as she cleared her throat.

Williams waved brusquely. 'Get off out of here, before I do you a grievous injury!' He noticed that Shirley had turned as white as a winding sheet. Scared of a half-wit? Williams, who had floored more bone-hard men in the ring than he had ever held lengthy conversations, saw red. He walked menacingly across the road, towards the shadowy lopsided smile.

'Stay here and I'll wrench the head off your scrawny shoulders,' he grated.

Dewi moved back a corresponding distance through a sea of ferns and into the dripping trees. 'I'll bring wrath down on your head,' he called.

Randy Williams made a rush at him but slithered on a polished stretch of leaves and went down on one knee, marring the immaculate whiteness of his cabaret trousers. 'I'll bring my boot down on yours, if I get half a chance,' he roared.

Williams was still swearing sufficiently for his cashier to wince as she tried to erase the last vestige of mud from his satin trousers. She was used to casual profanities, but he really meant it on this occasion: the vehemence showed in the way he clenched and unclenched his sledgehammer fists.

But a double gin calmed him down and, by the time the audience had been warmed up with a medley sing-song, a grin had returned to his broad face.

Shirley announced him from a microphone with a trailing lead, and some thirty young women cheered shrilly and drummed their heels in anticipation.

Throbbing music assaulted their ears to the tune of 'The Stripper'. Then Randy arrived: thrusting a bare hairy arm out from behind a curtain and flexing his considerable biceps to squeals of encouragement, then spinning into frontal view fully dressed. A spotlight picked out a thousand sequins on his clothes.

He began to dance, slowly at first, in time to the suggestive music. Gyrating hips propelled him forward in rhythmic thrusts. Nobody had time to look at his weather-beaten face; all their attention was on his jutting suggestive movements. The room was filled with noise. Music, clapping, hysterical laughter from breathless girls and some shrill wolf whistles.

Whenever he prowled towards the girls they shrieked with delight. He sat on a freckled girl's lap, and slid her hand slowly down inside his shirt-front. Deep down. She threw her head back with an expression of tortured pleasure, as much to entertain her friends as herself. But when he thrust the rest of her arm on down to his abdomen her mouth popped open in frozen surprise.

Nobody escaped his attention, and they loved it.

He stuck out his tongue long enough for them all to see, then inserted it in the ear of a girl who sat shuddering with laughter. He stood pressing his stomach and thighs into the face of another, ruffling her hair extravagantly and directing her face wherever he wanted it.

The women did not know where to look. They covered their eyes, only to stare with shocked delight through the bars of their fingers; they turned their backs but immediately peered over their shoulders so as not to miss a second.

Now he was ready to divest himself of some of the clothes. He jumped up on a chair and slid the jacket off provocatively. He twirled the item around his head and let go, so that it sailed into the audience. A large girl in a small striped dress caught it and buried her face into it, kissing the aroma voraciously.

He stripped off his shirt, flinging it into the gloom beyond the spotlight and then embraced an eager woman with an elfin haircut so ardently that her chair went over backwards.

Nobody minded them threshing on the floor, but there was uproar as others tried to see what was going on before he bounced back to his feet. Hands reached out from all sides, clutching at him.

He pulled one into the pool of light where she was transfixed while he wound his leg around her, snakelike, then unzipped her dress down the back to reveal a Marks and Spencer brassier size 36C. But almost immediately he relinquished his hold and pranced back into the centre of the floor.

He needed to shout to make himself heard over the thudding music. 'Two volunteers to help me undress. Come on!' He held up an appropriate number of fingers. 'Who's it to be? Come on, girls, for the chance of your lifetime.'

Two women were pushed, doubled up with laughter, from the security of the tables and Randy blindfolded them with chiffon scarves before directing their hands to work on him.

First they had to unfasten his thick leather belt and unzip the tight front, while he screwed up his face in imagined ecstasy. Then he got them to kneel down and gave each of them a trouser leg to tug down.

As the trousers slipped down over his hips the light went out to shrieks of protest. But when the spot came on again he was standing, legs splayed, clutching a hand of each woman over his private parts. Other than that, he was naked.

There was pandemonium, and he shouted to his two volunteers: 'How are you feeling, girls?' Then, flinging their hands apart, he revealed a silver G-string and dangling pouch.

A few moments later the G-string was discarded and he was waggling his big white bottom at them. Most of the girls were cheering themselves hoarse and one or two were on their feet shouting incoherent advice.

Naked at last, he advanced with wicked intent on the circle of females, one of whom seemed literally to be wetting herself with laughter.

'Make the most of me, you gorgeous creatures. It's first come, first served!'

Hands shot out even though their owners turned away and covered their eyes. The room shook with laughter and shrill screams.

Outside in the cold of the night Dewi stood listening intently.

Gusts of noise reached out and stirred dead leaves in an uncomfortable shuffle around his feet. There was something malevolent about the smile that spread slowly across his face. Pleasure to come.

After a while he turned and walked away up the hillside. The sky ahead was dark grey but, by staring hard, he could pick out the darker intensity of Snowdon herself.

He gave the diminishing clubhouse and discordant sounds a final glassy smile. I'll be back soon enough, he promised. But I won't be alone.

Eight

It was well after 11 p.m. when Randy Williams cut the engine of his big white Rover and glided to a halt outside the huddled row of miners' houses on the road to Betws-y-Coed. Billie Lewis, a shapely twelve stone blonde who had borne three children and who had the capacity for beer and bad language of a Cardiff docker, placed a restraining hand on his thigh. Her giggles died away with the motor.

'Oh God, I think he's back early. The light's on in the scullery.'

Williams mouthed a word not to be found in any self-respecting dictionary. 'But you said he never gets back from darts till midnight.'

She quickly produced a compact with a round mirror in the lid and stretched her lips in all directions, examining herself for obvious signs of male interference. 'Sorry, darling. You'll just have to keep the lid on your kettle tonight.' She patted the inside of his leg by way of consolation.

'Bugger me,' sulked the club owner, who had invested almost a bottle of gin on priming her. Talk about leading him on, then slamming a door in his face! He wouldn't mind so much if she seemed frustrated. But she was so bloody matter-of-fact about it.

He pulled the car door shut with ill-grace and revved up

noisily, little caring if it brought her husband to the window. Serve the bitch right.

He twisted the saloon into a tight turn and accelerated angrily back towards Blaenau Ffestiniog: eight miles to the south, including a plunge through a sheet of water well over two feet deep which drowned the road and made it inaccessible to all but reckless club owners intent on getting a bit on the side.

He was back at the club within ten minutes. He switched off the engine outside the club and the night closed in silently around him. Shivering slightly he locked the car door and slipped the keys into his pocket. The wind had died away and the rain had stopped. It was as if Nature was drawing a deep breath before deciding what to do next.

He glanced right and left before unlocking the main door.

His footsteps echoed across the dance floor, faintly lit by a half-obscured moon. He could even hear himself breathing. Odd. A faint prickling sensation began at the back of his neck and spread across his shoulders.

When the wind started up again it did so with a rush, and he jerked around. One moment there was silence. The next there was a moaning gust of icy air that swept down the unseen mountain and rattled doors. Close behind it came a more persistent force that jarred windows on their latches and banged for admittance. Within less than a minute it had developed a frightening intensity.

Williams ran into the kitchen, flicking on a light, and stared out of the window. At first he could make out only his own anxious reflection but then, beyond it, a line of sturdy elms bending under the force of the gale. Naked autumn branches streamed and flailed. Outriders of rain lashed obliquely down, harrying the dark countryside as they approached, and now drummed feverishly on the roof. The power behind its fall dissolved the rain into hissing spray which reared up several feet and almost obscured the building.

Williams pulled back, alarmed to the edge of panic. He was not a timid man; far from it. He had inherited a sense of truculence that had never before let him down in a tight physical situation. But this was different; it touched an unknown depth of fear.

As the storm raged, several slates lost their grip and slid down the roof: clattering and cartwheeling before smashing on the concrete forecourt. A door banged open and shut before an outraged force.

'That you, Sylveee?' he called, more in desperation than expectation.

A window pane split with an abrupt crack that made him jerk around. Another dissolved in a spider's web of pressure. Glass sprayed his trousers as more windows gave in to the raging wind.

Curtains flapped and snapped past his head in disarray, and a pelmet collapsed, just missing him.

The night had gone mad. He couldn't believe it was actually happening, even though his eyes were wide with shock. He stumbled against the piano, but there, at least, he found a pocket of shelter in which to huddle between the glossy 'T.G. Paine of London' upright and the wall.

There he might have remained until the storm abated, except that the back door was going wild, banging as if to escape from a maniacal pursuer.

He drew a deep breath, summoning a reserve of shuddering determination, and blundered through a scenery-and-storeroom at the back of the hall. He fumbled unsuccessfully for the lights and fell over an upturned chair, badly bruising his leg. In a haze of pain he kicked the chair unmercifully, venting his rage on something he could comprehend.

However, it was the adjoining kitchen that was almost his downfall. As he felt his way in, a high Welsh dresser toppled hugely across the darkened room. The crash broke several floorboards and he only narrowly escaped being crushed.

'Jesus Christ,' he moaned, stumbling over debris towards the banging door. His lips were gritty with a substance that tasted like custard powder: plaster dust from the ceiling.

He dragged the door shut – more easily than he expected now that the wind was dropping – but it sagged where the top hinge was torn from its frame. Through the triangular gap he was able to gaze dazedly at the persistent rain. Overhead the moon made a brief, scurrying appearance between the clouds. But it provided a glimpse of the road and a distant line of huge pylons which carried threshing overhead power cables south-east towards England.

Something in the wild night, in the other direction towards the satanic mountains, caught his attention. It was something moving towards the club. Perhaps somebody was coming to help.

He peered out into the gusting rain, straining to make out a shape. But whatever it was had already been obscured from view.

The club was a shambles. He tried the lights several times but the power had gone. Swearing did not help any more. Wherever he moved there was upended furniture and the crunch of broken glass.

He measured the distance from the back door to his car. If he could reach it, he could be on his way home.

There it was again!

A movement from the edge of his perception. Something swaying forward, detaching itself from the dense shadows of the mountains and moving against the lighter background of the sky.

He stared hard, concentrating on identifying whatever was approaching, but could not make it out. Yet now the whole building creaked ominously around him. He stared fearfully up into the rafters. It was not an old building but for a moment it seemed moved by a giant hand.

Animal fear stung up through his nostrils and brought tears to his eyes. He was trapped. He had to get out! He began stumbling into walls and doorposts and a trickle of blood worked its way down from the corner of his mouth.

One moment the moon was clear; the next it was obscured. The building gave a prolonged groan, as if it had been pushed sideways several metres on its foundations. Pictures fell from walls, lights from ceilings. It could not survive another such movement without the roof splitting open and brickwork caving in.

Randy Williams made for his car, the tail of his silk shirt flapping. He ran blindly through the downpour and across concrete that danced to the blurred drumsticks of rain. He fumbled frantically with the car door.

Then he stopped, and cowered. Some people experience moments in their lives when, without seeing a soul, they are suddenly and acutely aware that they are not alone. This was one such moment. As numbed rainwater seeped down inside his collar, dribbled along his arms and into his squelching shoes, he found that his legs would not move. Rigidity set in. It was an instinctive last line of animal defence.

For a while nothing else happened except that he grew cold, so very cold. The last thing on earth he wanted was to discover what was behind him. But the same fear that rooted him to the spot also forced him to face the inevitable.

His mesmerized gaze slowly left the car and, as he turned, his mouth opened and shut with little inarticulate fishlike movements.

They discovered Randy Williams the next day in what remained of his Rover 3000. He was trapped so tightly inside that, although the vehicle was discovered by a farm labourer at 7.30 in the morning, it took three men until mid-afternoon to prise him out.

Inspector apJones contemplated the wreckage with a pained expression, then turned away. He listened while Constable Henry Jarvis licked his stubby pencil and read out some notes from his pocket book.

'Must have been drinking, sir. Bloody hard, too, because he could take a pint or two in the normal way of things.'

'Why do you say that?'

'Stands to reason. First, why would he be out in the middle of a freak storm unless he was half-cut and lacking proper judgement? And, second, he must have been doing seventy when he came through here, yet there's no sign of any skid before impact.'

apJones could not deny it. His narrowed eyes followed the line the Rover would have taken when it veered off the road, across the concrete approach and straight into the back of the club, burying itself almost out of sight in masonry, splintered planks and collapsed window frames.

The car's long bonnet had concertinaed back on to the front seats, and one end of the front axle was twisted like spaghetti.

apJones chewed his lower lip while he looked at the buckled dashboard where the driver's head had rammed it. He noticed though that the sight did not seem to affect Constable Jarvis who peered inside with some relish.

'It's lucky he'd dropped his passenger off.'

'What passenger?'

'Well,' Jarvis confided with a discreet cough, 'he always took home a woman after one of his cabarets. It's a bit of glamour in their lives, see: walking out with the star of the show.'

apJones grunted and walked around the car. 'Know where he'd been?'

'Yes, sir. The club cashier says he took home Mrs Lewis from up near Bettws-y-Coed. You know,' he cupped his hands expressively ' . . . the one with the big assets.'

apJones pursed his lips. 'That big?'

'Oh, at least. She's famous around Bettws-y-Coed for her titties.'

'All right. You'd better get up there on your bike and have words.'

'Right, sir.'

Jarvis looped an elastic band around his notebook and slipped it back into his rear trouser pocket. He moistened his lips at the prospect of interviewing Billie Lewis. The flighty bitch wouldn't know yet what had happened to Williams. He'd enjoy bringing her down a peg or two.

apJones stayed on at the scene of the carnage for a while. It didn't make sense, but then nothing made sense to him these days. Perhaps he was in the wrong job.

He glanced at the mountains brooding silently in the distance. The circumstances of the accident left him feeling curiously uneasy, but the surroundings bore an air of impenetrable calm and told him nothing.

There was little further to be learned here. He turned up his coat collar and rubbed his arms. It would be night again soon.

Within a few hours the inspector was at the power station: off duty and as relaxed as a policeman can be. He stretched his legs out from a sagging leather armchair in Casson's snug quarters, and contemplated the chess board.

Casson, resting his chin on his hands, watched him. apJones was steadier in temperament than his twenty-six years might suggest. Somebody had made a wise choice when they picked him out at the promotion board.

The telephone jangled and the two men exchanged pained expressions before Casson lifted the receiver.

'Hello.'

It was Jarvis from the police station. 'Is the inspector there, sir?'

'Yes, he is. Hang on.'

apJones took over. 'Uh-huh?'

'Evening, sir. We've just had word from Meadows, up at Stonehill Farm, that someone's hiding in his hay barn. He saw a man weaving down the high ground a bit earlier. I think it's got the makings.'

The inspector was suddenly alert. 'Webb?'

'Don't know. But the same thought occurred to me.'

'We'd better get up there right away. Who's on duty with you?'

'Harmon, sir.'

'Right. I'll want you both. Lock up the station and bring a shotgun. I'll meet you in front of Meadows' place in . . .' he consulted his watch ' . . . ten minutes.'

'Doesn't give us much time, sir.'

'It's too dangerous to leave him any longer. And don't let Harmon hang back to comb his hair. Oh and, Jarvis, warn Division what we're up to.'

He put the phone back on its cradle and swiftly folded his trouser bottoms into his long socks. 'I've got to go.

One of the Gwynfa prisoners could be in a barn about a mile from here.'

Casson was already up and reaching for his own coat. 'I'll drive you in my car.'

'You don't need to get involved. If it's Arnold Webb, he won't like the intrusion. Won't be grateful.'

'I won't get in your way. Anything you want me to take along? We've got plenty of stuff here.'

'All right: a torch, some rope and something heavy to protect yourself with.'

'I've got an old golf club. Will that do?'

apJones nodded. 'Make it a driver. He's a big bugger.'

'Right,' gulped Casson. 'By the way, he killed two people, didn't he?'

'Yes, with a pick-axe. Here, you all right? You look awfully pale.'

Casson meant to say 'Fine', but nothing came out. He nodded instead. Much to Hetty's disgust they left her at the power station, and accelerated into the night accompanied by her barks of indignation. Quite soon they left the road and bumped on to a cart track which was treacherous with mud. Casson was unable to prevent the car slithering several times before they reached the two uniformed constables.

There was hardly any moon and a wind prowled restlessly across waterlogged fields, but for once the rain held off. Elwyn Meadows came out of the farm to meet them and whispered to the police, pointing and gesticulating while Casson hopped from one foot to the other, partly to keep warm and partly to cover his anxiety. When he had decided to come he had barely considered confronting a big mentally deficient prisoner who might rush murderously in his direction. He renewed his grip on the battered golf club that tourists had left behind at the power station the previous year and swung it in a reassuring arc. The swish of displaced air bolstered his confidence.

Casson and the equally apprehensive Constable Harmon were despatched around the back of the ramshackle barn, while the inspector led Jarvis and the elderly farmer towards squeaky double doors at the front.

Jarvis did some running on the spot and swung his arms like windmills, warming up with a determination that whoever was inside would come off worse than him. Indeed, when apJones dragged open the quivering wooden doors, the red-faced constable burst in shouting at the top of his lungs.

Bat shadows disintegrated in all directions, swooping and wheeling in confused squadrons and blinding them momentarily. A moment or two later there was an upheaval of hay on a ledge at the back of the dust-filled barn.

Casson knelt on one knee oblivious to the damp which seeped through his trousers, relieved that he was not involved. There was muffled shouting and grunting, then the farmer appeared and called them in.

Harmon was even less enthusiastic than Casson but, when they got into the barn, everybody else seemed comparatively relaxed.

'False alarm,' grinned apJones. 'Not a pike in sight. Only minnow.'

Casson could see Jarvis kneeling aggressively on the chest of a spreadeagled suspect. A writhing body was illuminated by the light of a torch. The eyes that blinked with pain seemed familiar, and a mass of unkempt hair confirmed it. Dewi.

'Don't hurt him, man,' somebody said.

Jarvis bristled. 'If you ask me, he deserves a bloody good going-over.' He took a handful of eccentrically overgrown hair and tugged the head into view. 'What the devil are you doing here, maggot?'

Dewi gave a distressed sob. 'Been up the mountain, haven't I.'

apJones joined the circle of dull yellow light. 'What, in the middle of the night?'

Dewi's eyes watered with pain. 'It's the best time to go. It's when things happen.'

Jarvis growled in his ear. 'Don't talk foolish. There are educated people here.'

'All right, Constable.' apJones leaned over their prisoner. 'You're soaked. How long were you roaming around up there?'

Dewi shrugged haphazardly.

'Did you see anybody?' persisted the inspector.

The eyes became slits. 'Up there? In the dark?' His head shook vigorously.

'You haven't been up to your old tricks, frightening people, have you?'

'Oh no. I'm a deacon now. I'm respectable.'

apJones straightened up and said quietly to Casson, 'Look, thanks for helping out. Perhaps it's just as well we didn't find anybody.'

Dewi made a funny gurgling noise as if the pressure on his chest was obstructing his breathing.

'Stop panting like a little girl,' said Jarvis, 'or I'll really give you something to think about. Shall I take him back to the station for a statement, sir?'

'Yes, please. But go easy.' He tapped his head. 'Give him a bed in an open cell. It'll give his clothes a chance to dry out.'

Later, as Casson strapped himself into the car, he heard the bedraggled Welshman yelp as Jarvis marched him off on tiptoes with his arm bent up behind.

'You'd best let me go,' Dewi whined. 'Or you'll regret it later, Mr Henry Jarvis.'

'Don't you Henry Jarvis me, you barmy bugger.'

There were several little gasps of pain as Dewi was directed back down towards the police station, too occupied now to threaten his tormentor any further.

Casson slipped the car into gear and the vehicle bumped slowly back towards the road. 'Poor sod.'

apJones was deep in thought, gnawing the side of his hand. 'I've got a nasty feeling in the pit of my stomach.'

'Well, he's your constable.'

'No, nothing to do with that. It's been there several days and it just won't go away. A premonition.'

Casson forced a smile. 'Oh, that again.'

The inspector responded with a tight grin that deceived neither of them. His feeling of deep unease was instinctive, but in this part of the world he had learned to heed his instincts.

Dewi was too exhausted to protest when pushed into a cell and the steel door was locked. It was not supposed to happen, but Constable Henry Jarvis had an extremely short fuse and he was furious at being called out in the middle of the night on a wild goose chase that left his normally immaculate black trousers and duty boots caked with mud.

A few minutes later the bull-necked policeman banged open the cell door and dumped a bucket of water and a scrubbing brush inside, crashing his boots down beside them. 'Clean these!' he snapped. 'And don't let up until you can see your ugly face in them. There's shoe polish in that cupboard. Got it?'

Jarvis had some supper, warmed his feet in front of a stove and returned to the cold cell after half an hour. Dewi, who was huddled in a corner, gave him an idiotic smile.

'Well? Finished my boots?'

The ragged Welshman nodded towards the bucket, and Jarvis was thunderstruck when he peered inside. His boots were submerged in water.

He kicked the bucket over, so that a muddy tide washed Dewi even further into his corner. The policeman's face was masked by a ferocious smile. 'Oh, I see. You're a comedian too, are you?' His hands were clenched and the veins stood out in his stocky arms.

'I want to go home now.' Dewi avoided the malice in the policeman's eyes.

'So you shall,' purred Jarvis. 'Just as soon as we get you smartened up. After all the trouble you've taken, giving my best boots a soaking, I'd like to do something for you. So take your clothes off, boyoh.'

Dewi was a frail youth, with only the sinewy strength he had developed from wandering about the mountains. Not that he would have stood much chance against the heavy-bottomed policeman at the best of times. He pressed back into the wall. 'What do you mean?'

'You heard me! Take your clothes off!' roared Jarvis.

'What for?'

The policeman cuffed his ear, knocking him off his knees, and Dewi rolled into a protective ball, burying his head into his chest. He started quietly to sob.

Jarvis was not to be deterred. In fact the very act of submission seemed to incense him, and he snatched the back of Dewi's shirt collar and jerked it towards him. In a few savage movements he had ripped the garment off the heaving shoulders and flung it aside. Underneath was a pathetic grey vest.

'Ooh? We wear woolly underclothes, do we? I suppose you got it from the Rev. Pryce-Jones's wardrobe? That right?'

He took a handful of hair and lifted Dewi's head for a reaction, then let it drop. ''Course you did. You've got the run of the place now, haven't you?'

He yanked at the vest but it refused to tear, and he snarled in frustration: dragging the groaning Welshman halfway around the cell before it pulled over his prisoner's head.

Dewi scrambled back into the corner, covering his chest with skinny inadequate arms. 'Leave me alone,' he panted. 'You'll be sorry if you don't. They've all been sorry when it's too late.'

Jarvis was breathing hard with exertion. 'I'll be sorry, will I?' he exclaimed, standing back and feigning surprise. 'Well, that's a stunner. But in the meantime you'd better get your bloody trousers down, boyoh.'

'I want to go home.'

The policeman leered down at his spindly victim. 'Plenty of time for that later.' He tore open the flies that protected Dewi's manhood. Buttons snapped off worn thread and as Dewi tried to stand up in haste, the shapeless trousers pleated down around his ankles.

Jarvis roared with delight, grabbed the turn-ups and yanked him around the cell in sweeping circles. Dewi clung to what remained of his clothes and pride, sobbing with despair as he was dragged about on his raw back.

Eventually, when Jarvis paused to rest and laugh derisively, Dewi scrambled to his feet; his matchstick-white legs wearing only an incongruous pair of black shoes. He covered his delicate, bushy black pubic hair with cupped hands.

'What do you want with me?' he asked desperately.

'You'll see,' panted Jarvis. 'Wait there a minute.' He backed out of the cell, holding up a restraining hand, and after a while there was a distant clanking and rattle. He reappeared dragging the brass nozzle of a thick canvas hose, which he aimed at Dewi's chest.

'Now, let's try and make up for all those little washes you've missed over the years, and get rid of some of that obnoxious grime. All right?'

Water pulsed down the thick tube and the nozzle came alive in his hands. A heavy jet of water hit Dewi with the kick of a horse. He was flung back against the wall with a thud that knocked all the breath from his body while a hissing spume of water hammered his mouth and nostrils and swam through his hair. In a few seconds he was both stunned and half drowned.

Jarvis seemed to lose all control, braying with laughter and spraying the whole cell with the exploding stream of water so that soon everything in sight, including himself, was soaked. Dewi was buffeted along the wall. There was no escape. Either he was directly assaulted or water fizzed off the walls in a fine, continuous spray.

Ironically, the final degradation was the least effective of all. Dewi was too far gone. Jarvis took a fresh grip on his hair, pulled the thin man up on to his bottom, and set to work enthusiastically scrubbing him with a long-handled brush and bar of green carbolic soap.

Harsh bristles raked cruelly across Dewi's back and thighs. Angry little weals burned his skin, but he was beyond tears. After a while the only sound was Jarvis's laboured breathing as he sawed obsessively with the scrubbing brush.

At last he was satisfied. He slopped the contents of the

bucket over Dewi for the last time, then fell back on the cell bed, grinning dementedly.

After a while Dewi became aware of the silence, blinked once or twice and sat up cautiously, leaning his weight on one hand. He seemed dazed and, when he swayed upright as if to go home, Jarvis pulled a grey blanket off the bed. 'Take this,' he ordered gruffly.

Dewi trailed to the door of the isolated police station but, once outside in the grey light of the pre-dawn, he dropped the blanket and walked unsteadily away.

He looked back from a long way off and saw Jarvis standing tiredly in the doorway. As the feeling returned to his arms and back, they began to smart agonizingly. He winced up at the massive Druidical shape of the mountain ahead.

'Surely you're not going to let them get away with it?' he whispered.

Nine

Casson sat up late into the night. He knew he would not sleep, and left all the lights on so that the interior of the power station was as bright as day. Outside, the reflection of the lights glowed off the still waters of Tan-y-grisiau reservoir.

Hetty frisked about with a rubber rat in her mouth and nudged Casson continually until he gave in and hurled it the length of the turbine hall. The boxer bounded after the toy with such zest that, on catching up with it, she skidded past the resilient rat and had to scramble back a few feet to snatch it up in her jaws. Then she loped back along the hall, ears flat and hind quarters wriggling with delight for Casson to wrestle the rat free and hurl it into the distance again.

There was plenty of room in the big hall which contained the top section of each of four vertical-shaft machines that did the work of Ffestiniog power station – pumping and generating in turn – and which reached down, through four basement floors, to bedrock. Along one long wall were panels of switch gear and, overhead, two hundred-ton roof cranes.

The sleek animal reappeared, wagging her stumpy tail. It was a game of which she never tired. But eventually Casson gave her silky ears a rub and returned to his snuggery. There the chess board awaited him.

He took off his shoes and fitted on equally gargantuan carpet slippers. Hetty, sensing another game, tried to take one in her soft jaws but he pushed her affectionately away.

'You'd have the shirt off my back if I gave you half a chance.'

The boxer did not deny it. She simply wagged her tail eagerly.

Casson circled the room, contemplating the chess board from afar as if the challenge it presented really had nothing to do with him. He fingered his chin thoughtfully. The policeman had left him pretty well tied up after half a dozen swashbuckling moves, but Casson was not too concerned. The faster a man moves the more likely he is to stumble. He had the patience to wait for a half-chance.

His hand rasped across his chin. He needed a shave, and that meant it was not far off dawn. He made a cup of scalding coffee and sipped it noisily, because that was the best way not to burn his tongue, while Hetty looked up expectantly. Their eyes met.

'What are you staring at? Haven't you seen me in a tight spot before?'

Hetty blinked her great brown, forthright eyes and readjusted the weight on her forepaws.

Casson grimaced at the chess board. 'Look, it's not that bad. I'll think of something. Just give me time. At worst I could accidentally knock the board over. Right?'

He scratched his head and crossed to a bookshelf. The selection included one or two chess volumes left by a predecessor with time on his hands. Casson took one down and flicked through the diagrams of master moves, but nothing remotely resembled the predicament he was in. Eventually, his attention was drawn back to Hetty, who was still watching him intently.

'All right, all right. I'm only looking at a few examples. There's nothing wrong in that, is there?' He returned the book primly to its shelf.

After that he drummed his fingers for some time before making a move. King's pawn to . . . For a while he hesitated, then finally made the move with jaw-clenching resolution.

Casson looked at Hetty with an air of smug satisfaction. There! he thought. That should do it.

The dog looked doubtful, and Casson raised his eyebrows questioningly. 'No?' But Hetty got up and made tight circles, wagging her tail.

'Good girl,' said the lanky engineer, rewarding her with brisk patting. 'I think we've got him by the short and curlies this time.'

Casson was still feeling pleased with himself when he made a final check of plant equipment and climbed into bed. Hetty jumped up beside him, snorting contentedly as she settled her weight against his legs. Casson sighed, gave up some space to the heavy-jowled dog and closed his eyes.

It was late morning by the time he had washed and eaten. There was not much to do in the power station, so he copied the chess move into his wallet set and summoned Hetty back from a distant administrative area where she had been snuffling and pawing. He let himself out by a side door and set off across the hillside for the police station, whistling.

It was a dry chilly morning and he stepped out briskly in the bracing air while Hetty ranged ahead over rocks and through stretches of decaying fern.

Within five minutes he reached a road that wound down to the isolated police house. Quite why the authorities felt it necessary to build a station there, a mile outside town, was puzzling. Except that perhaps it marked the boundary between two parishes.

A line of telephone poles led down towards the modest police house and marched beyond it towards distant hills. There was no sound but the abrasive wind grazing the slopes.

Hetty stuffed her head into a dark hole which probably once sheltered a lumbering badger and did not respond to his calls for some time. When she scampered to catch up, she did so in a sweeping arc, through fern and heather, and shaking off a great spray of water when she arrived.

Casson held her collar and turned his face away. 'You odious dog,' he spluttered.

There was now time to glance down at the little police house. It was unusually quiet. No sign of movement and, curiously, no wildlife to be seen or heard in the vicinity. Hetty caught his mood and sniffed inquisitively. Together they approached the whitewashed building and the closer he got, the more Casson felt uneasy. His steps faltered and he came to a stop. He felt foolish. It was broad daylight. But the feeling persisted.

He made a conscious effort to shake off his mood and swallowed hard.

'Hey,' he called. 'Anybody about?'

The words echoed emptily through the house and, without knowing why, he glanced quickly over his shoulder at the surrounding hills as if he half-expected something to have stolen up unseen. His eyes slowly traversed a distant fringe of grassy hilltop, stirring faintly under the coughing wind, but there was no one in sight.

The house itself was possessed by silence. The place seemed almost hostile, warning him not to go inside. The feeling was so intense that for a moment he felt his head was being held under water and his senses distorted.

Hetty whined, and that was enough to bring Casson back to reality. He rang the shrill bell, knowing there would be no answer and then pushed open the front door apprehensively.

Halfway down the narrow hall there was a long dark

smear on the wall. He touched it gingerly and sniffed his fingers none the wiser.

'Hello. Hello there.' His voice echoed ahead, up the bare stairs, without drawing a response. He edged into an open area containing a reception desk and, beyond it, the duty room. The disorder that met his eyes was unexpected but a peculiar stillness persisted and he did not react because of it.

The duty desk lay on its back, smashed by some unimaginable weight. A discordant trail of papers and files led back to a small kitchen where a half-glass door was shattered and hanging from a single screw. It appeared as if someone had been hurled bodily against it.

Casson picked his way cautiously through the wreckage, hardly breathing, and ventured up creaking stairs. A single bed had been slept in; its covers were thrown back and there was one slipper in the middle of the floor. But no sign of apJones or his two constables.

Casson stood paralysed with fear when a stair creaked outside, but it was only Hetty nosing her way in to find him. He went downstairs and lifted the phone. No dialling tone; nothing.

The air was oppressively close and he tugged open the neck of his shirt the better to breathe. He had to get outside for some fresh air and was thankful for the excuse.

His feet covered the distance to the top of a nearby slope more rapidly than he could have imagined. He brushed the hair out of his eyes, aware that his hand was trembling.

Damn! He had forgotten to leave the chess wallet for apJones! It was silly not to. After all, there still might be a logical explanation for the confusion.

Now that he was well clear of the house he felt foolish about his fears. The three policemen were almost certainly out searching for the prisoner from Gwynfa.

He considered returning guardedly down the hill and tossing the wallet in through the front door, but something inside screamed silently at him not to do it.

Don't go back there! it pleaded. There was no arguing. He shuddered with relief and returned to the power station.

It was noon now. He had plenty to do: routine checks on equipment and water levels. But his mind kept returning to the three policemen and what had become of them. He couldn't just leave the matter there. Every few minutes he found himself squeezing his hands so tightly that they felt bruised.

Finally he grabbed his heavy jacket, whistled to Hetty and let himself out. He'd go out of his mind if he stayed by himself much longer. Somebody must know something.

It was not far to the temperance chapel and if anybody knew what was going on, it would be Elliyn Pryce-Jones. Her congregation stretched thinly for miles in all directions and what they did not confide to her in whispers she could surmise after a lifetime in the shadow of second-sighted Snowdon.

She was standing in the pulpit when he arrived at the otherwise empty chapel: an imposing woman in a black high-necked blouse and trailing dress, slowly turning the gnarled pages of a massive bible. She smiled at him. A knowing smile.

'Hope I'm not disturbing you.'

'No, come in. I was expecting you.'

He ventured down the aisle, then turned to wave Hetty back. 'Outside! Go on out.'

Elliyn Pryce-Jones closed the weighty bible with a subdued thud and came down from the pulpit. 'Don't send your bitch away,' she said reproachfully. 'You can stay in here, girl. We're all God's creatures.' Hetty swallowed submissively and settled down near the door.

Casson was curious. 'You were expecting me?'

She contemplated him from the bottom step. 'I sometimes have premonitions.'

Casson's forehead wrinkled. 'You too? I didn't know I was coming myself until ten minutes ago.'

'It doesn't take long. Whenever I feel something specific is about to happen, then invariably it does. It's not very frequent but, when I feel it, it's usually with iron-hard certainty.'

Casson changed his weight from one leg to the other. 'I

don't think I believe in things like that. Perhaps you're just a good guesser.'

She did not argue the point. 'Perhaps.'

She moved towards the far door with surprising grace for such an awkwardly built woman. He was fascinated by her plainness, so common-place it almost made her riveting. He regarded her long enough for him suddenly to be aware that it had become obvious.

'You wanted to ask me something?'

'Yes. I'm having trouble finding a policeman.'

'Which one?'

'Any one. I've been looking all morning. There's no sign of them.'

'All morning? Must be important.'

He shrugged self-consciously. 'Well, sort of.'

She came closer. He felt stunned by her eyes, a strong mesmeric gaze that tried to dominate him. Then she let go.

'Don't worry. I saw them a couple of hours ago on their way to the Beddgelert Forest; that's past Beddgelert on the Caernarfon road.'

Casson felt a rush of relief. 'Are you sure?'

'Of course I'm sure.'

'Thank heaven for that,' he croaked. 'I had an unpleasant feeling that something had happened to them.'

She took his hand and gently squeezed it between her own strong palms. 'Don't let your imagination get the better of you. Engineers are supposed to keep their feet on the ground, aren't they?'

She led him to a pew where they sat and talked for several minutes: about the local power supply which she said was behaving erratically, and how much the more isolated families relied upon it. She asked if in future he would work much more closely with the chapel, which was the mainspring of the community.

Occasionally she touched his arm or hand to emphasize a point. At first he shifted fractionally away, but her eyes concentrated on him with a disturbing frankness and he began to enjoy it.

'You're all alone at the power station, aren't you?'

'No. Hetty keeps me company.'

She ignored the point. 'Not good for a man in the prime of life to live alone. God created woman for a reason, you know.' Again her fingers searched for his hand.

His mouth felt dry, and a disbelieving voice inside asked: Is she giving me the come-on? In church?

They were interrupted by the tortured creak of the church door opening wide enough to allow Hetty to wriggle out. A moment later they heard her growl menacingly in the porched entrance.

Elliyn withdrew her hand. 'That'll be Dewi. You'd better look out for your dog. He doesn't like them much.'

A startled yelp brought Casson to his feet. He hurried down the aisle and yanked the door open to discover Hetty crouching on the grey flagstone. Her ears were pressed back and there was an untypical snarl across her black muzzle. But he couldn't see the cause of her belligerence.

'Stop it!' snapped Casson.

A slithering movement overhead caught him unawares. It was Dewi, perched with his legs wrapped around a beam high in the pointed, perpendicular porch. Now he let himself fall backwards, his legs still hooked around the beam, so that he hung upside down with a grotesque expression on his face.

Casson responded with a flat stare, not yielding an inch. And the Welshman's wild upside-down eyes shifted past him to the boxer. 'What are you doing in this place?' he panted, addressing the animal. 'Do you want a whipping?'

'She's with me.'

Dewi swung himself down in a half-somersault and landed crouching. He swished a tapering birch cane intimidatingly at Hetty's face. 'No good letting him speak for you. It's wrong for you to come into a place of worship, and right for me to chastise you.'

Casson stepped between them. 'If there's any arse-whipping to be done, I'll do it.'

Dewi's eyes flickered briefly over the tall engineer but he continued to taunt the boxer. 'Dogs are like little people, see. They have to learn to be obedient. Otherwise, it's our God-given duty to punish them.'

Casson said in a dangerously low voice. 'Stop swishing that bloody cane in her face.'

The Welshman's expression barely changed. 'Scriptures say it's wrong to swear in church.' An instant later he flicked the birch viciously within an inch of Casson's unprotected face.

The taller man jerked back instinctively but Hetty was less tolerant and retaliated by snapping at the Welshman's tattered trousers. She got a stinging lash across the back for her pains.

'God Almighty!' said Casson. He grabbed Dewi's under-nourished shoulders, spun him around and booted him with enough bone-crunching force to lift him several inches off the ground.

Dewi cried out with pain and humiliation and tried to hobble out of range, but Casson caught up in the open, kicking him on the run with all his force.

'Oooouh!' groaned Dewi, clutching his backside as if grievously injured.

'Stop it!' Elliyn Pryce-Jones arrived and thrust herself between them. The bedraggled Welshman wore a pained but triumphant expression. 'You saw! He almost crippled me. I'll have him and that ungodly dog of his!'

Casson tried to duck under her strong restraining arm, but she held him off. 'Stop it, both of you!'

Dewi looked at her slyly. 'He struck me while I was doing holy work. You saw for yourself. That means it's out of my hands now.'

'Don't be silly, man,' Elliyn said with a sharp, hysterical edge to her voice. 'You're going too far.' She turned quickly to Casson. 'Tell him you're sorry.'

'Bollocks!'

Dewi's lopsided smile intensified even though blood trickled from his mouth where he had bitten his tongue on being kicked. 'It's too late for going back.'

Elliyn would not accept that it was inevitable and shook

Dewi by his lapels until he almost rattled. 'No, it's not!' she insisted harshly. 'We need him here.'

'IT knows,' Dewi said in a matter-of-fact voice. 'IT didn't like what happened, I can tell. Nothing can change that now. It'll come looking for him tonight. You'll see.'

Elliyn bundled her shabby disciple across to the house. There seemed nothing further that she could do. 'Get along inside, Dewi. Wash that blood off your mouth. I'll be in soon enough.'

Dewi pointed eagerly at Casson. 'Does he know?' He peered round the tall muscular woman. 'Hey! Do you know you've been condemned?'

Elliyn watched him vanish into her house, then swung back to Casson. 'You foolish man,' she said distractedly. 'You should never have struck him. I don't know what to do. You'd better go quickly. Do you understand?'

Casson shook his head in confusion, and patted the dog uneasily.

She shepherded him on his way. 'You'd best get as far away from this place as you can before dark.'

'Umm?' A feeling of dread crept back into Casson's stomach.

'Don't make the mistake of thinking he's joking. You leave this district completely.'

'That's ridiculous,' he gulped.

It was already beginning to get dark and her untidy hair was silhouetted against the streaky black-and-blue sky. 'You do understand, don't you?' she kept saying, and he could tell from the quaver in her voice that whatever it was that she feared was irrevocable.

He backed away nodding, his hand on Hetty's collar, and returned to the power station before dusk settled into night. All the way back he had a strange feeling that he was being watched from afar. But no one was in sight.

That night he took extra precautions. He walked around, talking loudly to Hetty in order to boost his treacherous confidence, and locked all the doors. It was a routine precaution but tonight he also dragged a fire bucket full of slopping water behind each of them: for additional warning in case anyone had got hold of a key.

Later he changed into his athletics track-suit and rubber shoes and lapped the corridors with Hetty padding at his heels. But his heart was not in exercising. He returned to his rooms, picked up a reassuringly heavy torch encased in rubber and whacked it across the edge of a metal table several times.

The dog was greatly interested in the activity and frolicked around until quite late.

He awoke with a start at about 2 a.m. in the awful silence of the echoing building and sensed that he was not alone. He had no conscious notion of what had aroused him, but now he lay rigid and unmoving, straining to hear through the impenetrable darkness.

He stared fixedly across the pitch black room, afraid even to turn on the light.

He remembered going to bed and reading until midnight, reluctant to switch off the bedhead lamp and trying to tire himself for a long sleep.

Hetty snuffled drowsily and settled again on the carpet beside his bed. But Casson was not reassured. Rather he strained to hear over the dog's noisy breathing.

Eventually he raised himself ever so quietly, and switched on the light. The room was still. Books, one or two pictures on the walls, discarded clothes . . . the half-open door to the corridor which led into the turbine hall.

Gingerly he got out of bed and rubbed his forearms quietly to warm away the goose-pimples. He knew he was quite alone in the locked power station, apart from the dog. It was ridiculous even to contemplate an intruder. Yet he had awoken with an overwhelming sense of something moving towards him.

He began slowly to convince himself that it was a mild nightmare which fled with the light. He even sorted out a headache tablet and dissolved it in a beaker in an inch of water. But as he tilted back his head to swallow, distant strains of music reached his ears.

Again he froze with apprehension. Music in the power station? How could there be? It didn't make sense.

But there it was again: the sound of a harp wafting eerily along the corridor.

Shakily he put on his slippers and dressing gown, slid nervous fingers through his dishevelled hair and edged out into the cold corridor. He did not want to go, but there was no alternative. It was either that, or remaining frightened and huddled in his room until daybreak.

Hetty stayed behind and slept disgracefully on with a blissful look on her face. Casson wanted to toe the dog awake, but it might cause too much of a disturbance.

He walked with infinite care on the outside edges of his foam-rubber slippers: a tall shadow moving cautiously along the faintly lit passage. And the farther he progressed the more distinct became the music.

The harp chords were chilling and he reasoned they had to be coming from a radio. Perhaps from his set in the control room. That was it! The realization lifted an enormous weight from his mind.

On the other hand, he clearly remembered switching off the control-room lights and surely he would then have noticed the panel glowing on his seven-band Ingersoll?

His heart was beating rapidly as he inched across the shadowy turbine hall and he held himself as taut as a violin string in case something should spring out at him from any of a dozen shadows, each dark as an abyss. All the time he drew inexorably closer to the glass-panelled control room.

There it was: a light over his desk in front of the main control panel.

Casson swayed back out of sight and pressed against the cold wall, breathing hard. He could feel agitated heart beats. But there was no way out of it now that he had come this far. He took a deep breath and reached for the metal door handle.

The music was 'Greensleeves' with the radio on a much higher volume than he had ever left it; almost as loud as it would go.

Casson reached into the dim pool of light and switched

off. A deathly silence descended as the glow faded away, leaving him in utter darkness. Nothing moved except the fear rising inside him.

He had to get back to the bedroom!

He turned and walked into the brutally hard edge of the door and blundered painfully on, with hands outstretched. A door snicked shut behind him and he listened in a panic to the slip-slap of his own progress across the turbine hall.

A scrambling, slithering noise almost gave him heart failure, but it was only Hetty, awake at last and coming to help. He had never been so relieved to see another living creature in his life. Casson hugged the sleep-warm boxer like a lost friend.

Back in the bedroom he leaned on the door before fumbling in a locker for a cigarette. He did not smoke but had noticed a discarded pack a few days earlier; and suddenly there seemed no better time to learn.

It took him some time to open a quivering box of matches and light the moving end of his first cigarette. After the second deep draw, the smoke went down the wrong way and he couldn't stop coughing. God, he almost choked. He squeezed out the glowing end and listened anxiously at the door, but the power station was encased in silence once more.

He sat at the chess board for some time but spent as much time watching the door as he did the pieces. Occasionally he tested his hands to see for how long he could extend them without shaking.

When the noise came back, it filled him with renewed terror.

This time it was an alarm bell ringing shrilly from No 3 pump in the pit, four floors below ground level. He knew precisely where; and that this was exactly what was supposed to happen when a major piece of equipment malfunctioned. *Except that No 3 pump was not in use.* So, it couldn't be.

He sat listening to the distant clamour. Transfixed and unnerved.

Hetty showed him what to do when she began barking.

Casson had, at least, to calm her down. Afterwards he filled the wash basin, rinsed his face and peered at his pale reflection. It was no more reassuring than the uncertain expression in his grey eyes, but he was obliged to do something.

He took a quick, tight grip on the heavy-duty torch and stepped back into the corridor, cleared his throat noisily and began to descend into the concrete depths of the deserted power station.

Ffestiniog station is built on five levels but only one above the ground. The remainder are set at varying depths in the bed-rock at the foot of Carreg Flaenllym, extending thirty-four metres downwards to the pump basement.

It was customary to take the two-man lift down to the lower levels, but tonight an inner sense beseeched him not to. He set off cautiously down rough concrete steps, occasionally glancing up at the high echoing space overhead and switching on banks of lights as he descended. More than half the power station was ablaze with harsh light by the time he reached the basement where the Swiss-made pumps generate a force of 500 lbs a square inch and can make even the surrounding concrete walls vibrate.

A notice warned 'Ear Protection Required When Plant Is Running'. But there is no machinery operating, he kept telling himself.

Waves of sound rolled towards him from the alarm bell. It was overpowering in the confined space between rough-cast walls and bulky machinery. He stood at the end of the row of massive pumps with their heavy glass inspection windows and glanced apprehensively along. His cowardly arms trembled.

As he approached he could clearly see a flashing amber light on No 3 pump. He opened a small inspection door and summed up the cause in a few seconds. All that was needed was the on-off movement of a switch and a push of the automatic-restart button. Nothing to it. The puzzle was: there was no apparent reason for the broken contact which had tripped off the alarm in the first place. Not unless . . .

Casson quickly glanced over his shoulder. Hetty was sitting dutifully behind him, unsure why they had crept through the building in the middle of the night.

. . . someone down here in the damp, unvisited basement had purposely set it off.

He flashed his torch at distant shadows before starting back towards the lift. Hetty trotted alongside. Gradually he quickened his feverish step and felt a great relief at arriving safely.

His finger was extended, about to press the lift button, when the mechanism started of its own accord. He was shocked. The lift was moving down towards him from ground level.

Jesus! He stepped back abruptly and stumbled over the dog. A pain started up in his side like a stitch. He had to get upstairs before the lift shuddered down to the pump basement.

Fear rose in his throat like bile and it was difficult to breathe. The lift was an old rattler and moved without haste. It gave him just enough time to reach the foot of numerous flights of concrete steps and stumble upwards, sometimes treading on the front edge of his own dressing gown and once falling over Hetty's scrambling form and swearing incoherently.

He stopped only once on his wild ascent, and that was on the third level as the lift passed him on its way down. He shrank back into the cold wall and watched with dreadful fascination a faint glow that penetrated a small frosted-glass window in the aluminium door. It descended thankfully out of sight.

When the lift door opened down on level five, he was thudding along the ground floor corridor back to his room. Hetty had caught the feeling of terror and raced ahead, stiff-legged and darting furtive glances over her shoulder.

Casson had no idea what to do next. He knew only that he must reach the temporary haven of his room, barricade himself in and buy enough time to think.

He fell asleep. It was the last thing he had expected to do

in the circumstances but he must have drained himself of nervous energy, stumbling upstairs from the lowest level. Whatever the reason, he slept for more than an hour.

When he came to, he was in the middle of a nightmare.

Casson was back down at the bottom level, walking towards No 3 pump, which had again gone haywire. He was limping and dazed, as if sleep-walking. His stomach ached with fear over what lay ahead, along the dimly lit gangway between shadowy pumps and steel chambers. Great thick pipes stretched and twisted overhead and metal ladders glinted with dark, malicious pleasure as he passed.

He was alone. Yet he knew in the pit of his stomach that something fearful was waiting for him at the end of the long passageway. The shrill noise of the alarm had gone beyond the point of discernment.

Hetty brought him back to reality, barking frenziedly somewhere behind, somewhere in the direction of the lift and the stairs. The lithe heavy-shouldered boxer raced across the concrete, covering several metres with each bound, intent on reaching Casson.

Instinctively he reeled around towards the familiar sound, only to feel the blur of her passing. The boxer raced on towards whatever had awaited Casson in the gloom ahead. As usual with Hetty, she reached her destination with too much speed and frantically scrambled to reverse her momentum at the last minute. Only now, she sensed an acute danger and was barking defensively as she slid forward.

Casson fell over heavily on his way back to the lift. He was weaker than he realized. One knee was numb, and even hobbling became intensely difficult. Every step he took towards safety was in slow motion. He could feel the danger behind as if it was almost close enough to grab him by the throat.

Hetty had saved his life. He was crying but he knew there was nothing he could do, other than stumble as far away as he could possibly manage.

There was no longer any reason to avoid the lift. The

real danger was unseen, but IT exuded terror and its location was unmistakable: immediately behind him.

The lift door clanked open and a dull yellow bulb welcomed him. Inside he pressed a shaking index finger repeatedly onto the button marked 'ground floor'. As the dilatory door slid shut he glimpsed the gloomy passageway between pumps and wall at the end of which Hetty's barks echoed with less frequency until they were reduced to an extended and bitter whimper. She was in desperate trouble.

Casson closed his eyes and kept them squeezed shut until the lift door rumbled open and he could lurch across the entrance hall. His trembling hand pulled back the top and bottom bolts and, suddenly, he was out in the shivering grey drizzle of the dawn.

He tried to call out for help, but all that issued from his mouth were inarticulate noises. His legs were made of stone and it seemed an inordinate time before he reached the long-deserted ruin of a slate cottage where he slumped to his knees in the shelter of roofless walls.

Silence closed in around him, and he was sickeningly aware that this was not a dream. Thank Jesus Christ our Lord he was safe.

PART 2: Razorbill

Ten

Casson stared fixedly ahead as the undulating ribbon of road unfolded across the Yorkshire dales. Dry-stone walls divided fields of black-faced sheep from others with cows bulging with cud and well-being. A prosperous wool town slid by. Small bridges hump-backed in stone. But his eyes barely registered. He had not slept properly for days and his remaining concentration was focussed ahead.

He had to find her again. She would know what to do; she always knew. He remembered, as a boy, looking back along the lane in order to store a picture of her finely drawn face in his memory. Eyes glistening. He had been bound for London and the future.

The parish of Ottley was signposted for the first time, winding into the West Riding, off the main Ripon road. He pulled on to the grass verge to contemplate the name and stood resting his chin on the top edge of the car door while a damp breeze stirred his tousled hair. It was like coming home after a long absence. He felt better already, in the knowledge that the welcome he would get was time-proof.

Overhead, the sound of a plane hurtling north reminded him that the American Air Force had built a base on the moors in the intervening years: to guard the radar installation at Fylingdales and scurry like sheepdogs up and down NATO's Arctic flank.

But at ground level, so far as he could see, little else had changed. The interlocking hills of the Pennine Chain stood patiently awaiting his return like reliable friends.

Winding flintstone walls enclosed the schoolyard.

Bicycles were propped against an enormous, gnarled oak. His initials were carved there somewhere.

The house where he was raised had been converted into a post office. Inside he half-expected to see familiar faces, or hear someone gasp his name. John, is it you? But nobody did.

Memories. Mother Frost, he called her at first. Mother, later. She was never forthcoming with strangers. You had to prove your worth and make an effort before she responded. A quiet, tolerant woman.

Memories. Everyone called her Mother Frost, even those who mistrusted her affinity with nocturnal animals and folklore. Some daring boys, who decided she had a dark side, hurled stones from a distance and ran for their mortal souls when she appeared in the doorway. But with shards of glass at her feet, she laid a calming hand around his narrow shoulders: understanding both the culprits' brittle courage and Casson's trembling indignation.

He had his first dog in those far-off days. A particularly ugly old bull terrier named Sam with a black patch over one eye, who developed a limp so badly that people said the kindest thing was to put him down. Mother Frost soothed the damaged limb with a lotion, produced by simmering the chopped inner-bark of an elm tree in boiling water, before compressing it in a soft-leather sock. Sam hadn't liked it but, within two weeks, he was walking cautiously without a limp. And in a month he was racing pudgily across the dales once again.

Memories. Saturdays were best, when he wound squelching sheets through a dripping iron mangle while she rocked Hannah in the cot and told him tales of yore. He remembered listening with particular fascinated horror to 'The Devil at Tyke's Farm'.

He watched while she tinted her hair dark red using berries from the elder trees, much as the Romans did. If there was an interruption it was probably somebody at the back door with a hand cupped over a throbbing ear or tooth, which she would ease with a pad of cotton wool soaked in parsley juice. For fevers and chills he was sent to pick lilac leaves, which she boiled and left to infuse for ten minutes. Thereafter small cupfuls throughout the day brought remarkable results.

Now he was back after nearly twenty years and, although he had sent no photograph of his lean and hungry face, he knew her shrewd old eyes would recognize him in a moment.

A postmaster, newly arrived from Ripon, knew no one of that name. 'Frost, you say? Nay, can't say as I do, lad.' But he obligingly produced an electoral roll and discovered a Miss Frost, spinster and teacher, with an address on the Dewsbury road.

'Thanks. Thanks a lot.' Casson drove on with growing excitement.

No one answered his knocks at the small, leaning property called Spindle House and he left a message next door. 'Tell her, please, that an old friend is back. John Casson from a long time ago. She'll remember. I'm staying at the King Harry. Tell her I'll call later. Thanks.' He backed off, reluctant to leave now that he had found a reassuring warmth again.

He was in the lounge bar, later, when a military Jeep scrunched to a stop on the gravel forecourt.

An immaculately dressed U.S. Air Force officer with a derisive expression, and the two silver bars of a captain on each shoulder, held open the door with fingers which drummed as he waited. In a moment a young woman ducked unamused under his extended arm. They looked as if they'd been arguing.

Casson returned his attention to a gluttonous slice of cold pork-pie alongside his pint of best bitter. There was hardly anybody else in the pub, apart from a barman coming and going.

The woman tilted her chin in his direction. Unsmiling, watchful. She was tall, slender and pale as winter. Casson had already noted a senatorial nose and intelligent mouth. No pushover.

She spoke to the barman; heads leaned together. The latter nodded across the room in Casson's direction and she walked over, leaving the American sorting through the numerous banknotes in his wallet. He seemed to have trouble finding one small enough to pay for their drinks.

Casson smiled politely and noted that her skin was drawn with transparent tightness over high cheekbones which accounted for some of the paleness. She seemed oddly resentful.

Finally she said, 'I never liked you.'

He glanced behind him, puzzled. Perhaps he had misheard.

'She always treated you like a son, which you weren't. I remember thinking how unfair it was that she loved you just as much as she cared for me.'

'Hannah?' He got to his feet, hardly believing it.

She nodded and he would have grabbed her joyfully, but she was an adult now and unaccommodating. A different person.

'Well, it's good to see you again.' He manufactured a smile and made as if to touch her arm familiarly, but did not quite make it. She had moved imperceptibly out of range.

'I'm afraid I can't stay more than a moment. We've a prior engagement.'

'Of course.' He clenched his teeth. What a prig she'd turned out to be.

'You do understand?'

'Absolutely.' Casson glanced out at the empty vehicle. 'Where's your mother?'

'I can't say categorically. But of the two obvious alternatives, I like to think she's in Heaven.'

Casson's mouth opened and closed drily. Oh God. Not dead. His one hope of finding out what it was all about. Not dead. He touched the depths of despair at that moment. It must have shown in his haunted expression, for something almost melted her reserve.

But she kept it in check by swallowing heavily and glancing at her watch. 'Heavens, is that the time?' She left her drink and went outside. The American glanced curiously at Casson before following.

He was left in a shrunken world. He struggled half-heartedly to unbutton his collar. Dead? His mind slid hopelessly over the possibilities left open to him.

Outside there was some sort of fuss going on, but he barely noticed until feet crunched hurriedly on the gravel and the American burst back inside.

'Where's the barman? Hey you! Yes, you! She's fainted. Help me get her back in here.'

Once on the long leather window seat, she raised her head dazedly and repeated 'I'm all right.'

Casson returned her firmly but gently to the horizontal while the American went off to find some water. She held his hand with slim fingers which made grateful little movements. Vulnerable and breathing shallowly, she seemed a different person from the woman of a few minutes before.

'Was I out for long?'

'Only a minute or so. You relax now.'

She smiled wearily. 'I heard something that upset me.'

'Did you?'

'I heard a dog barking a long way off like an echo.'

A shiver of cold wrapped itself around his shoulders, like a chilling intrusion from another world, but before he could respond the American bustled back and elbowed him aside. He slapped her face repeatedly; unnecessarily, Casson thought.

'This isn't like you, darling. Come on, don't frighten me. Take a sip. Feeling better now?'

She sat up and nodded gratefully. 'J.J., I heard a dog barking. In a dark, remote place a long way from here. It sounded distraught. It wanted me to hear.'

The American put his arm around her shoulders. 'You fainted. You're all right now, darling. Put it right out of your mind.'

Casson who had been standing to one side, moved forward. The palms of his hands were clammy. 'What sort of dog?'

She shook her head forlornly. He knelt in front of her, gripping her by the shoulders to focus her attention. It was suddenly vitally important. 'What sort of dog?' he insisted. She met his eyes directly and somehow he knew – beyond the edge of doubt – that it was Hetty.

But the perplexed American was not having any. 'Move aside, fellah.' He thrust Casson away. 'What sort of dog? Are you crazy? She just fainted. What sort of question is that?'

After lunch came another jolt. He was casually turning pages in the *Daily Telegraph* when he came across an inside-page lead, 'Three Policemen Killed by Lightning.' He hardly needed even to read the first paragraph to confirm that it was Rhys apJones and the others. 'Their three crumpled bodies were found in a patch of badly scorched hillside at the foot of Snowdon,' it said. 'The sad tragedy of a freak of nature.'

And only he knew: that wasn't how it happened at all! There was nothing natural about their deaths. They'd all been slaughtered.

He badly needed help to sort himself out. He ordered a whisky and ginger but his hand shook so much he spilled most of it. He was too late. The only woman who could help him was dead.

The American rang before dusk and invited him to dinner with the two of them. Hannah was much better and he, Air Force Captain J.J. Andretti, would be bringing a first-class meal over from the base, pre-cooked, by way of thanks for his help.

Casson could do without patronage. He accepted for her mother's sake and later wished he hadn't. It was an uncomfortable meal. Not that the food was unpalatable. Boeuf Strogonoff followed by a delicious raspberry cream gateau. But Casson was not to de drawn. His fears were locked inside him, and not to be prised open in casual conversation.

Andretti was an Italian-American, narrow-nosed with a tightly curled head of hair. He was too aware of himself for Casson's liking. For instance, he got them talking about family backgrounds and then proceeded to describe his own lineage, which came either from pure Roman nobility or straight from his imagination.

It was impossible not to make a comparison with poor modest Rhys apJones.

Andretti's nasal voice droned on, and the engineer smiled agreeably at all the right places. But his mind gradually slipped back to the hunchbacked mountains of Wales, gloating over their victims. They would be content to sit through the incessant rain, wrapped in their wrinkled spite, waiting for the next unsuspecting creature. Whether man or dog.

'John.' He heard her voice floating in the distance, although his attention was locked hundreds of miles away.

'John.' Her hand touched his forearm, bringing him suddenly back to this particular evening. He immediately became aware that the captain had stopped talking and they were both staring at his right hand.

In it was a dessert spoon, the silver handle of which had bent slowly back on itself in a loop in his desperate, unconscious grip. 'Uuh? Oh, I'm so sorry. I was thinking of something, someone far away. Excuse me. I haven't got over the drive yet. I'm still rather tense.'

She relieved him of the spoon. 'Doesn't matter a bit.' She laid a hand gently on his taut wrist, and the frustration was soothed away.

Andretti gave him an understanding smile, as if forgiving him for interrupting a particularly interesting part of the conversation. 'Whatever's bothering you, relax. You're among friends. Good friends. Anyway, we've all got our secrets. Take me. I'm as superstitious as any person you ever met. I guarantee it.' He took a pinch of salt and dropped it over his shoulder to make the point. Right hand over left shoulder, as you would expect from somebody who took his foibles seriously.

Casson laughed and caught Hannah's eye. It was little more than a shrug, but he enjoyed sharing even a small understanding with her.

He was able to tell them about Hannah's gifted mother, things that even she didn't know, who would avoid getting out of bed on the Devil's side: the left-hand side. But, if there was no alternative, she would counteract the consequent bad luck by putting on her right sock and right shoe first.

The American was intrigued. So Casson related to them her habit of slipping a coin in the pocket of any new item of clothing. It was said to ensure a plentiful supply of money thereafter.

Andretti responded by admitting that whenever he flew he wore a silk scarf in which he tied a double knot. The theory was that if the Devil was nearby he would be so intrigued by the shape created that any thought of interfering would be forgotten.

Most of the tension gradually slid from Casson's shoulders, and he found himself sufficiently relaxed to enjoy the rest of the evening. They sipped their way through three bottles of deliciously refreshing white wine before the captain glanced at his watch.

'Damn, I'm duty officer at the base from midnight. I have to go.'

'Me too.' Casson was quickly on his feet.

Hannah collected the military overcoat and peaked cap. 'Take care, darling.' Casson stood back and noticed the way she kissed with her eyes open, and even momentarily caught her attention in mid-embrace.

The American half-turned. 'Can I drop you off?'

'No, I'll walk. I just want a word or two more with Hannah. Then I'm away.'

'Of course. Well, in case we don't meet again.' Andretti proffered a hand and was gone.

Alone together, Casson and the girl smiled at one another slightly awkwardly and returned to the lounge for coffee. He said, 'I wanted to ask you about the dog.'

'Please don't.'

'Why not?'

'I don't know. I don't like what I sensed. There was something almost evil in the background. Nothing I could put my finger on.' She shivered a little and fidgeted with the bone-china coffee set.

They lapsed into silence, which she eventually broke. 'What made you come back?'

'Your fiancé rang and invited me.'

'No, I mean why come back here after so long away? We thought you'd forgotten us. That was why I was so angry when I saw you again. You left it too late.'

He smiled sadly. 'I know. I needed her advice.'

'Oh? What about?'

'Believe me, you don't want to get involved.'

'I see.' She stood up briskly, drained her cup and looked as unamused as when he first met her. 'Time I was in bed.'

'Yes, I must go.'

But it had begun raining, heavily. And, after inspecting the downpour from the protection of the porch, she screwed up her face and said, 'I think you'd better stay the night. You can sleep in the spare room, if you like.'

In the stillborn hours before dawn the next day, when the house was cloaked in darkness and silence, she screamed. Piercingly.

Casson was in bed two rooms away. He jerked upright, his eyes suddenly wide open. Fear, which had been lurking in the shadows of his mind, flooded back. An ache returned to his chest like an old illness and reminded him that he had not distanced himself from the Moelwyn Mountains at all.

He dreaded what was to come.

The sound of her snagged breathing reached him clearly as she groped along the creaking landing towards him. Towards him!

Cold with fright, he put on his bedside lamp and took an unsteady sip of water from a beaker.

The tapping on his door was unexpectedly subdued. One, two, three. Almost polite. But what shocked him most was the expression on her face as she edged slowly around the door. A *lopsided* smile. Not at all the look of a terrified woman; rather that of a sly, demented person.

The impression it gave was hideously familiar. Dewi. His grin and his idiotically shining eyes in her face.

Casson's feet moved frantically under the sheets in an effort to push himself farther back, but the wall blocked his progress.

She began to speak with a Welsh accent; in a macabre sing-song voice that did not belong to her.

'So! Where have you been, boyoh? Frightened is it, you are? Well you're not the only one. I've got your dog here, see. Terrible to be alone, especially for a dog that doesn't understand why she's being kept in a coffin in total darkness. And if you're not back soon I'll nail the lid down. For good.' She dribbled with laughter.

Casson grabbed her wrist and tried to shake the imbecilic smile off her face. 'Stop it! Wake up!' He almost tugged her bare arm from its socket. It must have been painful yet she continued to smile vacuously.

'Stands to reason.' The voice was pitched higher than Dewi's but there was a grotesque similarity.

Casson smacked her face hard and then immediately pulled her to his chest protectively, apologetically. At the same time he talked to her endearingly with words which, later, he would not be able to remember.

He gulped with relief when eventually she recovered enough to speak in her own mild North Country accent. 'I had . . . I had an awful dream,' she stuttered.

'I know. It's over now.'

'What am I doing here?'

'Never mind. Just lift yourself into bed and I'll cover you up. You're shivering. That's it.'

She was docile and obedient now, but still trembling. 'Did I make a fool of myself? Did I do something silly?'

'No,' he breathed and kissed the top of her head.

She felt for his hand and held it painfully tight. 'I have to tell you: I heard the dog again through inky darkness. I don't know how I know, but I just know it was your dog.'

'Did you?' he said quietly, and prayed she would say no more.

'Someone was trying to strangle her in a place that was dank and echoing. Gurgling with pleasure, he was, as he half-throttled the poor creature and then threw her aside to recover as best she could until the next time.'

Casson gulped and did not trust himself to speak.

'I couldn't do anything to prevent it,' she said, her eyes brimming with tears.

'Don't worry about it.' Casson promised himself he would repay Dewi agonizingly when he got the chance.

Her fingers scrabbled against him. 'There was something else, something hideous standing in the shadows behind them. I couldn't see it clearly, but I heard . . .'

'Look, try to put it out of your mind. You had a nightmare.'

But she was not to be put off. 'I heard it breathing. It was awful. I can't describe it, it sounded bestial.'

Eventually Casson said, 'Wheezing? Strangulated?'

She stared at him distractedly. 'How did you know?' But he turned his back to her and the silence that followed was filled only by her snatched breaths. 'That accounts for it,' she said.

'Accounts for what.'

'That thing in the darkness. I had an odd feeling I wasn't in immediate danger because it had already singled out its next victim.'

Casson squeezed his cold hands together until they ached, then tried hard to sound casual. 'Oh. Who?'

She swallowed quietly. 'You.'

She was her usual brisk, assertive self in the morning. Or at least that was the impression she tried to give. 'Of course you won't go back. Be silly to do that, wouldn't it?' She laid a breakfast tray across his lap in bed.

''Course not.' He rubbed his hands in anticipation over the fried egg and mushrooms followed by crisp toast and marmalade.

'Look, you've got to face the unpalatable truth. Hetty is probably dead by now. I know it hurts to hear that, but you must face up to it.'

He nodded at length. 'I suppose so.'

'You could stay here for a while. I'd be glad of your company.'

'No, that's kind of you, but I think I'll make tracks for London and bury myself in work.'

'I'm glad.' She was as nervous as an autumn leaf when it was time to say goodbye. He tried to make light of it and promised to write before another twenty years elapsed. They even kissed.

He was a long way down the road when she shouted anxiously after him. 'Don't forget! Let me know when you arrive in London. Right?'

'Right.' What else could he say in the circumstances? But he was not fooled by his own words as to his destination. Nor was she.

Later, Hannah rang the air force base and got through to J.J. It took a long time and he sounded exasperated.

'Sorry, darling. I've been with the goddamned colonel. He's not amused that I was two hours late getting back through the goddamned floodwater last night. Says he has to make an example of me to other duty officers. Next week he's putting me on the milk run to Germany. Isn't that ludicrous, putting his best pilot back on ferry work? He's never really liked me. Seems to resent my background.'

'I'm sorry to hear that. Look, I'm awfully worried about John.'

'John?' snorted Andretti. 'John who?'

'Casson, of course. I'm afraid he might do something silly.'

'Look, darling, we've all got problems. Colonel Kolowski's mine. After next week I won't be seeing you for a while.'

'What's that?' The consequences of what he was saying opened up a glimmer of opportunity in her mind.

'Must be a bad line. I say, we won't be able to see each other for a while after next week.'

'All right, J.J.' she responded almost eagerly. 'Don't worry about me.'

There was a pause at the other end of the line, then

Captain Andretti said in a puzzled voice, 'I'm not. I'm worried about me. Goodbye, darling.'

She was filled with a sense of rising fear and excitement. She did not know precisely where she had to go. But it was somewhere in North Wales and she had been there once before, in the depths of the night.

If John Casson could go back alone to such a dank, inhuman place, then she could too.

Eleven

He found it more of a struggle getting back to Tan-y-grisiau than it was getting out. Floodwater sprawled over further tens of thousands of acres westwards from Chester, and he had difficulty in finding passable roads threading along the high ground.

He had been absent too long as it was. You can only leave an automatic power station for a few days before it gives up fending for itself.

He submerged his fears by working himself into a state of fierce determination: vowing that he couldn't wait to get back to face whatever it was that made him abandon Hetty.

But the closer he drew to the mountains and the isolated power house concealed in their shadows the less sure he became, and gradually a feeling of dread descended upon him once more.

The car got stuck several times and he did a lot of wading to fetch help. When eventually he reached Tan-y-grisiau village, he was wet to the waist.

There were no people about as he drove cautiously up the tilted, winding street eventually to emerge with a clear view of the distant reservoir. His caution was justified. The moment he saw the low unaltered shape of the power station he was aware of a change.

Nothing moved. The grey impenetrable waters of Tan-y-grisiau reservoir gave no indication of welcome. The sky was leaden and the mountains heavy with hostility. Nevertheless, something had altered. There was an atmosphere about the place that prickled the back of his neck. A sense of perverted animosity, as if something unnatural was now in occupation.

As he approached the power station, silence descended. Even the breeze that ruffled his hair now stealthily withdrew. The distant lapping of water and skittering of birds faded. Likewise, he let the car roll downhill in neutral, without switching on his engine.

Something up ahead had suddenly become aware of his presence, something unseen that was now watching him just as intently as he was staring. He was certain of it.

Casson dared not move. A chill gripped his arms and crept down his legs.

He was trapped in a corridor of silence; as if underwater for so long that his ears were blocked. A reverberating silence encompassed and pressed in on him. And in the half-distance, for the first time, he heard the menacing breathing of the Demon. Coming inexorably closer, along the corridor towards him.

Terror seized him and instinctively he started the engine and wrenched the car into reverse. Someone was shouting his name. The car whined backwards, lurching up first one pavement and then the other, but putting as much distance as he could between him and the power station. He careered off into an inevitably soggy patch of grass and the wheels spun helplessly as they bogged down. He switched off and still heard the persistent voice through a half-silence.

'Mr Casson! What's the matter? Are you all right?'

Hazy words penetrated the corridor and restored his awareness. Elliyn Pryce-Jones was hurrying towards him with concern in her eyes. 'Careful, how you get out. You look ill.' Her strong grip closed around his arm until he was secure on his feet again. 'You poor man. You're soaked. How far have you come like that?'

Casson stared at her dumbly.

She took charge of him like an intolerant schoolteacher with a pupil. 'What is it?'

'The silence,' he stuttered. 'Something was coming towards me. Through the silence.'

She frowned impatiently back up the slope whence he had come, but the power station was hidden from sight. She was dressed in the forbidding manner of a Welsh extreme Non-Conformist: a long black dress with high-buttoned neck, dark shawl and small black bowler hat tilted forward on her leonine head.

'You've got a fever, Mr Casson. Better come back with me.'

He shook his arm free, staring back up the scrubby slope. 'It was uncanny. I heard a . . .'

Her eyes narrowed. 'Don't be silly,' she scolded.

'I know what I heard,' he said angrily.

She recited some Welsh at him. It was unintelligible until she repeated the words slowly in English. 'The Demon is ready to dance: a silent dance to the death with any who intrude into the Land of our Fathers.'

'What? What do you mean?'

'Come on.' She brooked no further interference; turned him by the arm and accelerated him towards the chapel cottage. Inside, she gripped his boots one at a time between her strong thighs and tugged them off.

'What was that you said about a demon?' he asked shakily.

'I didn't say it,' she responded, stone faced. 'Somebody else did, a long time ago.'

He sat in a deep, worn leather armchair, shivering and rubbing his arms while she prepared a hot drink. 'Did you at least hear the silence?' he asked, after avoiding conversation for as long as he could.

She made a contemptuous dismissive sound. 'How can you hear silence? You'd best close your eyes for a while.'

'It was almost as if IT was glad to see me back.'

'Glad?'

'Gleeful and vindictive.'

She put a hand on his throbbing forehead, testing its

temperature. 'You've overdone it today. By far, I'd say. Shut your eyes a while.'

The drink made him drowsy. Later she sat alongside, took his hand and talked quietly in her persuasive sing-song voice about the valleys and the people there who wanted nothing better than to live at peace with the past. She was incredibly plain; a great slab of woman, and yet she possessed the most soothing and manipulative voice he'd ever heard.

Day receded into dusk.

She cleared away the crockery and the chink of plates and cups brought him back to reality. 'The power supply has been awfully erratic since you left,' she was saying. 'Lack of attention I suppose. You'll want to get back and put it right as quickly as possible. But not tonight. You're not up to it. Right?'

Casson was not in the mood to argue. He certainly did not want to venture back into the nightmarish world outside. 'Would it be imposing on you?'

'Not at all.' She slapped his shoulder boisterously. 'I can't get over the fancy way you talk. There's a bed waiting right now. Mind you, a big chap like you, people will start talking. They'll ask what we're up to, I shouldn't wonder.'

'I wouldn't want that to happen.'

She squeezed his arm reassuringly. 'I was only teasing. Look, you just relax and I'll do the rest.' Her fingers lingered.

Later, he listened to the occasional boom of her laughter reverberating through the house and the comfortable tock-tock-tock of a grandfather clock in the hall, and relaxed.

Logs were piled on the fire and, as darkness crept in from the corners to share their warmth, she uncovered a tall, shrouded object by the window. It was an ornate harp, taller than the seated Elliyn and fashioned from superb light-golden yew. She made herself comfortable on a stool, leaned the triangular bardic instrument back against her shoulder, and played.

At first, Casson was extremely tense. It was reminiscent of the chilling harp music he had heard at night at the power station. But when she sang 'David of the White Rock' in a deep Welsh voice as melodious as velvet, he gradually relaxed.

It was a cumbersome instrument but she handled it deftly, making each note as clear and pure as a drop of water: occasionally dampening the rich sounds with the flat of her hand.

When she raked over the embers and said that it was now time for bed, he glowed from the music and the subdued heat of the fire. The shock of the early part of the day had faded. He was distanced from everything by a warm haze.

She stood over him, a tall dominating figure. 'Can I help you undress?'

'No, no,' he slurred. 'I'm fine.'

'All right. Leave your clothes down here. I'm going up.' She hesitated. '*Nos da*.'

'Night.' He stretched and smiled wearily. 'Oh. Where's my room?'

'Top of the stairs. You can't mistake it. It's the only one.'

'Fine.' He didn't take in the implication; he was already swaying exhaustedly from one foot to the other, pulling off his socks. Her eyes coveted him possessively before she disappeared up the creaking, steep-angled stairs.

When he arrived in the low-ceiling room, which was three-quarters filled by her handsomely carved Edwardian bed, she was on her knees with her hands steepled in prayer.

It was obvious that her voluminous linen shift had not been tailored to stimulate masculine interest. Nevertheless he was dressed only in a vest and stood blinking, with no time to cover himself.

'God, I'm sorry. I didn't realize you'd be in here.'

She took a pious but protracted look before returning to her prayers then got up. 'Never mind, lovely. Close the door.'

He attempted to pull the diminutive vest down over his

embarrassment, although inches short of success. Even in the intervening second or two he was beginning to swell.

'Close the door,' she murmured insistently.

He did so and sat heavily on the bed, pressing his folded arms down into his lap. 'Look, I'm dreadfully . . . I don't know where to start.'

'Don't you?' she chided.

'No. I mean . . .' He tripped over his own words. 'Look, let's talk about something else for a minute. I mean, your voice,' he gulped, 'was magical when it combined with the harp.'

The momentary change of subject seemed to please her. 'A woman's voice is the most valuable thing she possesses, apart from her religion.'

He nodded earnestly but it didn't make him feel any less foolish. 'Don't be embarrassed,' she said, searching for his hand. But he shook his head urgently; if he uncovered himself he was lost.

'What a fine, lovely man you are,' she laughed. 'You mustn't be nervous of me.'

'Me, nervous?'

She smiled conspiratorially, took off her shift without a moment's misgiving and walked heavily to the slate-topped dressing table to blow out the candle. Leaning over the flame she glanced around at his amazed reaction.

She was superbly built. A sculptured white carthorse. Long untutored hair, massive breasts and enormous marble thighs. He gave a small involuntary grunt as she stood directly in front of him. Overwhelmed: stunned by her massive beauty. Her plain face vanished into the shadow of inconsequence.

'You're not too tired to make love?'

He shook his head eagerly.

'I'm glad.' She depressed the bed hugely, getting in. 'And don't look so furtive. There's no sin in a natural God-given act.'

'Amen,' he gulped as he got under the covers and rolled helplessly down the incline into her. From then on, nature took its urgent course. Later, gasping and drained of energy, he lay grinning up into the darkness. She was powerful and insatiable. The epitome of womanhood; regal in her awareness that this was her supreme moment.

It didn't matter that he wore himself out the first time. Inexorably she coaxed a further excess.

At first light they were again locked mountainously, and the room was filled with delighted gasping sounds until both were incapable of moving another inch.

They slept on, long after more distant and respectable folk were up and about.

Sunshine. Not from a wholly clear sky, but enough to squeeze between a procession of clouds, a gap in the curtains and then prise open his eyes. The huge walnut bed was deliciously warm and he basked in its comfort.

Life was blissful, right up to the moment she planted the flat of her large foot against his unsuspecting buttocks and shoved him to the very edge of the mattress.

'Get me a cup of tea,' she ordered drowsily.

Before he could respond, a second thrust propelled him out on to the floor which he struck with his knee entangled in blankets. 'Aaah! Careful. What are you playing at?'

His indignant face reappeared over the edge of the bed, but there was no endearment in her expression. 'Plenty of sugar,' she yawned, 'and hurry up about it.'

Casson sighed and set off downstairs, picking his way gingerly down the dawn-cold steps like a moth with sore feet. The scullery flagstones were equally inhospitable as he filled a big black kettle and set it on the stove.

After gargling the overnight taste out of his mouth, he sorted out cups and saucers and found some brittle ginger biscuits. Upstairs she sat up in bed, like a whale erupting from the sea. She clutched a sheet to her formidable breasts as she took an exploratory sip.

'I distinctly said plenty of sugar, my love.'

'I put two in.'

'Well put in two more!'

He muttered and set off downstairs, this time staying long enough to pull on his trousers and tuck in the shirt.

Elliyn helped herself to the sugar bowl and stirred remorselessly.

'You snore,' she said eventually.

'So do you.'

'Another time, I'll make you sleep on the landing.'

He nodded again and pulled the tie from his pocket. 'I think I'd better be going.'

'What do you mean?'

'I want to get back to the power station.'

The frown vanished. 'Yes, you'd better make sure it's running properly, love. But be back here well before dark, mind.'

He squashed his feet into still damp shoes, 'What do you mean?'

'I mean, I don't want your tea standing about getting cold until all hours.'

'Oh.' He relaxed his taut stomach muscles. 'Look, I won't want any tea. I'll be making my own from now on, at the power station.'

'But surely you're coming back for more?'

'More what?'

They exchanged searching looks and each knew perfectly well what the other meant. He put on his jacket and rubbed his hands with an air of awkward finality. 'Well, I must be going. Thanks for . . . everything.'

She got out of bed which, relieved of her weight, rose several inches. 'But we're affianced now. Bonded.' The curious thing was she said it without affection: rather as if he was an acquisition.

'You're joking.' He started for the stairs. 'I'm my own man, and always have been. All right, I appreciate last night. It was incredible. You certainly know how to get the best out of a man. But there's nothing more to it than that. So let's forget it before it begins.'

'It's too late.' She clenched her fists anxiously. 'I want some wood brought in, love. Put it by the fire, and stop being silly. If you want to survive in this part of the world, you need my patronage. Need my protection too, I shouldn't wonder.'

Casson cluttered downstairs. 'I'll leave it by the fireplace.' He rapidly collected some logs, piled them up and walked away. He did not look back although he was conscious of her at the upstairs window. A dominating woman, accustomed to getting her way. If he made an enemy of her, he was really on his own.

'You know you can't stay at the power station, don't you?' she shouted. He refused to turn, slow down or show even that he heard.

'Dewi will find out and it will be completely out of my hands. You won't be able to avoid IT. You know that, don't you?'

Cold invisible hands held Casson. Fear of the unknown gripped him anew. *IT?* He turned and shouted into a rising wind. 'It? What do you mean by that?'

Elliyn glanced up at the clouds, cascading overhead in a silent landslide. She pointed up and around. The Moelwyns, the sky and the weather. All as one. The omnipotent force of Nature. Then, almost as if there was nothing more to say, she slammed and bolted the window.

Casson cupped his cold hands and breathed warm air into them. He was going back to the power station in broad daylight and if he hesitated, for even half a step, he was lost.

He forced himself to walk on, imagining the conversation continuing.

'But you said there was no such thing.'

'Did I? Well there is. I've seen it make men's flesh creep and heard it crossing the mountains.'

'That's ridiculous.'

'Look, boyoh, no matter what you say, once it starts there's no stopping it. You'd best get back here quick, while you still can.'

Casson continued on up the slope, swallowing repeatedly. Now all he had to protect himself was animal instinct, and his increasing sense of fear.

Twelve

The power station was as quiet as a church on a Monday. Nothing stirred inside as he unlocked and tentatively pushed open the squeaky door. Nothing moved to intercept him and, if there was anything waiting, it held its breath. Simply white walls and static machinery, as you would expect in a pumped storage system during the idle hours of the morning.

His instincts were on a knife-edge: feeling ahead, anticipating hostility. Listening for the monstrous breathing once again. But still there was nothing. His fingers brushed the wall and he sniffed suspiciously at the moisture they picked up. Harmless enough.

A glance through the plate-glass window at the control console showed lights glowing faintly, as you would expect, and dials registering normal levels. He walked cautiously to his quarters and edged inside. The bed was just as he had abandoned it a week before, rumpled covers flung back.

He was beginning to relax when the main door slammed far behind him. And echoed. He twisted around, listening tensely. When he finally ventured outside he found the wind had picked up and was teasing the tops of distant trees. The door again banged shut and he pulled a face, feeling rather ridiculous at his own jumpiness.

Later, after bolstering his self-confidence with a mugful of tea, his thoughts returned to the two women continually jostling into his mind: alluring Hannah Frost and the magnificently plain Elliyn. He admired one and desired the other and he was a little in love with both.

But he forced himself to concentrate on the real reason for his return: to discover what happened to Hetty when he abandoned her. He felt ashamed as he ventured down to the generator floor. He even stood halfway down the next flight of concrete steps and bent to peer at the turbine floor on a level deeper. But that was as far as he could manage. The memory of the night on which he awoke in terror, and found himself in the pump sub-basement in the bowels of the building, was still too raw to be re-opened. He left it at that for the time being and returned to ground level rapidly.

That same evening he began to carve a piece of elder. He had always enjoyed shaping wood. At first his hand shook, reminding him of his latent fear over what lay far below him in the building. Perhaps tomorrow he would flood all the floors below ground with electric light and look for Hetty.

The idea did nothing to calm him. Instead the knife slipped across his thumb and sliced a deep welt in the table. But he stuck to his whittling, determined to occupy his mind, sometimes using a gouge and sometimes his wickedly sharp knife on the eight-inch block of wood. And, gradually, he formed the rough shape of a spoon.

The practice of fashioning love-spoons was widespread in Wales some three hundred years ago. Casson had read about it in a weathered book which contained spidery sketches of the intricate patterns once cut into the handles of wooden cutlery.

He propped the flaking pages open in front of him and, as the day wore on, pared away at white wood, absorbed in the shape he was creating. It was eerie; almost as if someone had control of him who had fashioned such a spoon before.

The custom, by which a man just once in his young lifetime carved with infinite care a wooden spoon to indicate his love for a Welsh maiden, had lasted nearly two centuries before fading away in Victorian times. Mechanization took over and the need for rapt attention to culinary detail was at an end.

It was the detail which had been such a powerful and unmistakable symbol of a young man's love and on which he worked with endless patience during the evenings, while light lasted, before mutely handing the elaborately carved profession of his love to the girl of his choice. It invariably spoke louder than words.

If the girl accepted his spoon, she accepted him and from that moment they were betrothed.

What if the girl was Hannah?

The thought spurred him on. He worked over the puritanically narrow spoon throughout the day and, by ten at night, his fingers ached. Then the gouge slipped and he took a shallow trench from the whorled pad of his thumb. Shocked white flesh quickly filled with blood which he sucked ruefully, grimacing at its flat taste before abandoning the evening's work.

By now a chilling wind was stealing down from the Moelwyns and beginning to whisper around the walls of Ffestiniog power station, seeking entry. A Non-Conformist wind bent on chastisement.

Eleven o'clock and he walked from the control room through the long turbine hall, switching off lights, ready to turn in for the night. He was particularly drowsy, having swallowed two sleeping pills to deaden his apprehension of spending another night in the echoing building.

In the zig-zag corridor, just a few steps from his own quarters, he heard an echoing snick, as if a manual override had been pulled back among the gunmetal-grey equipment. Then a second distant click followed by a familiar subdued hum.

He twisted round, almost unable to believe his ears. Two of the four big generator shafts had gone on to spinning reserve.

It couldn't happen. Not without someone pressing out a pattern of commands on the controls at the end of the building which he had just left.

Cradled in the Ice Age lake of Llyn Stwlan, up there in the darkness behind a buttress dam between the Big Moelwyn and Little Moelwyn peaks, were 375 million gallons of water, an enormous pouch of energy which had been laboriously pumped up from the reservoir alongside Ffestiniog power station days before.

Under control, the massive force was no problem. But if it ran amok anything could happen.

He walked quickly back. Never run in Station Emergency situations, they'd taught him. Better to keep calm and lose a second or two. The steady hum of machinery was anything but reassuring. Fifty-five seconds was all it normally took for a duty engineer to trigger off the mechanism and bring the icy waters of Llyn Stwlan thundering down steel-lined tunnels.

Casson burst open the control room door without pausing even to switch on the main lights. Dull red bulbs were all the illumination he had as he yanked the radio-telephone microphone towards him and depressed the talk-button.

'Manchester One, this is Ffestiniog Power Station. Manchester One, this is Ffestiniog,' he said anxiously. 'Are you receiving? Over.'

There was no immediate reply and he turned, listening tautly to the modulate throb of the twin generator shafts outside. A good many of the fifty-five seconds had already been eaten away.

'Manchester One, answer please. This is Ffestiniog in an emergency situation. Are you receiving me, Manchester? Over.'

The silence seemed interminable until a calm nasal Manchester accent filled the room. 'Hello, Ffestiniog. This is Manchester. Receiving you strength three. How can we help? Over.'

'John Casson here. What the hell's going on? I've had a two-shaft switch-on without warning. Are you expecting me to generate tonight? Over.'

'Hold on, Ffestiniog. I'll check for you. Negative. That's a negative, Ffestiniog. No request has been made for your power.'

Through a separately listening part of his ear, Casson heard a deeper gear engage somewhere behind him. *Christ.* It was the turbine lock snapping into the generator shaft, ready to govern the shaft's speed because it was about to receive a concerted deluge through all four huge stainless-steel pipes which bored down through the heart of the mountain.

Casson abandoned the microphone. There was nothing Manchester could do now. He broke the rules and sprinted, veering off down the concrete steps. He deliberately ignored the lift because of what happened when he last went near it.

He was panting when he reached the dimly-lit alternator floor well below ground level. His footsteps echoed eerily, giving the impression he was being chased. The noise increased the farther he progressed. No windows here; simply claustrophobic walls and machinery.

He was heaving for breath and the noise was excruciating, but he had almost reached the manual-control section. Only seconds left now and it could tear out the heart of the power station. Come on, come on, he urged himself as perspiration stung his eyes. Almost there.

Then it happened.

Something caught him a full-blooded blow in the throat. He was stunned and momentarily blinded. For a while he seemed to be floating on a velvet sea.

Although he couldn't see it, a heavy chain had been stretched tightly across the aisle and fastened to machinery on either side. Casson was pulled off his feet and carried forward by his own momentum into a metal stepladder.

Winded by the jarring impact, he found himself on his knees and making little whimpering noises. Blood ran from his nose, his neck was bruised and he was badly dazed.

How on earth could it have got there? He stopped floating and tried painfully to pull himself up; his thought processes flickered back into action. It was impossible. Nobody could get down here into the power station . . . he'd left the building locked tight and checked every conceivable door and window.

Only a maniac would have set up such a lethal trap and then made sure he came running along the ill-lit passage. A madman with keys.

'Oh, dear God!' His head swam as he remembered that the machinery was reaching a critical point. If it wasn't immediately shut down, water would arrive in the basement with the force of a runaway locomotive. The turbines were not in a position to cope, valves were closed. The lake up in the mountain would empty itself into an unprepared power station and he would either be crushed or drowned.

He was almost there. Just a few yards now and he would be able to reach the manual controls. His legs buckled but he dragged himself forward on his knees until, gasping and straining, he got his hands on the flat control wheel: ten inches wide, it had the facility to shut off the danger.

Grunting with effort he twisted it clockwise; a full turn, then again, until the wheel locked against solid metal and the remaining strength ebbed from his arms.

Remotely he heard a clunk of valves closing and the waves of mechanical noise receded. The water had been held back by a hairsbreadth. For a while the main shaft spun freely but, without motivation, it gradually lost momentum. The stillness that now descended was absolute.

The power station became a cathedral of silence once again.

All that moved was the solitary figure of John Casson, making his way back along the dimly lit aisle between the rows of machinery and sobbing as he held his throat. For the moment he was vulnerable to whatever the intruder chose to inflict on him.

Someone or something wanted him out of the power station. Out of Tan-y-grisiau. Alive, if he went right away. Otherwise dead.

He lay back full-length in the bath, soaking up to his lower lip in an extravagance of water, letting the exhaustion and tension expunge itself in the steaming heat.

Yet it wasn't that easy. Hetty could still be down there somewhere, relying on him to come back and save her.

If it was a man, how the devil did he get in? And if it was not a man . . . For the moment he was too tired to think; too shattered to do anything. He glanced at the door. If anything came for him now, there was nothing he could do to stop it. A flimsy lock. That was about all.

Later he dragged himself to bed. He was still sitting up when sleep overtook him and he did nothing to resist its welcome attention.

He awoke at about 3 a.m., perspiring. Sat up, aware that something remorseless had disturbed him, although he could not remember what.

There was nothing untoward about the half-visible shapes in the room although his throbbing neck reminded him of what had happened. His jacket hung hunch-backed across a chair. In the distance he could hear heavy rain hissing diagonally down, soaking into the very pores of the mountains.

In the interim he had dreamed of Hannah. Surprisingly, nothing at all of Elliyn. The girl from his childhood achingly occupied his mind. Her wide mouth and cool eyes. Light blue, weren't they? But the more he strove to recall her face the more difficult it became to remember all the detail. Oh God, why hadn't they met six months earlier? She was on the verge of marrying her superstitious American pilot.

Beyond that, something else disturbed him, and he wasn't sure what. Perhaps it was something to do with the basement . . .

A thud echoed dully along the darkened corridor outside. It came from a long way off within the elongated building: In the deep basement.

He ignored it purposely and gently felt his injured neck.

A second and slightly louder bang echoed along the main operating floor. And again! As if someone was regularly slamming a distant door. He turned on his side to ignore it. Prayed that it would go away.

Eventually he had to get up and crossed silently to the door, but listened without opening it. The noise alternated between two slightly different sounds which were repeated every ten seconds. Remorselessly. Thud. Thump. But they were too loud and evenly spaced simply to be a window harassed by the wind.

Every echoing thud made him start. It had to be a heavy door off its latch. Damn! It really was too bad! The thought of leaving the warm sanctuary of his room to search for the cause made him clench his teeth in nervous anger.

When, reluctantly, he felt his way along the corridor, his anger shrivelled. He reached for the light panel and swept down all the switches, but none responded. The whole bank of lights must have fused. God Almighty! He had started shivering again, but reminded himself sharply not to be foolish. He was alone in the building. Whoever had fixed the chain downstairs had almost certainly done so in the daytime, he reasoned, and would be far away by now.

As he ventured into the turbine hall the noise increased in volume. *Thud. Thump.* What the devil could it be? It seemed to be coming from below ground.

He hesitated behind each of the generator domes which were spaced along the centre of the hall. By the time he reached the stairs he was breathing painstakingly.

The intermittent thudding was much clearer now. Somewhere below, but so close it gave him a headache. Fear was a flat, metallic taste in his mouth.

He found it painful even to swallow as he descended the concrete steps, dreading what he would find. One floor below, the noise resounded all around. Then a basement second floor. He paused halfway and crouched, straining his eyes to make out what awaited him.

The cause of the noise was now apparent: the lift. Its door was closing automatically every ten seconds but, on banging into an obstruction, immediately jerked back into its recess.

After a pause the door rattled across in another frustrated attempt to close. The process would go on indefinitely until the power ran out.

Casson kept well back at first, trying to discern what was blocking the lift. But, still too far away to make it out, he was obliged reluctantly to edge closer.

It looked like a sack. A coarse, bulging sack containing something solid enough to withstand a constant bludgeoning from the lift door.

Each thud against the pliant contents made them change position slightly, almost as if there was someone inside.

Don't go near it! Don't be a fool! And for Christ's sake, don't touch it! Advice panicked across his mind.

He quickly glanced behind him. There were shadows in all directions, deep and impenetrable. If he ventured any closer to the agitated lift, God knows what he would find grinning maniacally in the darkness.

Yet, incredibly, his feet moved forward; cautiously, down one step at a time. His mind groaned in protest, but the treacherous common-sense in another part of his brain reasoned it was no good remaining rooted to the spot.

Just be careful, that's all, he warned himself. Frighteningly careful.

He stepped over the sack with fearful precision and stood awkwardly, with his other foot wedging the door open. Trapped in its recess, the thudding ended. All that could be heard now was the distant routine hum of the power station and his own tight breathing.

Yet it was far from normal.

Casson's face twitched. A flat, oddly familiar smell reached his nostrils which he recognized with a feeling of dread. Blood. The bottom of the sack was soaked in it.

He swallowed painfully with rising terror. If there was a body inside, he did not want to know! He simply wanted to get away, far away. But his foot was trapped behind the vile, sticky weight of the sack.

He shuddered and shifted the leaning weight just a few inches. It was enough to open the top of the sack, revealing something white and pallid inside. An unhealthy, blood-drained trunk of flesh.

With fascinated horror he eased the sack open and tipped the contents away from him. The leg, hooves and the carcase of a fully-grown sheep emerged. He might have leaned back against the side of the lift in trembling relief, except for one thing. There was no head. The animal had been decapitated.

Casson was sickened. What sort of person could hack off a sheep's head, and then go to the extremity of stuffing the gory remains into a sack, leaving them in the middle of the night to be found where any normal person would jump out of his skin at the sight?

It had to be someone with a deranged mind. Someone still in the building. Any doubts in that respect fled from his mind.

Decapitation was a repugnant practice used by Druids living in a barbaric world of ritual slaughter. He had read somewhere that the wisdom of the savage Celtic priests was also held in such esteem that their word could stop tribes in mid-battle.

One of their brutal trademarks was the stabbing of a random victim in the back in order to deduce the omens from his death throes, then cutting off his head. Centuries old and it hadn't died out. Casson shivered and looked around anew.

The wheezing, laboured breathing he had heard on the hillside the previous day came back into his mind. Cold fingers crept across his body and they made the hairs stand up on the back of his neck.

What now? He couldn't leave the carcase there. It took a lot of courage to step across it, back into the dank lift. But it was the only way he could get at the pungent, twisted body. Screwing up his face in distaste, he dragged the slippery remains into the cramped aluminium lift with him.

God, it was heavy. The door closed on them and silence descended. By now Casson was perspiring heavily. He stabbed a numb forefinger onto the button marked G, and all that happened was that the dim bulb went out.

An expletive stuck in his throat. It was unbelievable! He jabbed again and again, but there was no reaction from the lift. It would neither move nor open its door. He was trapped claustrophobically in a pitch-black lift with the awful weight of the headless animal pressing against his legs.

He tried every button on the panel, depressing them frantically one after the other. Swearing, sobbing. Until the machinery started with a jolt. The movement came as such sweet relief that he didn't care where it was going.

Down instead of up. As far as it would go. It quivered to a halt in the pump sub-basement and the door rattled open. Here the darkness was intense: so thick it almost smothered him. But he had little choice. If he was to escape the malicious lift, it meant plunging into the envelope of darkness ahead.

He dragged the mutilated body of the sheep out on to the concrete floor, prising up one of his fingernails agonizingly in the process but not caring. Anything to get away from the lift.

How he dragged the obscenely sagging carcase back up endless flights of hostile steps he never knew. Bathed in sweat and, at times, almost doubled up with back-breaking effort, he tugged and grunted.

But he had a purpose which pushed all other considerations from his mind.

Only one person was demented enough to have done such a thing. Dewi! It was all that cretin's fault. Everything bad that had happened. The terror in the shadows, the half-seen movements at dusk must have been Dewi all the time. There was no need for any deeper explanation.

The focussing of his suspicions lifted an enormous weight from Casson's mind. Dewi. He fed on the name and ground it between his teeth. That demented disciple of Non-Conformist bigotry had crept through the building at night, scaring him witless, and had battered poor, defenceless Hetty.

Casson chuckled with feverish delight as he manoeuvred the savagely hacked sheep into the main hall; delight at how he would avenge himself on that sly bag of bones. No remorse now. That mad sod deserved all he was going to get. But to an outsider it would have been difficult, at that moment, to decide who was the more unhinged.

Thirteen

His car wouldn't start. But, even if it had, he doubted it would have got him as far as the chapel. More water lapped across the road during the night, and that would mean driving along the grassy ridges and high ground. It would be difficult to judge just what was firm and what marshmallow.

He re-tied the neck of the sack, sucked in a deep breath and heaved it up on to his shoulders. Casson was a tall man without the benefit of the forklift arms of a typical Welsh shepherd, yet he had a certain stamina.

Despite the stale-offal smell of the carcase and the increase in its deadweight with every step, he kept going. Occasionally he glanced at a rope coiled around his waist, reassuring himself it was still there. He would need it later.

He dropped the awkward load more than once, and soon his mouth sagged open with effort. It was a nightmare, but he forced himself to a point beyond strain and almost past caring.

Pasty grey clouds scuttled overhead, unsure of themselves. Once or twice they even changed direction as if disconcerted and not at all certain of what to do.

When he staggered up to the chapel porch, brushing enquiries aside, someone hurried inside to find Elliyn Pryce-Jones. But she was not to be found. He stood bent-backed and eased the sack slightly on his aching shoulders. His arms were numb with strain but he was afraid that, if he let it down, he would never be able to raise it again.

'Find Dewi!' he croaked. 'Get him out here, right away!'

Dewi finally emerged, halting suspiciously in the back of the porch and calling, 'What is it you want, boyoh? Try anything here and you'll be in terrible trouble, that's the truth.'

There was no answer.

'Look we don't want no trouble at the chapel, see? Not on the Sabbath. If you've a mind to pick an argument, make sure you've got the right person is all I can say.' He ventured a little farther, but there was no sign of Casson or the bulging sack.

Dewi glanced both ways, then frowned back into the chapel. 'Where is he then?' he demanded stridently.

'Right here,' said Casson as he stepped quickly from a shadowed alcove inside the porch and swung the blood-soaked sheep from its sack. It caught the unprepared Welshman high in the chest, flattening him.

Dewi lay full-length with all the breath knocked out of him, squirming faintly under the dead weight. When eventually he wriggled over and on to his hands and knees, Casson dropped his own weight on the thin back and the stunned Welshman collapsed again.

'Jesus have mercy,' he gasped. 'I can't breathe. I can't . . . I'm choking!'

Casson grimaced mirthlessly down at him. 'Mercy? Didn't know you knew such a word.' He unwound the rope with one hand, gripped Dewi by the back of his collar and dragged him to his knees.

When the Welshman began threshing, Casson transferred his grip to the long, tangled hair and twisted it agonizingly. Dewi yelped and arched his body to ease the pain. Little streaks of remorse washed down his grime-stained cheeks.

Casson heaved the sheep carcase firmly on to the man's skinny shoulders and looped the rope around them, levering it tight. Then round again, trapping his arms and forming criss-crosses. The carcase squashed into Dewi's neck and around his ribs. Tighter and tighter it was jerked, despite his whimpering, like a great pack on his back.

Finally Casson stood back, breathing hard. Now he unbuckled his own belt and swished it through the air. 'Get up.'

Dewi sobbed and made an effort but the weight defeated him and he sank forward in a huddle on his knees.

'On your feet!' Casson lashed his buttocks with the leather strap.

Dewi yelped. 'You're mad! Bloody crazy.'

'That's right,' snarled Casson, relishing the moment. 'This time you've picked on somebody just as vicious as you are.' He raised another welt on Dewi's backside.

Dewi hyenaed with pain and stumbled to his feet, but the dripping bulk of the sheep bent him over like a hunchback. He staggered head-first into the wall, then backwards into the chapel where several startled people milled out of their way.

'Right, show them how bible-clever you are, Dewi! Let them see the corrupt sheep you slew. Butchered it, didn't you? And left it for me to find, you vile man.'

He lashed down with the strap so many times he lost count. Sweat dribbled into his eyes, stung and almost blinded him. Dewi scrambled and staggered to avoid the endless beating, knocked over pews and brought collection plates crashing down.

'Slaughtered it for me, did you?' Casson heard himself pant. 'Only now it's returned like a prodigal, and you'll need a bloody miracle to escape what's coming to you!'

The organist hung on to Casson, anchoring his arms. The engineer could not recall what happened next but, amid the confusion and utter exhaustion, Dewi scrambled outside.

He got an impression of the Welshman staggering towards the cover of distant trees, pursued by barking dogs, before he himself slumped down on the porch bench.

'That was a silly thing to do.' The deep, calm voice of Elliyn Pryce-Jones penetrated his thoughts. She stood contemplating the havoc.

Casson wiped his face. 'What he did to me I've returned with interest.'

'He'll make trouble for you.' She glanced at the swirling clouds. The air felt humid and unsettled. It still couldn't make up its mind. 'As soon as he gets free, he'll call down the weather.'

'Let him,' Casson said contemptuously. 'I've been wet before.'

'Not like this, you haven't. You'd better get going. I've seen what he can do when he puts his mind to it. You'd be surprised what happens when the blood runs to his head. Being born up in the mountains where the weather comes from, he thinks he's a half-brother to the storms.' She shrugged. 'Of course, a lot of people say he's just off his head. But I wouldn't take that chance if I were you.'

Casson felt she was getting her own back over the tiff that followed their night of love, but he set off nevertheless.

Within ten minutes he'd be back in the power station. He didn't believe Dewi had any influence, other than over susceptible people, but it left him with an uneasy feeling and he began to hurry just the same.

It was the storm to end all storms. Something he would never forget.

It caught up with him halfway home after he had squelched through the waterlogged meadow and was picking his way between rocks scattered up the hillside.

Spears of rain attacked his shoulders and he was soon soaked through. He was breathing hard when the first flickering trace of lightning danced along the ridge ahead of him.

The next blinding flash struck the ground and hissed down the hill towards him: following a murderously erratic path which left the air sizzling in its wake before giving up. There was nowhere for him to shelter.

He hesitated, wrapping his shivering arms tightly about him. God, perhaps there was something in what she said after all. Thunder exploded overhead, deafening him, and the rain fell in sheets on to harassed earth and made it almost impossible for him to see.

Clouds bloated with the rain blundered in low and emptied their contents, as if by order. The dark, gloomy countryside was in turmoil.

A jagged blue-white bayonet of lightning lunged into the rocks ahead of him. He was stunned by its proximity and stood mutely contemplating some brittle ginger hairs on the back of his hands which had been singed in the heat.

A few random steps in the wrong direction were all that separated him from death at that moment; all that divided him from the fate of Rhys apJones and the two other policemen.

The rain fell with increasing fury so that he no longer had any idea where he was going. He went down on his hands and knees at one stage simply to make gasping progress; cut his hands on razor-edged slate; and got up only to step heavily into a choking dewpond, disguised by a beautifully intricate green coverlet of duckweed. He floundered blindly up to his armpits before finding a firm footing again.

Noise rumbled across the sky and light split into ten fingers of crackling energy. He was crouching down, with his hands shielding his bare head, when he saw an even closer flash of lightning followed by trailing tendrils of electricity. They twitched like lethal lengths of barbed wire only inches past his outstretched arm.

By the time he reached the narrow winding lane that led up to the power station he was talking incoherently to himself. Stumbling, he urged himself on but most of his cohesion was gone.

The vehicle that came along at that moment saved him. Without it he might have been bludgeoned or burned by the storm, even decapitated.

Brakes squealed and tyres locked as they skidded. He subsided wearily in front of the approaching truck which veered broadside to avoid hitting him. Even so, he found himself under its protective bumper.

He had a hazy impression of words stencilled in white along the side. United States Air Force.

Captain J.J. Andretti turned the collar of his lightweight Service raincoat up against the worst of the weather and groped under the front of his vehicle.

Recognition dawned in his face and, despite the teeming

rain, he said ironically, 'Well . . . fancy bumping into you.' He straightened up and called from behind a cupped hand, 'It's him!'

Hannah Frost's face was distorted behind the briskly-sweeping windscreen wipers. She put a fuzzy hand to her ear.

Andretti raised his voice against the frantic rain, then waved it aside with a disparaging sweep of his hand. He lifted Casson out from under the oil-warm belly of his Jeep. 'You all right? Didn't hit you, did I?'

'No, just stunned,' Casson grimaced with relief. 'My fault.'

'Okay, I'll get you inside.' He paused. 'Or would you rather I left you here and just run over you? I know how self-reliant you British are.'

'I'll take the lift.'

Casson was helped into the haven that was the back seat of a military vehicle. He blinked and tipped his head to allow the driving rain to run out of his ears. Hannah was there, twisting round anxiously from the front seat. When he recognized her it seemed like a miracle to him.

'Is he hurt?' she asked.

'He says not. Couldn't have missed him by more than a whisker. Look, Casson, when you feel like it you just indicate the way home and I'll get you there.'

Casson smiled wearily and pointed ahead, without once taking his eyes off Hannah's face. It was wonderful to see her again, and the feeling of relief that spread through him was indescribable.

The American started the engine and smiled tightly over his shoulder. 'Okay, let's try to get out of this screwy storm. It only seems to be affecting this side of the hill.'

'Straight ahead. The power station is the big building you'll come across. Main gate's open.'

Hannah smiled reassuringly and reached awkwardly back over the seat to grip Casson's hand. New hope flowed from her touch, but she didn't speak until Andretti ducked through the lashing rain and opened a distant door for them.

'I had to come,' she said quietly and for his ears only.

He gulped with joy, mistaking her meaning.

'I prayed you would.'

'I had another dream,' she said. 'This one was frightening.'

'Oh, I see.' Was that all? he thought. For a moment or two all the light and life drained out of him.

'I'd like to stay here with you for a while.'

'If you like,' he said dully.

She looked at him questioningly but by then Andretti was back, gesticulating wildly. 'Come on, you guys. Hop out. Don't let me drown in vain.'

Hannah slid out, showing her long slim legs. She kept a firm grip on his hand and ran with him through a gauntlet of rain to the sanctuary of the reception hall.

The captain took off his Service hat and ran relieved fingers through his tight curly hair. 'Phew, we almost bought it twice, I've never known anything like it for sheer intensity.'

Hannah was busy with practicalities. 'Get the bags from the boot, J.J. I'll help John along to his room.'

The dripping officer hesitated as he looked out at the unrelenting rain. 'Why not?' he said sarcastically. 'I mean, if I can only get my right shoe full of water, I'll be completely waterlogged. There's no point in doing things by half measures.'

Casson, still a little unsteady, walked on ahead with Hannah. 'I feel a bit of a fraud.'

'No need to. You had a nasty fall. What happened?'

'I thought something was chasing me.'

They walked along the corridor in silence, listening only to the squelching of their wet feet. 'Silly, isn't it?' he said.

'Not necessarily.'

He stopped and reached for her hand. 'I really am glad you're here, but you mustn't stay. You don't know what you're letting yourself in for.'

She searched his eyes. 'I know this much. The unknown can play some macabre tricks when you're alone. But they are easier to see through when there are two of you.'

'Look I don't want both of us to get hurt.' He sighed and relaxed his tense shoulder muscles. 'The real reason I'm here is I've got a dog to find, and I'm going to find her dead or alive. Ridiculous, isn't it? I don't expect you to understand.'

She reached with sensitive fingers to touch the edges of his mouth; storing a braille memory without taking her eyes off him. 'I understand. You love her.'

He nodded numbly.

'I wish somebody loved me like that,' she said indistinctly.

Casson fought down an urge to close the few inches that separated their mouths. 'You've got him,' he croaked, nodding towards the main entrance.

'J.J.?' She pulled a sad face. 'Sure I have. It's just that at times I feel he deserves someone better than me. He's got such high standards. Occasionally I think he regrets I'm not more intellectual.'

'You mean, you're not intellectual?' Casson whispered, making it sound ludicrously important.

She shook her head and grinned, and he was awfully close to kissing her. But J.J. came briskly around the corner, dripping wet, with a grip in each hand. 'Come on, come on. What is it about you Brits that you have to discuss every finite detail of the weather? Haven't you ever seen a storm with a mind of its own before?'

'In here.' Casson led the way. 'These are my quarters. This is home.'

In turn they changed their clothes while Casson put on the kettle for tea. Hannah discovered where he kept the bread and cake, and set about preparing a meal. It was all reassuringly cosy.

Andretti laid an arm around Casson's shoulder and whispered to him while Hannah was out of the way for a while. 'Look, I don't pretend to know what's going on here, but Hannah says you invited her to stay for a day or two while I'm out of the country.'

'Un-huh,' responded Casson non-committally.

'You two have always been close, like a brother and

sister?' The Italian-American watched him closely and nodded when Casson nodded. 'Fine. Another time, you ask me first. Capito?'

Casson cleared his throat. 'There may not be another time.'

Andretti examined his eyes suspiciously but could find nothing to indicate that he was being misled. 'Right,' he said emphatically.

Hannah returned and said brightly, 'What are you two up to?'

Her fiance smiled tightly. 'Just man talk. Nothing for you to worry about.'

Hannah stretched her neck, listening. 'I think it's stopped raining.'

'It stopped just after we got inside. The odd thing is that when I looked out just now, I saw the clouds banked up about a mile off: holding back as if they're watching the place. Perhaps they're getting ready to start again whenever we show our faces.' Andretti laughed uneasily.

They had tea and, afterwards, Casson told them about Dewi and the troubles. He purposely left out any mention of the butchered sheep, so as not to upset Hannah.

Andretti fingered a heavy family ring on his finger. 'That's incredible. I'm superstitious, but I've never been this close to the supernatural before.' He turned to Hannah. 'What do you think, darling? You know a lot more about this sort of thing than I do.'

Casson turned to her with a flicker of hope. Any light she could shed would be a step forward. But she shook her head. 'I'm sorry. I'm out of my depth.'

Andretti patted her hand. 'Nothing to be sorry about, honey. The reason I love you is that you've got your feet on the ground.'

Hannah nodded but her eyes stole into a silent conspiracy with Casson's. She did know more, a great deal more. He was sure of it. They were partners in a tentative understanding.

'Well . . .' The captain stretched and consulted his

multi-purpose flight watch. 'It's going to be dark in an hour or two. I have to start back.'

'He's gone,' Casson said needlessly as the sound of the Jeep's engine faded around a curve of the mountain.

She said absently, 'I hope he'll be all right.'

Casson listened to the building creaking faintly as it settled at the end of the day. 'We're the ones you should be worried about.'

She lifted her head slightly, sniffing a higher layer of air like a vixen at dusk. 'No,' she said matter-of-factly, 'that's not so. I had a premonition about J.J. yesterday.'

Nearly two miles along the road, Captain J.J. Andretti scythed the high-wheeled vehicle through a sheet of water and accelerated up the far slope. He was the sort of driver you would expect an outstanding pilot to be. Strong and firm-handed at the wheel. Mind alert and ready for almost anything – which was just as well in the circumstances.

As he swept around the next bend he saw Dewi standing in the middle of the road, hands stretched out as if beckoning the Jeep towards him. His face wore an imbecilic smile of welcome.

There were less than thirty yards of open road separating them. Andretti swung the wheel hard over one way, then back just as abruptly: making the Jeep slew off the road, bump along a dangerous verge and shudder back as its wheels screeched for a grip on the far side of the scrawny figure in the ill-fitting suit.

Andretti stopped, wound down the window and shouted back. 'What the hell are you up to, mister?'

Dewi took his time turning around and, when he did, he said vacuously, 'I'm here to punish you.' He extended a tapering finger at the air force captain. 'It's your fault. You should not have helped a sinner.'

Andretti realized he was talking to the local idiot. He backed his Jeep until he was level with the thin Welshman. 'You realize I could have killed you?'

Dewi did not seem to be listening. 'You brought it on yourself. I shall make an example of you.'

'If I didn't have my wits about me, you'd be dead by now, fellah.'

'You must get out of that car.'

'What's that?'

'You're to be sacrificed.'

Andretti's hands tightened on the wheel. He saw there was no point in arguing. Perhaps he should find a constable; the man obviously belonged in an institution. Instead he put the Jeep into gear and pulled quickly away. Soon he was lost to sight.

Fourteen

Captain Andretti bit his thin lower lip as he drove. He was accustomed to discipline and order. Oddities made him feel ill at ease. There was no obvious way in his carefully regulated life of dealing with them. He thought back through the episode to make sure he hadn't left the impression that the Welshman had gained the upper hand, particularly in view of the Jeep's squealing departure.

Already night had begun to fall, seeping down the grim slopes of the Moelwyns. Drifting insidiously across the road and pulling its gloomy shrouds around the fast-moving vehicle.

Although his eyes were on the road, Andretti kept part of his attention on the mountains that towered over him. A glint of light, perhaps a watery reflection of the setting sun, caught his eye on a peak away to his left.

He was still slightly disturbed at the thought of Hannah staying at the power station with Casson. She was sensible enough, but a lonely man and a single woman thrown together like that . . .

Andretti drove on, fixing the spot in the corner of his

eye. Now it was moving. About a mile off, but keeping station with him.

He wasn't sure about marriage. Of course he loved her. Who wouldn't? At times, given the right moment, she was breathtakingly beautiful. At open evenings at the base he sensed the envy of bachelors and married pilots alike. It was just that marriage inevitably meant children – and tedium.

There was no road running parallel to his left, and it could not possibly be an aircraft that close to the rockface. Perhaps a reflection cast by a quirk of the fading light?

He stopped, wound down the window and peered out. Oddly, the glint also came to a halt.

The air was gently oppressive and he tugged at his collar, opening the top button. A sense of unease was triggered in his mind; not enough to unsettle him, but as a trained observer he ought to have identified the object by now.

It was ridiculous! He reached for a pair of powerful Service binoculars on the back seat. He'd settle the matter once and for all.

But before he could take any action, the light intensified as if it realized there was no longer any need to be surreptitious. A tight corridor formed between Captain J.J. Andretti and whatever it was.

He was trapped in reverberating silence. It seemed to paralyse him and made his eardrums ache. He was reminded sharply of a college visit years before to a coal mine on the Allegheny, near Pittsburgh, when the cage dropped like a stone and painful pressure blocked both ears. Only this was worse. For, through the throbbing silence, came the sound of laboured breathing.

Andretti's eyes widened and perspiration formed on his upper lip. The binoculars were in his hands, still unused, and now he raised them unsteadily.

The distant object sprang into focus. Not one but two closely-set patches of white light. The impressions he got were nightmarish: an enormous shadowy face in which only the eyes could be seen. They mesmerized and compelled him to stare into their horrific depths despite himself. Blind, linen-white eyes.

Casson was instructed by Manchester to generate that evening. At a time when millions of housewives were lighting electric fires and cooking evening meals for late-home families, who in turn leaned forward and switched on television, the demand for power from the National Grid soared.

Manchester needed to call on the muscle that was flexed and waiting in the ancient mountains of north-west Wales: and in particular the power it could harness from the high-level lake of Llyn Stwlan.

Casson pressed a sequence of buttons in the control room, starting the mechanism which released the first gushing deluge of water down steel-lined tunnels towards the power station.

The water would pound down, uninterrupted, for four hours; its raw force penetrating valves six feet wide and, in turn, activating turbine and generator. The spent water was released into the lower reservoir. In the meantime, overhead cables sizzled with power that now surged eagerly from pylon to pylon eastwards into the night.

After an hour or so he left the controls on automatic and wandered quietly back to his bedroom where Hannah was sleeping. He felt a pang of remorse that the foot of the bed, where Hetty liked to stretch out, was empty. It was his fault she wasn't there, loyal as any stone dog at the feet of a Crusader.

He went into the adjoining room and arranged a spare mattress on the floor, wedging the door open in case he was needed in a hurry during the night. He had an idea that once he settled into the bed's foetal warmth and closed his eyes he would not stir again until morning. But he was wrong.

A distant bark reached him over the subdued hum of machinery. Casson was not yet in bed. He stopped pulling off his shoes, and raised his head instantly. Hetty?

There it was again. Three distinct staccato barks from a

long way off. Casson got up and moved lightly out into the turbine hall, buttoning his shirt and straining to make out the direction.

He paused by the lift, breathing hard. Come on, girl, he urged. Come on now. Let me hear you once more. There it was again, from far below! He raced headlong down the concrete steps, jumping the last half-dozen to a landing and doing the same on the next descending flight.

Any dread he harboured of the sub-basement was submerged by the prospect of finding Hetty alive. If she was there, he would get to her.

Dim night-lights gave him just enough illumination to reach the bottom of the building. Here enormous pumps rested on bedrock. He took in their thick inspection windows and heard the drip, drip, drip, of perpetual water.

There had been no bark now for nearly a minute, but he was sure of his direction. There was no other way. Down as far as he could go, then straight along the narrow gangway until he found her, or reached the concrete wall at the far end. More than once he whistled, knowing that she would normally respond. But she did not.

Quite suddenly he stopped and melted into the shadows. Ahead of him was a single bright light. That meant that somebody else was in the deepest corner of the power station. His hands trembled, but he quickly occupied them in slipping his shoes off. From here on, he needed to move silently.

He gripped his tongue lightly between his teeth and moved cautiously over the last thirty or forty feet; listening intently and then edging forward again.

Beyond the last pump, the floor widened to provide just enough space for a table and chair: somewhere for an inspection engineer to make routine maintenance notes before returning upstairs. But the sight that met Casson's eyes gave him a jolt. He almost felt the cold and clammy hand of death grip him by the throat.

Someone was sitting, leaning into the table. A human outline completely covered in a white sheet. Elbows bent. Unmoving.

Casson sucked in his breath but was quite unable to control his shaking legs. A dread of who might be under the sheet urged him to run, but the very same fear rooted him to the spot.

There was no sign of Hetty. He was breathing shallowly and desperately fast as he tried to pull himself together. He was going to have to lift the edge and find out who was underneath. Despite his terror, he knew he had no option.

God, how he wished he was somewhere else! He screwed up his courage, and side-stepped a little closer and thought about snatching up a corner of the sheet. But suppose something reached out and grabbed him?

Casson cleared his throat. 'Look here. Who are you?' he heard himself say. But there was no answer from the pyramidical shape.

Tensing himself in a supreme effort he lifted the cover in horrified anticipation. Underneath was a dressmaker's dummy, sitting with her hands folded primly in her lap. Headless.

Casson stared at it speechless and let the sheet drop. His hands were trembling uncontrollably.

Somebody had lured him down into the silence. But why? In order to attack him? Casson jerked around, but there was no movement along the entire floor. Somebody had gone to a lot of trouble in order to entice him down there. It had to be Dewi.

The reason for it all came to him a split-second later. Hannah. Upstairs, asleep and unprotected. Her door left ajar.

Casson sobbed as he ran pell-mell back towards the lift. He had been hopelessly fooled. The indicator showed the lift to be at the ground floor. He flung himself full-stretch at the stairs, leaping three and four at a time. Dear God, don't let anything have happened to her.

Panting up flight after flight. Frantically he plunged along the turbine floor. His mouth was a lather of saliva as he burst into the room. But the sheets had been ripped back off the bed: she was gone.

Fifteen

Razorbill was classified as the most secret U.S. airplane based in Europe. It specialized in flying fast and low, homing in upon its target more accurately than any of its predecessors.

One of the reasons it was named after a Welsh seabird was its deadly skill against shipping. It could appear over comparatively small targets as if from nowhere. It had, like its namesake, the ability to pick out quite distant, unsuspecting fish while skimming the waves.

The attack plane stood ready in a hangar at the Nato base near Fulda, close to the East-West German border. There was something sinister about its deceptively dull-black finish. A killer at rest. A vehicle packed with enough armament and electronic equipment to make it the most fearsome flying object since pterodactyl.

Captain Andretti was woken at dawn by a yawning corporal in overalls offering him coffee in a mug. He would have much preferred a cup and saucer in keeping with the niceties of life, and frowned as he walked crisply to the met. room for a pre-flight briefing.

There was fog drifting in a broad swathe down from Denmark, which was nothing to a sophisticated plane like Razorbill. He zipped up his green flying suit while recalling a disturbing dream of the previous night. He barely listened to the met. officer. He had imagined an horrific face with cloth-white eyes. Coming to inspect him and standing frighteningly close, as if about to claim him.

Soon he was crossing the runway to where the lethal black warplane was standing waiting, primed with fuel and ready to be ferried to England. On his way across the tarmac, through clinging tatters of mist, he dropped a glove but did not glance back. If you drop a glove, never pick it up yourself. Not unless you want bad luck.

He nodded to a ground-crew master-sergeant who caught up and handed it back. 'You dropped this, sir.' But a moment or two later any gratitude was overtaken by exasperation.

'Jesus Christ, Sergeant. Who painted this green thing on my plane?'

The beefy non-commissioned officer locked his jaw and gazed at the four-leafed clover on the fuselage without comprehending what was wrong. Most of the planes had a personal marker. It was accepted squadron practice.

'Why, I did, Captain. Knowing how you are about keeping your fingers crossed and carrying a talisman, I got the boys to put it on for good luck.'

'When I want your help, I'll ask for it. Until then, you keep your ideas to yourself. Got that?'

'Yessir.'

Andretti nervously massaged his hands. He was in two minds about asking operations to delay his flight and ordering his ground crew to paint it out.

'Something wrong with a four-leaf clover, sir?'

'Nothing, Sergeant,' he gritted. 'But it's bright green!'

'Sir?' Bewilderment was written all over the man's face.

'It's an unlucky colour. In fact, it's *the* unlucky colour.'

A senior technician tried to put matters right. 'Excuse me, sir. I believe there's really nothing to fret over. She's a real smart-ass airplane.'

'It's not the plane that bothers me,' seethed Andretti. 'It's my ground crew.'

After that sort of hard-nosed reaction he was bound to swallow his pride and get aboard. He checked the instruments, got clearance and was scudding down the runway within minutes. The Razorbill scythed up into cloud and burst through, a moment or two later, into a peaceful world above the weather.

He checked with Fulda base and then listened with ill humour on his head-set to a distant intercept pilot whooping as he swept up on the tail of a Soviet Bear reconnaissance bomber somewhere over neutral Arctic waters. From then on he was alone in a world of dials, reassuring pinpricks of light and an occasional glimpse of the earth through cottonwool clouds far below.

Razorbill hissed across Europe and he momentarily noted waterlogged Dutch fields before a strip of beach and the start of the North Sea. Soon afterwards mist settled around him with an air of sullen permanence.

He did not give it a second thought. There was little the high-technology jet could not do. Radar scannings were fed to automatic controls. Neither of them needed to see what lay ahead.

He passed the time thinking about Hannah. She had excellent taste and an elegant appearance. But one day he meant to be an air force general and she would have to match up to it. If she had a fault it was in not being fastidious enough. For instance, she let slap-dash waiters off the hook far too easily. He relaxed. Don't be so supercilious, he told himself. She would make a splendid wife . . . if he decided to marry.

He looked out at the impenetrable weather and then glanced at speed-height indicators and radar, which all showed he was still over the North Sea. Still?

That was odd. Andretti raised an eyebrow: he rarely questioned a cockpit reading. Yet it was Friday – always an unlucky day to start a journey – and that numbskull had painted a *green* clover on the fuselage. He gnawed the inside of his mouth and rolled the plane over and down.

Razorbill's controls responded immaculately to the lightest touch. Rolls-Royce engines took him smoothly down through the cloud. He broke into clear view beneath the low ceiling and blinked rapidly in disbelief.

The plane was less than 500 feet over the granite spine of the Pennines and closing with it at 500 miles an hour. Christ! The instruments couldn't be that wrong!

Captain Andretti somehow hit the ejection button and survived the colossal impact. Although not for long. When they found him, his green flying suit and neatly-tailored shirt had been ripped open from collar to waist, exposing his body as it twitched in its death throes. Whatever looked down could have read the omens. In the way of the Druids.

PART 3: Retribution

Sixteen

Arnold Webb lay back on some musty sacks in the cellar and let his close-set eyes follow a crack that climbed erratically from dislodged foundations to the cobwebbed rafters of the empty cottage. In his own dim way he felt pleased with the roof over his head.

Not bad, he thought laboriously. Not bad for an escaped prisoner.

He had been given special treatment at Gwynfa and nobody bothered him. His blunt, closely cropped head gave credence to the story that he once butted a neighbour to death in the badly lit prison chapel during the singing of a hymn because the man tittered when Arnold steepled his hands to pray.

Even hard prison officers treated him with deference and allowed him to eat alone. Their consideration stemmed from an incident which he repeated on several consecutive days after arriving at Gwynfa: he swept food off a communal dining table and then swung a tubular chair high over his head and brought it down on the table with a strangulated roar, presumably to register his opinion of the cuisine.

Thereafter he remained in his cell at meal times. A tray of boiled fish and rubbery bread, followed by water-thinned custard and wizened prunes, was slid gingerly across the floor into his cell, first through a limited opening in the outer bars and then through a flap in the heavy door.

A psychiatrist regularly questioned him but rarely received a reply. The only object to arouse a response was a hypodermic syringe. His belligerent manhood was all he possessed and the blurred knowledge that it might be taken away through the gradual application of drugs made him dangerous to handle.

When left alone, sitting on the edge of his bed, he made a curiously sad figure. Observers could only guess what occupied his thoughts. Perhaps he was re-living the day when, handcuffed in the dock of Number One Court at the Old Bailey, he heard Mr Justice Winchmore pronounce sentence.

Even the cynical Central Criminal Court reporters raised their eyebrows when the judge described him as a mad dog. The only person unmoved was the lumbering prisoner, who mutely studied his scuffed shoes. The judge's high and precise voice carried crisply across the lofty courtroom to the raised dock opposite. To one side of the bewigged figure rested an incongruous posy of sweet-smelling garden flowers, which Old Bailey judges carry by tradition to ward off jail fever. But there was little fragrance about his words.

'Arnold Webb, you will be incarcerated for the rest of your natural life . . . or until such time as your faculties have declined and you are physically incapable of harming man or child.'

Webb remained impassive with his eyes lowered. The only indication that he even comprehended was the occasional restless rattle of the steel cuff against the dock rail.

Journalists had a field day. They called him 'Mad Dog Webb, the pick-axe killer who struck with terrifying ferocity,' and they reported the judge's inescapable intention that this man should die in jail.

He was destined for Broadmoor Secure Mental Hospital where isolated quarters were being prepared specifically for him. But temporarily they took him to Gwynfa . . . from which he had broken free.

Cold and uncomfortable, but feeling pleased with himself, he hummed tunelessly and recalled his biggest achievement at Gwynfa.

A psychiatrist penetrated his unreceptive mind almost by accident. He had suggested Webb taking up a hobby, although the big man barely glanced at the selection of books and games offered. He had, however, paused and reached for the least likely of the items in front of him: two blunt knitting needles and a ball of wool.

From then on he was completely absorbed in his new interest. Ponderously he would wind, loop and lift off stitches. For hour after hour, whenever the officer on Landing C3 checked the observation eyehole, Webb sat engrossed with the tip of his tongue gripped lightly between his teeth.

He worked intently up to the very moment of lights-out, then carefully put away the misshapen sock he had knitted. He refused to let anyone catch more than a glimpse of it and tucked it down inside his shirt, using it as a comfort in the loneliness of the night and rubbing his mouth absently against the lumpy knitting, which seemed to meet a need stretching back further than he could remember.

Punishment for jail misdemeanours normally meant little to him. But when, one day, his supply of wool was cut off, he pounded on the door so that reverberations shook the entire unit. No more wool was forthcoming that day or the next, and he took revenge on the Establishment by wrenching his iron bed from its wall fastening and battering it into an unrecognizable shape. He smashed his shelf and made a million snowflakes of an old feather mattress.

They came for him in force: five prison officers with short, thick truncheons. The punishment for his rebellion was humiliation; that is, if it is possible to shame a man who doesn't care. He was stripped and sedated, and kept for three weeks in a dark cell without bed covers. The only emotion he showed was to screw up his face in silent anguish.

When, at last, he returned to his own cell his fingers immediately closed around his shapeless knitting. He showed no reaction, other than blinking constantly in the unaccustomed light. But from then on the crumpled sock never left his side. The heavies on the landing joked that he would kill rather than allow it to be prised from him again; and no one ever put the matter to the test.

Arnold Webb lay there, remembering the noise of the approaching flood. Could he ever forget? At first he had imagined it was prolonged thunder. But it went on too long; more a heavy ball rolling down a bowling alley.

Hundreds of tons of water careered down the winding valley, sweeping aside boulders the size of buses and lifting up startled, scampering sheep like grey corks. The head-waters broke against the obdurate walls of H.M. Prison Gwynfa and foamed all around.

Flattening doors, gushing along corridors, gurgling down spiral staircases, there was hardly anywhere it did not reach. Webb quickly found himself up to his waist in paralysingly cold water.

An alarm bell sounded, followed by a shatteringly loud order on the loudspeakers for absent prisoners to be returned immediately to their cells. But no sooner had it been announced than the governor's befuddled voice cut in and countermanded it.

'This is the governor speaking. Get all the men out of their cells and up to top-floor level. Hurry please.'

Arnold Webb was bundled into the corridor with thirty other men, having had no time even to struggle into his trousers. They were pushed and cursed through swirling water and up half-a-dozen steps to comparative safety.

But when the lights flickered out, and the governor shouted at warders to check each cell in case anybody was still trapped, there was confusion. Arnold Webb suddenly clutched at his chest and rummaged under his vest. His beloved knitting was missing!

He turned one way and the other in desperation.

A prisoner stood on a wobbling table and tried to force open a trapdoor to the roof; anything to escape a claustrophobic death inside. An officer tried to drag him down and succeeded only in getting himself trampled.

Webb went in the opposite direction: threshing back towards his cell. Somebody in uniform blocked the corridor and shouted 'Get back, you silly bastard!' A fist clubbed into the face and it vanished backwards.

Arnold Webb fought into his cell, where two wood-framed pictures of dismal religious scenes were floating close to the ceiling, and groped distractedly for his cherished sock. At last his hand closed around a bundle of soggy wool. Sobbing with relief, he pressed it to his face. Nothing else mattered to him now.

But all that was days ago. He made himself more comfortable on the damp sacks and contemplated his other and more significant achievement, which had happened when he arrived at the cottage. He was desperate to get in out of the relentless rain and used his unthinking brute strength to kick down the rotting back door.

His pockets were wedged with bread rolls lifted from a bakery on the outskirts of Blaenau and, although most of them were beginning to turn blue with age, they were agreeable enough when dipped in water and accompanied by a potato or two.

Once inside he heard something whimpering beneath decrepit floorboards. It was a boxer bitch in pitiful condition, which he lifted out by the loose skin on the back of her neck, half-starved and frightened out of her life.

He realized that where there was a tethered dog there must be a man. But, although he sat in the shadow of a dislocated upstairs window and kept watch all day and most of the night, no one approached. He gave the dog some bread and, in return, it licked his hand. Later it snuggled against him and, when he awoke, he found its soft head snoozing on his lap.

The double-killer had a friend at last. It cast a dull ray of light through the dungeon of his mind. And, although he cared little for his own life, when he laid his hand gently on Hetty's jowl and gave an encouraging grunt he was, in effect, giving her his formidable protection.

Less than two miles away Dewi unlocked the stable where

he had incarcerated the startlingly attractive young woman overnight, and found her sitting up wincing at a crick in her back.

'Still here then, I see,' he said facetiously.

Hannah, who soon discovered there was no easy way out of the barn, had spent much of the night planning to browbeat him into releasing her. But now the moment had arrived her instincts warned her to treat him extremely carefully. 'I told you I wouldn't run away, and I always keep my promises.'

'Sensible that. I don't like deceitful people.'

'Please can I go home now?'

Normally Dewi would have gloated in such a situation. But she was considerably more sophisticated than the slate-working women he was accustomed to, and he was not quite so sure of himself.

'No, I want to take you somewhere. You see, three heads are better than one.' His mouth sagged slackly as he laughed.

'Please . . .' she begged. 'Please don't do anything we'll both regret. It's not too late to forget the whole thing.'

Dewi said slyly, 'You've been crying.' Slowly he sorted out a handkerchief from the disordered contents of a shabby brown Gladstone bag.

'Frightened of me, are you?' he asked without looking at her directly. 'Think I'm loose in the head?'

'Not especially,' she lied.

'That's good. Unless you're lying of course,' he added craftily.

She forced herself to smile, trying to play on his better nature, and indicated the grubby handkerchief. 'Is that for me?'

He blew his nose on it and tucked it away. 'Could be. Yes, it could be later, if you do as you're told.'

There was no point in running. She was too cold and tired and it would only incense him. 'What do you want me to do?' she asked forlornly.

He pointed to the mist-shrouded upper reaches of the mountain. 'Come with me up there.'

'But I can't,' she said in a voice trembling with tears. She knew too well that the farther he took her from Casson and the power station the less chance she had of ever getting back.

Dewi left her to it and went outside where sunshine, reflected on the early-morning dew, had covered the face of the mountain with a glistening veil of spun gossamer. It's not everybody who could see the veil to be worn at their own funeral, he thought.

It was yet another sign confirming that this was the day he yearned for. He was already a chapel deacon, but today would bring a confirmation far beyond that. Once he had performed the sacrifice, his destiny would be fulfilled. He would become a living Druid. Not a foolish Stonehenge charade, but one touched by fingers reaching out from the past.

Stands to reason, he told himself. Stands to reason there has to be a sacrifice.

He smiled uneasily at the sky. Together they would start to restore the old order and basic beliefs. Those who followed him would revere his name, and no one would ever again poke fun.

He'd always had an affinity with the weather. Living in abandoned buildings or old slate workings on the edge of Snowdon for as long as he could remember, he invariably knew what sort of day tomorrow would be. He knew from the speed and density of the clouds and from the activity of insects at dusk. It became instinctive, second nature, until it seemed in turn as if he could make the weather do as he wished.

He had always known in the rambling corridors of his mind that he had an appointment with destiny.

Halfway up the mountain was the best place; ideal for the purpose. The very thought made him twitch with excitement. Best she didn't know.

Dewi forced her to climb the slope. In his eagerness he grew angry when she fell down exhausted several times. He was carrying the heavy bag and bathed in perspiration, but he felt inspired. Once, when she tried to run away from him along a horizontal goat track, he threw her to the ground and jumped his knees up and down on her until she clawed to be let up.

'Look, I don't want to hurt you!' he said, desperate with anger.

'Then why are you doing this to me?' she asked despairingly.

'Because it's written.'

It was hopeless. She closed her eyes to stem tears that streaked her face. 'But I've never harmed you.'

He stubbed the hard ground with the tip of his right boot. 'No, but *he* has.'

Hannah looked back down the impossibly steep slope and had no idea how they had managed to climb even this far. There was no sign of John Casson or any sort of help. She wondered why she had thought of Casson and not J.J. She felt pathetically vulnerable; there was no telling what this maniac had in mind. 'Who?'

'You know who.' Dewi stretched up in order to see the top of a derelict cottage set back in a *cwm*, a little recess in the mountainside. Almost there. 'Did you know he had a boxer bitch once?'

Hannah nodded. Anything that occupied his attention and allowed her to catch her gasping breath was worth exploiting.

'Well, I've got it now. Up there under lock and key, see,' Dewi rubbed his hands gleefully. 'So, he must be running out of friends.'

Quite soon Hannah got her first glimpse of what was once a hermit's cottage. The weather had taken its toll; there were cracks in the exterior walls and the thatched roof had collapsed completely at one end. But the impoverished Welshman looked uncommonly pleased as he rummaged for the key.

She kept a close eye on Dewi. His motive for abducting her was still obscure. If he planned to assault her, she would suffer it. She had no intention of being strangled simply to deny 'a fate worse than death.' The extent of her planning was that there is no fate worse than death. Beyond that she was too weary to contemplate.

Dewi propelled her into an empty, echoing room and sat her down. Then he tied her hands firmly behind a chair, facing out through a grubby window with a view of the holy mountain. For a while he shuffled about with his voluminous bag in the hallway.

He returned almost surreptitiously to put something on the tilting mantelpiece. But when she tried to look round, he slapped her head hard. 'You mind your own business!'

She did so but with an awful premonition about what he was doing behind her back. He tightened the rope, which cut cruelly into her wrists and the more she struggled the harder he pressed his hands down on her shoulders. When she gave up, Dewi remained behind her and slid his thin hands down over her straining breasts.

He turned his head away, as if it was nothing to do with him, but his mouth opened in appreciation. Then with an excited gasp he thrust both hands up under her blouse to fondle the breasts frantically.

There was nothing she could do but shudder in a room that seemed filled with his hoarse breathing. Eventually he released his grip and left her alone. But not once throughout the abrupt encounter had either of them uttered a word.

Hannah sat fighting for breath before darting a glance behind. On the warped ash mantelpiece stood two round shapes on plates. She was aware of a wave of nausea, even though she had to blink hard before the objects came into focus.

Fear welled up into her mouth.

On one plate was the severed head of a tailor's dummy; on the other the head of a butchered sheep. The animal's neck was stained with blood where it had been hacked off.

Between them was an empty plate; and she remembered his words, 'Three heads are better than one.'

Dewi struggled his bare arms and shoulders into a white robe which he had stolen from Elliyn's washing line, his confidence growing as he kicked away his own clothes.

Druids wear white robes. Druids converse with God and call down their strength from the sky. He fingered the flannel nightshirt with awed pleasure. Druids were repositories of law and custom; they conducted religious ceremonies and sacrifices. He untangled a circle of mistletoe, shook off some dust and put it on his head. Then went outside and grinned in through the broken window at Hannah's strained face.

After a while he turned to Snowdon and closed his eyes in order to concentrate. He squeezed his hands until they throbbed. There was a ritual, an ordered way of going about things, and first he must clear his mind.

When he looked, he searched the sky for a sign. Perhaps something carried on the wind, or signalling from the shimmering reservoir far below. But for a while he saw nothing exceptional. In fact it was so close that he almost missed it: a diminutive brown bird perched on the swaying baton of a branch.

Dewi backed, without taking his eyes off the bird, and rapped on the window. 'Look there,' he insisted.

Hannah stared out without seeing the bird, so small it could be encapsulated in his hand and still emerge unscathed, and without comprehending. 'Where?'

'There, woman! There! A little beauty.'

'That's a wren, isn't it?' she said doubtfully.

He nodded elatedly. 'Sacred bird of the Druids. It's been sent specially. Stands to reason.' He imitated its brisk tic-tic-tic call.

The bird responded with a vigorous chirping which belied its size, then flew away. They watched it fly into the distance.

She ran her tongue nervously around dry lips. 'Why are you dressed like that?'

His eyes widened and brightened. 'I wondered whether you'd notice. It has to be white . . . for the ceremony. White for purity. I expect you know all about that, purity.'

Hannah nodded dumbly.

'That's good. I'm glad. Because once the ceremony begins these two hands don't belong to me. They might as well be cut off for all the control I have over them. One hand caresses and the other brings retribution.'

'I'm frightened.'

'No need to be. No one's going to harm you in my temple.'

She swallowed heavily and glanced around the sullen, cobwebbed room. 'Your temple?'

He leaned back against the broken window. 'All these mountains were holy to the Druids, and I've chosen this place to be my particular temple. I thought everyone knew about the Moelwyns. The Celtic people have their roots here. They should never have left in the first place. But, when they did, they entrusted their shrines and ritual to the Druids; to people like me. They knew that one day each of them would return and claim the right to an everlasting life, and on the strength of that promise they endured every kind of harshness. Did you know we're the oldest surviving race in the world? And it's all here just waiting for them to come back. I'm like a caretaker.'

She shook her head wordlessly.

He whispered, 'Some people think it's a joke. People like you and that donkey at the power station.'

She shook her head. 'Not me.'

He smiled hideously, as if he had known all along when she was lying. 'It's too late to change your mind. But you'll like the ceremony. It's beautiful. Nothing personal, mind.'

'What are you going to do?' she stuttered.

'I'm going to bring down the wrath on you and the dog.'

There was an awful, extended silence. 'I don't understand.'

'There is to be a ritual cursing.'

'But I haven't done anything.'

'My forefathers didn't do anything either,' he said slyly. 'But they were still driven out by yours.'

'They'll catch up with you and punish you severely.'

He looked at her pityingly. 'I'm immortal.'

'Nobody's immortal.'

'A Druid is. It's written. His soul is indestructible. No one can laugh at me now.'

She covered her ears in anguish. 'Why do you want to hurt me? What have I ever done to you?'

He stroked her hair with delighted anticipation. 'I'm not going to hurt you or the dog. Not me personally. I'll simply call down the wrath on this house and all inside it. All right?'

He eyed her breasts, wanting to touch them again. But to force himself on her now, in a state of grace, would be profane. Slowly and frustratedly he massaged his hands.

It was more than an hour before Dewi returned and when he did he looked frighteningly zealous. Hannah was slumped forward in a daze, and only the fact that her hands were tied behind the chair prevented her falling over.

He was disappointed she did not share the moment with him.

All was arranged. The reckoning would be at dusk when the cold hand of death would reach in and touch all those within the walls. It would happen because he, Dewi apDafydd, had summoned it. He was a true Druid now, and this first bitter-sweet sacrifice would acknowledge the fact before the world.

He glanced out of the cracked panes, hoping for another glimpse of the hallowed wren, but it had flown off. Pity.

A scuffling noise in the cellar made him turn quickly. He had almost forgotten Casson's boxer bitch. Hetty was aware of the Welshman framed at the top of the cellar steps and her growl turned to a whine of despair in the gloom. Deprived of food and water, she knew there was no compassion in him.

Dewi shuffled down, groping for the rope that tethered her. Then stopped. In the further darkness something other than the dog moved. Just a fraction.

He froze. 'Someone there?' he asked sharply.

No response and he began pulling in the reluctant rope. There it was again! A foot crunching on rubble.

It had to be Casson! Somehow the man who had humiliated him at chapel had discovered his whining dog.

Well, it was too bad for him. He was in a place of Druid sacrifice.

'That you, mister?' he asked obsequiously. But in the darkness he grinned to himself; he was on familiar ground. 'I know you're there. Might as well show yourself . . .'

A fist the size of a granite brick hit him in the mouth with stunning force, breaking two teeth and carrying him back off his feet. The word on his lips was already half-formed and came out in a hissing bubble of blood. '. . . Sais!' ('Englishman').

Arnold Webb grunted with satisfaction as he stepped over the twitching body, cradled the trembling boxer in his arms and walked up the steps.

Hannah stared open-mouthed at the new shadow which emerged into the tiny hall. The man's visage was not one to inspire confidence, but anybody was better than the demented Welshman.

Suspiciously, Webb took in the fact that she was tied to a chair with no one else in sight. He put the dog gently down and took up the snapped leg of a table: ready to club the woman if she became hysterical. Women often did in his presence. But Hetty ran to her, stumpy tail wagging deliriously, and there was mutual recognition.

Webb hesitated. She was a friend of his own new-found friend. His expression of mistrust gave way to resignation. He sought out a folding knife from deep in his pocket and sawed through the tarred rope around her wrists.

Within seconds she was able to stand up unsteadily and exercise her cramped joints. 'Thank God you arrived,' she said gratefully.

Webb grunted and backed awkwardly into the cramped hall. Doubt crossed her face. 'Where's the man who tied me up?'

Webb refused to break his silence but he understood and ground a huge fist into his palm, indicating that Dewi was no longer a problem. He patted his leg and whistled to the dog, but Hetty remained with the woman. It was a quandary for Webb, who wanted to get as far away as possible before someone else discovered what he had done.

In the meantime, Hannah picked up the brindle bitch and buried her face in its flank with wordless relief.

Webb stood undecided before digging in his pocket for his faithful hand-knitted sock and rubbed it reassuringly to his mouth. He turned and was making for higher ground before she recovered.

A few minutes later Hannah and the boxer were scrambling anxiously in the opposite direction, down the incline, towards the power station and the one man they both needed.

Whatever vilification had been laid on the cottage remained there, ready to come to life with the advent of dusk.

IT came out of the dead shadows of the mountain as night gathered and moved tentatively downwards in a manner that gave it hoarse pleasure. At last it had a purpose and direction.

ITs mind reached out ahead with grotesque care and touched the only intellect it could detect inside the lackadaisical cottage: explored Dewi's schismatic thoughts . . . and re-created the same empty grin on its own frightening features.

The mind belonged to an unconscious man but that gave it no protection from intrusion. Slowly the figure absorbed the experience and adjusted itself to more of a human shape.

Beyond the place of sacrifice, in the smug comfort of the valley, it sensed numerous unguarded minds. From a long way off IT gingerly trespassed their sub-consciousness and delighted in the sensations of fear which welled up.

Easy enough to snap the twig of sanity in each. But for the moment, in the chill of an October evening, it would have its way with just one.

Seventeen

Elliyn was a dominant preacher whose sermons were sometimes so powerful they made women faint and the blood run to strong men's faces.

On a good day when she stood in the pulpit, bracing herself like Boadicea in a chariot, she was invincible. She scythed her way through an argument with exaggerated rhetoric and occasional thrusts of logic. In a moment she could switch from gentle persuasion to unbridled scorn and more than once, when she brandished a fist, the front row of pews swayed back, convinced she would topple out.

It was not just a sermon. It was also stimulating entertainment. Even now, mid-morning on a working day, the chapel was practically full. Of course most of the congregation were women and children. Their husbands and brothers were burrowing into the hunchbacked mountains, hacking a livelihood out of the hard dark-blue rock which they would later cleave into thin sheets and use to put a roof on the world. Slate was their life, and even chapel knew well enough when to take a back seat.

Although this morning her theme was a familiar one – the Day of Judgement – she weaved an almost hypnotic spell with her beautiful resonant Welsh: shaping the air to emphasize a point, only to bring them up with a jerk when she banged an outraged fist down on the pulpit.

Outside it was raining again. A north-easterly wind had been running the fat off the rainclouds like an untrained collie most of the morning. Nothing special one moment, then a gust the next which blew in the doors at the far end of the chapel.

Elliyn was not normally one to be distracted from a sermon, but even she paused and her eyes narrowed as an eddy of wind attacked the porch and brought a swirl of leaves into sight. High up along solemn windows either side of the building the tips of elm trees rapped the glass to attract attention.

There was a rustle of unease along the pews. Something was going on.

Elliyn signalled to a sidesman without interrupting her flow of words. The man, who had retired from the quarries prematurely with grit-filled lungs, limped to the doors. When he reappeared, and stood waiting to catch her attention, Elliyn noticed consternation in his lined face and raised her eyebrows questioningly. He cleared his impaired throat.

'The rooks are leaving.'

There was a stir among the congregation as everyone turned to stare at the source of information. Elliyn's brow creased. 'What's that?'

'Rooks are leaving, meistres. It's a sign, isn't it?'

She nodded briskly, as if it wasn't that important, put her hands together and said the closing prayer. She knew what it meant clearly enough. Someone connected with the land was about to die. Sometimes, if there were enough rooks, more than one person died.

Within a few minutes she was standing at the main doors nodding goodbye to her congregation as they filed out and hurried their separate ways. Eventually only the sidesman was left with her in the solitude of the chapel.

He fidgeted about collecting psalm books. 'Would you like me to stay, meistres?' he asked, using the old Celtic form of address to denote respect for a woman.

'No thank you, indeed. Were there many of them?'

'Never seen so many in the sky at one time.'

She stood in the porch looking out at the mountains for twenty minutes or more and then a distant figure appeared on the lower slopes. Whoever it was seemed to be meandering, but there was something about the scraggy silhouette that held her attention. It was Dewi, although the closer he drew, the slower his rate of progress seemed.

Elliyn went out to meet him over the last fifty yards. He was staggering aimlessly with both hands hanging loosely at his sides. 'Whatever's the matter with you, man?'

He turned, as if suddenly aware of her, grinning lopsidedly and with blood see-sawing slowly down from his mouth.

'Good gracious, man, what's happened to your teeth?'

He simply stood there, swaying slightly and sharing his secret with no one. She guided him firmly inside.

He was still wearing her brother's suit, but it was in tatters. An arm had been dislocated at the shoulder and hung on only by a few stretched stitches. Once-creased trousers were now baggy with mud. The upper segment of his shoe had parted from the sole, gaping like a fish out of water with every step.

'Are you all right?'

He allowed himself to be sat down, but continued to stare vacantly into the distance. 'All right, boyoh?' he repeated. 'Certainly.'

She busily wiped away the blood and examined him for further injury. 'Well? Speak up, man.'

'He came.'

'Who did?'

Dewi moistened his lips and took his time answering. 'Answered the summons, he did.'

'Who?' She eased off his jacket and he sighed with pain. He was massively bruised from his shoulder to his waist, as if he had fallen heavily on his way down the mountain.

'The Arch Druid.'

'Oh yes?' she said sharply, since she had never believed in spoiling people. 'There's no such person. You know that as well as I do.'

His smile spread slowly until it extended from ear to ear. 'I was there. I'd know, wouldn't I?' It faded as he recalled the moment of truth. 'I had to beg him to recognize me, and not to kill me like the others he was meant to. It's me! Dewi! I pleaded. Don't you know me? I couldn't properly see his face. Cunning he was. Just his eyes watching me. White as linen . . .'

Elliyn had enough to do holding his twitching shoulders steady.

'It was like going to Jesus, except that his eyes burned

into me and I found I couldn't look away.' Dewi sobbed and reached unsteadily for her blouse, feeling the material and gripping it tightly. 'Elliyn, this means I really am a Druid, doesn't it?'

She felt no dismay for him; only a shuddering elation for herself. It was the second omen of the day. There was no doubt at all now. Just as her and her brother's sermons prophesied: the Demon was coming to recognize those who had kept the faith for so long . . . and to seek retribution from those who had not.

The wide intensity of his eyes and the quaver in his voice made Elliyn prise his hand from her blouse and fold it with its partner in his lap. Then, acting almost on a whim, she moved her fingers backwards and forwards in front of his unblinking eyes, and felt a fierce surge of exultation. There was no doubt in her mind. He was blind.

Eighteen

John Casson tiptoed back into the bedroom and looked at Hannah for the umpteenth time in the past hour. She was sleeping heavily, arms thrown wide and snoring lightly.

A half-starved Hetty awoke at last on the foot of the bed and welcomed him anew. Her stumpy brown tail wagged delightedly at being safely back with him.

A farm worker on his way to milking had spotted the two of them wandering tiredly in the early hours, lost among waterlogged meadows at the foot of the Moelwyns, and dropped them off at Ffestiniog power station by tractor. Hannah had not said a great deal on seeing Casson, simply sank her head into the hollow of his shoulder and gripped his hand with pincer-tight fingers.

When he saw the pitiful state they were both in, Casson had an almost irresistible urge to storm over to the chapel and wedge his toecap forcibly into Dewi's mouth. But he could not risk leaving her alone again.

Casson went into the control room and spoke briefly to Manchester on the radio-telephone and then returned to the love-spoon he was carving. He progressed with infinite care, working whirls and flower patterns into the handle; it served to keep a lid on his rage and reflected the awakening love he felt for Hannah.

The soft wood had a superb grain and he knew she would enjoy both the shape and its feel. Something for her to keep always; more articulate than any love letter.

A bell shrilled at the front entrance but again he glanced in at Hannah before answering it. She seemed calmer now and he tucked restless hands under the coverlet and brushed distraught hair from her eyes.

Who was it? He had few callers.

The door opened to reveal Elliyn's strong face lit with a smile. Behind her was a pony and trap.

'Hello, John,' she said breathlessly.

'Hello. Something wrong?'

She shook her head and appeared overjoyed. 'On the contrary. Look, I can't stop more than a moment or two. I just wanted to give you some sound advice.'

'Oh?'

'Something marvellous has happened to the valley. And I've been in town explaining what it could mean to people. Something's happened that a few of us were hoping and praying for . . . a return to the old ways.'

Casson looked bewildered. 'I don't understand.'

'You're not expected to. This is part of our religion, part of our heritage. The trouble is, some people don't like change and that could mean a spot of bother here and there. So what I'm saying to you is: stay in the power station for a day or two. Don't go into town, and keep yourself to yourself.'

Casson stepped outside and glanced around. 'Well, what happened exactly?'

Her eyes slid off him in a clever and secretive way that close-knit Welsh people would recognize. 'It's to do with our salvation. Something peculiar to the people who live here. Look, all I'm saying is, you keep away from town for a while. I don't want you hurt.'

Casson had the almost-completed love-spoon in his hand. As he watched her clamber back into her two-wheeled carriage and gather the reins, he felt grateful she did not bear him a grudge and he waved the spoon in farewell. 'Take care of yourself.'

'You too.' Her eyes fell on the spoon. 'What have you got there, John?'

Casson gave a deprecating laugh and held up the love-spoon apologetically. 'Oh, just something I've been paring away in the evenings. It's a . . .'

'A love-spoon.'

He looked sheepish. 'That's right.'

'May I see?' She stretched out a powerful arm and examined the carving with undisguised admiration. 'But you're not a Welshman. How do you know about such things?'

'I'm not sure. I just had a profound feeling that it was the right thing to do . . . not long after I met you.'

She looked up quickly and met his eyes: boldly and with a sudden strength of purpose. He certainly did not mean to mislead her. And yet . . .

'For me?'

He loved the girl who was sprawled asleep inside the power station, but that was no reason to hurt Elliyn. Casson was embarrassed. 'It's for whoever wants it. Anybody,' he said awkwardly, not yet having declared his feelings for Hannah.

The ungainly woman preacher tucked the spoon in the neck of her straight-laced dress. 'Nobody ever gave me anything quite so beautiful before,' she gulped.

'Well . . . it's not quite finished.'

'I like it as it is.'

'I think I ought to finish it properly.'

She seemed disappointed, but nevertheless withdrew the spoon and handed it back, letting her big fingers brush lightly, gratefully across the back of his hand.

She alerted the pony, which snorted and jerked its head,

ready to leave. 'Stay here, mind. Things are going to happen, and I want to know that you're safe.'

He forced a smile but thought, damn! What a ridiculous, unthinking thing to do. Why had he allowed her to be misled? If she decided later that she had been scorned, she would make a formidable adversary.

Elliyn Pryce-Jones continued to get a mixed response to her news as evening drew on. A hastily arranged meeting at the Baptist Hall in Blaenau itself left those who attended in no doubt of the .Coming. Her exhilaration and the unshakeable evidence of Dewi, sitting there freshly blind and yet nodding ecstatically, sent them home white-faced and expectant.

She spoke powerfully from the two street corners as well as from the top window of a hardware shop, after propping up the sliding window with her sheathed umbrella, and none questioned her oratory. She exuded the burning conviction of a latter-day John the Baptist.

Yet there were still pockets of cynicism. She reached the Prince and Ferret in Blaenau's main street at almost eleven. But by now her hymn-singing procession of mainly elderly supporters, accompanied by an accordion, was drifting away.

Dewi shivered with cold and she asked the last two helpers to see him home before tackling single-handed 'this rancid den of beer-swilling debauchery'.

There were fewer people in the public bar than usual. Some had heard she was coming and they had surreptitiously slipped away. News had got around that Dewi had been struck bat-blind. They were not fools; they understood that some things are inexplicable and cast shadows even in the sharp light of modern knowledge. If retribution was rolling heavily in their direction, most of them would not stand grinning in its path. They were well aware of the occasional boulder which rumbled down without warning from the Moelwyns, flattening all in its path: sent perhaps as an indication of the greater force poised over them. So one or two more drained their glasses and left. No point in inviting disaster.

She hitched up her long, heavy dress and stood on a chair, making herself so apparent that her head almost touched the undulating plaster ceiling.

'Redemption is nigh!' she called over the babble of voices and constant music from an out-of-tune piano. 'It's on the move through this land of ours. On its way here to this very town. Do you hear me? It's even coming right into this very establisment.' She stabbed a finger at the polished wooden bar and the ornate Victorian mirrors, which threw her angled reflection back at her.

Her finger moved on to identify one of her audience. 'It's coming to see you, Berwyn Lewis!' Piano music faltered as the bespectacled man at the keyboard rose, startled, from behind a line of froth-stained glasses. 'Yes indeed! So pay particular heed to what I have to say.'

But Elliyn did not get all the attention she wanted. Among the noisiest regulars were the Roberts brothers of Little Maentwrog: three big men in their surly forties who quarried slate for a living and washed down the fine dust every night with best bitter, which then flowed, chastened, down the latrine drains behind the Ferret, into an uncomplaining stream and thus back to the land from whence it came.

So far as debauchery is concerned, there was usually no more going on there than can be wrung from a set of dominoes, three darts and a dog-eared pack of playing cards. Gallons of tangy beer gurgled down dozens of throats from the moment the doors opened until a second before the bolt was slid shut. The language grew more boisterous by the hour. But sin is thin on the ground in Wales; always has been. The exceptions at the Ferret were Megan behind the saloon bar, and her friend Hester from Tantypool, who were rumoured to be available.

Megan looked through from the other bar and pulled a face. 'The Jesus Woman's in again,' she reported back to the harassed landlord. There was a pause while she looked over her shoulder. 'No, I'm damned if I will. Remember what happened last time? She punched me in the sodding eye. I was black and blue for a month. Do your own dirty work.'

The pianist hurriedly collected up his tatty sheets of music ready to leave, but Idris Roberts, crossing the room with three full pints held aloft in one hand, pressed him back down on his stool.

'Don't go on my account, Berwyn.' Rock-hard fingers squeezed the pianist's shoulder, and in a moment the discordant music resumed. A noisy syncopation filled the gaps between laughter and general hubbub.

But it took more than mere noise to deter Elliyn. 'Quiet now! I want to ask you all a question!'

She was a fine-looking woman when roused. Idris Roberts smirked up at her. Her body was as straight and strong as a pit prop, and he'd run his rough hands up and down enough of those to know what it was all about.

She outshouted the din. 'I want to know how you'd feel if your Saviour came in here right now, and saw you with a full pint of beer in your hand?'

'Bloody choked,' responded Idris swiftly. 'Specially if he was buying.'

'I think you'd feel ashamed.'

'Never.'

'Well you should! You've never heard tell of Jesus drinking to excess. You've never heard of a disciple staggering home top-heavy as many of you will tonight.'

'No, but then they didn't have many pubs in Galilee, did they?'

His equally muscular brother, Trebor Roberts, banged a glass on the slate-topped table and tapped metal-tipped pit boots in time with the piano. The third brother, Powis, regarded the din with a permanently vexed look. He never ceased to complain about something or other: carping about the mine bosses or the acrid taste of the beer or whatever happened to cross his line of vision.

'Do you know what I want?' called Elliyn to the half-attentive regulars. She was already getting slightly hoarse.

'Do you know what I want?' she bellowed, before her voice gave up for the night.

'Well I know what she's going to get,' Powis said from the side of his mouth, 'specially if she goes on flaunting herself on that chair. I'm only human.'

Elliyn was in full spate. 'I want you to come to me one by one, and ask the Lord's forgiveness. To get down on your knees in front of everybody here and ask for absolution. And I promise you . . . you'll never regret it!'

Idris, who had dark curly hair and florid cheeks, leaned towards his elder brother, Trebor, and gnawed his lip. 'I'd like to get my knees either side of her, boy.'

The older brother contemplated the view and nodded. 'Better than banging your head against a wall. I wouldn't mind giving her one myself.'

Idris burped and wiped his mouth. He had consumed more than usual and the niceties were beginning to blur. He contemplated the woman preacher and raised his eyebrows questioningly at both his brothers.

He knew from their unspoken response that they had an understanding.

Idris swayed to his feet and beckoned her down from the chair. 'A private word in your ear. The three of us were thinking it's time we came back into the fold . . . But not in here in front of everybody. It's too public. Come out the back and we'll talk it over.'

She shook her head until Powis said, 'I told you she'd say no. There's too much sweat and grime in our family and not enough cash. Not worth saving.'

Elliyn hesitated no longer. There were no other immediate takers. She indicated that the brothers could lead the way.

They crossed the cobbled yard and Idris pushed open the latched door to a little room where there was a broken-down sofa and a spare dartboard, a place where members of the pub team could quietly practice. It was empty and Idris meant it to remain so.

'How about in here?'

'What's the matter with out there?' she asked suspiciously.

'Too public.'

'Mr Roberts, you do intend to repent?'

'Absolutely.'

She shrugged and bent her head to walk inside. All three brothers crowded eagerly after her. Idris frowned heavily at Powis. 'What do you want?' he muttered. 'You're supposed to make sure no one comes in.'

'What, and miss all the doings?'

Trebor stretched his arms and even looked casually behind the dartboard. 'Stuffy in here, isn't it? I'll just take my shirt off.' He unbuttoned his jacket and slipped the grubby shirt over his head, then a high-buttoned vest which looked allergic to soap and water. He was extremely hairy, and the black mat continued over his shoulder and some way down his arms.

'What's this?' Elliyn's eyes darted from one to the other. 'What are you up to?'

'Just relaxing,' smiled Idris, taking off his broad leather belt. 'Why don't you do the same on that sofa there?'

She stepped back to the far wall, closed her substantial bible and gripped it around the edges. It would make a dreadful weapon.

Idris meantime slapped the belt across his open palm, grinning wickedly. 'We all think you're a strapping girl. Every one of us thinks that, don't we, boys? Question is, are you up to us? To all of us, I mean?'

Three pairs of eyes devoured her.

She glanced at the encroaching night through a single window. 'I wouldn't do anything silly if I were you. Especially not tonight. See, if you had given me half a chance, I'd have told you: there's someone else coming to see you.'

'Is that right?' said Idris matter-of-factly, as he removed his boots and unbuttoned the front of his trousers.

'The Old Ones have sent him to assert order and discipline. Things we can rely on.'

Powis tried to touch her but she brushed his hand away. 'What's she on about?'

'I don't know. Grab her arms, quick.'

Elliyn was breathing fast. 'It would be quite wrong to harm me now.'

Idris confronted her, now that her arms were pinned, and slowly unbuttoned her dress front from the neck down. 'We're not going to harm you. Just give you an idea of how we feel about you.' He dipped a hand into the sagging flap of dress and sucked his breath in sharp admiration. 'Gracious me. What do you want to keep a thing like that to yourself for, girl?'

He thrust his weight forward and Elliyn was toppled on to the sofa and almost out of sight over the back, in a cartwheel of flailing limbs. Her balled fist caught him squarely in the ear and left him deaf for two days. But there was no stopping the panting miner who wrestled on top of her and began feverishly exploring what was under the heavy dress.

They grunted and perspired like two heavyweights until the tussle ended in a forced coupling. She arched her back and gave a great breathless gasp at the moment of penetration, after which Idris rolled aside and pretended to have enjoyed himself. But the way she resisted and twisted had caused him acute discomfort.

Trebor flung himself on top next, and mated almost before he was ready for it. And while she lay back, dishevelled and panting with disbelief, Powis spreadeagled himself over her for his share.

Each of the brothers lusted and satisfied himself. Then, sheepishly, they got her up on to the sofa, straightened themselves out and asked if she wanted a gin, or fancied a lift home, and was she feeling all right?

Elliyn Pryce-Jones regarded them speechlessly as she fought to regain her shocked breath. She had come to this place to help them . . . to warn them and their uncaring friends, who were still laughing and singing to discordant music in the half-distance, but they had scorned the new

Coming. And outraged her. They were no better than beasts.

All right! If that was the way they wanted it . . . Elliyn staggered across the cobbled courtyard and down a narrow alley to the road, clutching her torn dress around her shamed body.

As she stumbled through the gloom, towards Tan-y-grisiau village, tears welled into her eyes. It was rare for Elliyn to cry, but these were tears of rage. 'If you can hear me,' she sobbed up into the utter darkness that cloaked the mountains. 'If you care anything for me and the ways of the people, come down upon this place with a terrible vengeance and scour it anew.'

She stopped and felt a breeze lapping interestedly around her. An understanding silence surrounded her.

Quite how long she stood there she could not be sure. A curious feeling stole over her that she was being observed from the unseen Moelwyns. She half-imagined that something approached with ghost-like stealth from the night and contemplated her. Almost in a trance, she imagined it feeling out her mind. Although she could not clearly tell fact from fancy, it seemed to come to a conclusion which made her jerk with sheer pleasure: experiencing an orgasm that the multiple rape had failed to engender.

Perspiration ran in rivulets down her face and across her shoulders. There was no one there, nothing to see or hold. Yet, when she had given herself, she felt able to ask its help.

'Extend the strong hand of discipline to this shameless land,' she implored the darkness. 'Bless the righteous and punish the profane. Let there be a voice in the land so terrible that those who hear it will never again doubt.' She reached out beseechingly. 'If you were meant to come, come now!'

In her imagination she pictured a hideously grinning figure in a dark crease of the mountain. But when she opened her distraught eyes and strained into the darkness, there was nothing. No one.

Eventually she turned for home, limp and exhausted.

Hours later a misshapen outline, twice the size of a normal person, emerged from a gully. Blind eyes in a face which bore a lopsided smile. Already it was relishing the day to come.

Nineteen

That day brought the worst storm in memory. It was not forecast, but that was not unusual; much of the ill-tempered weather that regularly came out of the mountains appeared without warning.

Although only a few hundred miles away in drizzling London people were grimacing up at the sky and groaning 'Not again!' few knew or cared that ten times as much rain had cascaded on the distant Moelwyns. Yet there is a limit to what people can endure, and it seemed to have been reached in Blaenau Ffestiniog that morning.

A flock of sixty sheep was killed by lightning as the ewes huddled together, trapped in the strait-jacket of their sodden fleece. But nobody ventured out to check their fate while rain gushed down from a plague-black sky and each suicidal spear dashed itself to spray. Heavy shutters were pulled to, and no one left cover until late afternoon when the rainclouds finally lost their way and disappeared back over the mountains.

Trebor Roberts frowned out at the downpour before squinting anxiously upstairs. Rain beat noisily on the warped roof tiles, which should have been replaced two or three years ago. Much more of this and they would slide out of position, leaving him with an attic full of water.

He was anxious for another reason, and returned to the window to peer obliquely down the deserted street, which was swathed up to waist height in a girdle of spray. No one was likely to venture out on such a day; just the same, he was relieved not to detect any movement. The only people out and about would be the law: perhaps stirred into action by an outraged woman evangelist complaining loudly of an enforced rutting.

There was no doubt they had gone too far: stupidly far. But they had been swept along by the ale and Idris's insistence that they teach her a lesson. Not that a magistrate would take his word for that; not an older man's word that he was forced unwillingly into the situation by his younger brother.

He recalled again the moment of carnal truth. It was bloody over-rated and all over before he'd realized; anyway, he had a sneaking suspicion she was more worldly-wise than all of them.

No sign of a patrol car. The longer the better. Every passing minute lessened the chance of her seeking the retribution she threatened.

He did not hear the brass knob turn slowly. The steady rush of rain drowned a creak of pressure as someone tried to open it despite the bolts, locked top and bottom.

Trebor glanced along the hall and through the drab kitchen. There was nothing unusual in sight but he advanced hands in pockets. Someone there?

If it was a policeman, he'd have a long wait. Trebor stood sideways to the back door, listening. Then, quite suddenly, he was aware of a hideously grinning face through the faded lace curtains.

He jerked back. God! What was that? The horrific visage so shocked him that the breath stuck in his throat.

Unnerved and hardly believing it, he looked once more. Despite muzzy patterns on the rain-washed glass and the blur of lace curtaining, he saw clearly the lopsided grin and cowled head of some monstrous apparition staring in at him.

Trebor Roberts was an unimaginative man. Something of a bully but by no means a coward. He remained where he was, pressed back against the wall, and closed his eyes disbelievingly. When he opened them again, the image had vanished.

'Deeew!' His mouth sagged open. What was that? It was much too real to have been brought on by the ale.

Therefore, somebody was playing a trick. Perhaps Idris. Shakily he slid back the bolt. Wouldn't put it past the daft bugger!

Trebor opened the door and peered both ways. Rain drummed down on his head and quickly soaked his nylon shirt. There was not a soul in sight. He hoped his daft brother was hiding out there, catching pneumonia. Serve him right.

He slammed and locked the door, and a wave of relief passed through him. It had been a nightmarish moment and his heart was still hammering away but, if it wasn't his brother, it was a hallucination. A consequence of too much on his mind; he was past the age when he should be fretting about women complaining to the police.

Trebor trudged upstairs to run himself his fortnightly bath. Afterwards, refreshed, he would lie on the bed and have a smoke. But when the time came to dip his grubby foot in the white bath he sucked in his breath sharply. The enamel had corroded into unappetizing blue and green streaks beneath steadfastly dripping taps, and the water was too hot. Almost scalding. Yet he gritted his teeth and tried again. He was reluctant to add too much cold water; there was a lot of him to get clean and the heating was expensive.

He knelt in the water like a suppliant, soaping his thick hair before plunging his head under the surface. He didn't like soaking himself much, and screwed up his big face before each immersion. It made him feel childishly vulnerable.

A creaking noise caught his attention above the steady hiss of rain. Perhaps just the house settling, adjusting itself to the chastisement of the weather. Then again, to a person with too much imagination, it could have sounded like someone moving stealthily upstairs towards the bathroom.

He lifted his head and let the water stream off. But no more sounds reached his ears and, after a moment's hesitation, he ducked under the surface again . . . submerged and defenceless in an eerie world of watery echoes.

Unknown to him the door handle turned. There was no

lock. A bathroom floorboard protested as weight transferred to it.

A split second of realization allowed the Welshman's mind to fill with terror. But, before he could emerge from the water, a hand clamped down on the back of Trebor Roberts's head and held it down.

Suffocating with fear, his cheeks ballooned while his hands splashed frantically for relief on either side. But his struggles were matched by the vice-like grip. A great bubble surfaced. Then another and, eventually, a stream of expended air was replaced in his lungs by shuddering gulps of merciless bathwater.

It was nearly time to eat. Idris Roberts and his second brother, the crotchety Powis, had been arguing furiously over whose turn it was to cook high tea. At the end of a back-breaking week blasting and hauling slate, they liked a long lie-in on Sunday, after which they loafed about the rooms they shared: leafing through the *News of the World* or playing desultory darts until opening time at the Ferret.

'I got it yesterday, as well you bloody know,' said Powis in his usual hectoring manner.

Idris twisted his once-handsome face. 'Call that a meal? More like a burnt offering. Fried sausages are supposed to be succulent and forkable. Not black and crunchy. And I'm not going to eat any more congealed baked beans.'

'Not my fault you let them get cold.'

'Look, boy. Yesterday doesn't count in my book. Either you take your proper turn today or shove off and find your own flat. Right?'

Powis got up with ill grace and slammed the door to the small kitchen behind him. 'Sod you for a brother!'

Idris crossed to an unbalanced sideboard where he kept several quart bottles of stout. Pouring the rich, smooth liquid into a dusty glass and watching the head of froth seemed to calm him.

Still, it was high time his brother found separate accommodation. Idris might then persuade Madge, from the Ferret, to move in instead. Never mind her sharp tongue, she had a good bum and could cook a damned sight better than his sullen brother. Anybody could!

He drank deeply and gazed reflectively out at the dancing rain, performing handstands on the pavement.

On the other hand, the Roberts family had always been close. They needed to be in a supercilious, sanctimonious community like this. Better he and Powis stick together.

Idris poured some conciliatory stout into a second glass.

'Here!' he said, worrying the kitchen door with his toecap, 'get some of this down you. I don't want you bearing a grudge. Your cooking tastes bad enough even when you're in a good mood.'

The door did not budge. 'I've got a drink for you! Open up.'

A peculiar gurgling sound filtered through. He could not quite identify the noise; rather like the last of the water swirling down a drain, except that each gurgle was followed by a tortured gasp.

'Powis, boy!' He rapped urgently with his blunt knuckles. The door seemed to be wedged shut, which was odd in itself. Idris measured his weighty shoulder against it and barged. It barely shifted.

'Hey, what are you up to?' he called anxiously. 'Don't mess about. You all right in there?'

The gurgling had stopped and there was nothing to be heard for a while but the steady hiss of rain. Then a creaking noise: a protracted creak followed by a second or two of silence. It was repeated three or four times, rather like a reluctant swing moving backwards and forwards.

Idris, extremely disturbed by now, set down the drink and attacked the door with his shoulder. It gave way and he stumbled into a heavy object hanging sacklike from a rafter.

'Ooohhhh!'

He stared glassily up at his brother, in collarless shirt and familiar crumpled trousers, hanging by the neck. Throttled by a cruel length of electrical flex which stretched tautly upwards into the gloom. The cheeks in his unshaven face bulged like horrific blue plums and his lifeless eyes protruded with incredulity.

Idris gave a long and desperate wail of disbelief. He turned, fumbling across the untidy table for a bread knife. Cutlery cascaded aside until he gripped what he sought. Up on a shaky chair he sawed with feverish haste through the wire-hearted flex.

His brother's unsavoury sixteen stone crumpled to the floor as the cable snapped, bringing Idris down with it. He raised Powis's head and slapped the cheeks frantically in a vain attempt to restore life.

'What have you done?' he sobbed in disbelief. 'You daft bugger, I didn't mean nothing by it. What would your mam say, if she knew?'

He hugged the still-warm body, letting out great sobs of emotion and burying his face in Powis's shoulder. Then stopped. Stopped as his fingers discovered something quite unexpected.

Powis's wrists were bound tightly behind his back with a length of similar flex. How could that be? Confusion flooded his mind.

Idris leaned forward awkwardly to gaze over his brother's shoulder at his frightening discovery. You can't tie your hands behind your own back, then commit suicide. It's physically impossible, he told himself slowly.

Meanwhile there was nothing around him but silence.

Except that at the far side of the ill-lit room was the shadow of an open cellar door. Nothing moved there, yet just the same his eyes were drawn inexorably towards it.

Somebody was watching him.

Idris's arms twitched, and all his instincts urged him not to stare, but he could not help it. A lopsided smile. A look of imbecilic pleasure took shape and regarded him from the indistinct shadows.

Instinct is a remarkable attribute. Although his mind stampeded with fear, Idris assessed instinctively that the figure facing him possessed neither human remorse nor compassion.

He bucked away from his brother's corpse and stumbled

into the other room, crashing the door shut behind him. Certain he had only a few seconds respite he grabbed the end of a towering Welsh dresser and dragged it screechingly across the doorway. Four Coronation dining plates that had stood on end for as long as he could remember shattered on the floor, making him wince.

Idris rested for a moment against the protective façade of the dresser, arms trembling. His hair flopped into his eyes but he no longer had the co-ordination to prevent it.

Sudden movement in the adjoining kitchen brought him up rigid with terror. Whatever was in there was now just a foot or so away on the other side of the door, and trying to get through.

Whimpering with fear he braced himself. If only he could keep the door shut! Idris closed his eyes and pushed frantically. But in his self-imposed darkness he was unaware that the centre of the wall was arching towards him, under maniacal pressure from the other side.

His body was discovered later that day buried under more than a ton of rubble and brick debris, but those who examined the scene saw nothing sinister in it. They came to the conclusion that part of the building had collapsed after the foundations were undermined by constant rain. They also concluded that his brother, Powis, had come upon the gruesome accident and hanged himself in a moment of self-reproach. There was no sign of any flex around his wrists.

What other explanation could there be?

The moth of death that flitted through Blaenau Ffestiniog that day progressed unnoticed by nine tenths of the inhabitants who had drawn their shutters and were sitting out the storm in their homes, oblivious of any other danger.

At Little Park School, only six of forty children turned up for lessons next morning. Not even the headmistress had managed to arrive and so they sat about, laughing shrilly at the proximity of the thunder and wondering what to do.

Betty Thomas, of Tredore, hissed the others into silence

when at long last the latch clicked on the assembly-hall door. The headmistress was a martinet when it came to observing the school rules and acting with decorum at all times.

'Look out! It's Miss!'

All the pupils, down to five-year-old Dylan Edwards, of Aberdynny, scrambled to their desks and sat straight-backed with flushed cheeks and breathing hard. Long black hinges squeaked as the heavy door swung open behind them, and someone stepped inside.

None of the children looked round. The headmistress did not approve of inquisitiveness and insisted that their eyes should, at all times, be on either the blackboard or their books.

Betty had dusty golden hair and frail shoulders inside a sunflower pinafore. One day, if she survived, she would be a remarkably attractive woman. A hand touched her back, and slid up and over the small round contour of her shoulder.

Madge, the barmaid from the Prince and Ferret, smiled down at her. 'Hello, children. All alone?' Her own hair, scooped into a bun, was glistening with dampness. There were great wet patches on her blouse where the pelting rain had penetrated the shawl and seeped through to her plump arms.

'Hello,' Betty responded shyly.

'Hasn't Mrs Griffiths arrived?'

'No, miss.'

Madge consulted her watch. 'Not surprising in this weather. Been washed right off her bicycle, I shouldn't wonder.'

The children were at first surprised that a grown-up should joke about their mentor, then giggled delightedly.

'Well, never mind, we'll find something to do until it stops. You certainly can't go home in this, now can you?'

'No, miss,' they chorused, eager to find out what a barmaid felt was appropriate work to occupy them the rest of the morning.

‘Right, Betty. You read the first chapter of that book out loud, please. And I’ll look in Mrs Griffiths’ room.’

She left the children for the worn parquet corridor which led past the caretaker’s empty room to an end door. The word *headmistress* was inscribed in faded letters.

It was locked and the barmaid from the Ferret would have left it at that but, along a side corridor, she spotted Mrs Griffiths’s padlocked bicycle.

Madge returned to the door and knocked tentatively. ‘You there, Mrs Griffiths?’

She cleared her throat, feeling silly, and tried again. A firm rap. ‘This is Madge Evans, Mrs Griffiths. Are you in there? You feeling all right?’

She fancied that she heard a muffled movement within. But there was no answering voice, and the distant shuffle of rain made it difficult to be sure.

Madge glanced back along the corridor to ensure no one was looking before stooping to peer through the keyhole. At first there seemed to be nothing coherent to make out, then she recognized the base of the headmistress’s desk, a wastepaper basket . . . and a sensible shoe.

Nothing else was in sight, and her view was strictly curtailed. Yet a discarded shoe in the middle of the floor? In a room belonging to a meticulous headmistress?

Madge ran her tongue undecidedly around dry lips. Eventually she called out with a slight tremor, ‘Are you quite sure you aren’t in there, Mrs Griffiths?’

The silence that followed seemed slowly to encompass her. As if reaching out and containing her in a stealthy world of its own. She had experienced a similar sensation once before: going under anaesthetic for an operation. Odd how memories crowded nervously back.

The assembly-hall door opened tentatively and Betty Thomas piped, ‘I finished reading, miss.’

Madge returned to the percipient world, nodding uneasily. Ahead of her the girl waited for instructions while she now had the distinct impression of someone breathing close to the other side of the door. A hoarse, wheezing inhalation.

She forced down a feeling of rapidly rising panic for the sake of the schoolgirl and led her back into the reassuring atmosphere of desks and perky faces. She leaned back on the door and with some relief heard it click shut.

Outside the rain drummed down as fiercely as ever. Madge forced a bright smile. 'I think the storm's quietening down. I want you all to pick up your satchels and make your way quickly and in line to Mr Cadoc's shop. It's not far. He's a governor and he'll see you all get home without getting too wet. I don't think the headmistress is well. So there'll be no more school today.'

There was a squeal of delight and considerable milling about until the pupils formed pairs. Madge cautioned them with a finger. 'Right now, follow Betty and don't go running off alone.'

The senior girl peeked out at the battering rain which awaited them at the school entrance, then looked back for confirmation that they were doing the right thing.

'All right,' Madge smiled with a confidence she did not feel. 'On your marks, get set . . . Go!'

They scuttled across the asphalt playground, laughing shrilly. One fell on the way and Betty Thomas hesitated when they reached the road, realizing the barmaid was not following them. Madge stepped out in the wet, gesticulating.

'Go on, go on. Don't wait for me! I've forgotten something.'

The last thing she wanted was to go back inside but, if Mrs Griffiths had suffered some sort of fit, there was no one else. At least the children were out of the way. Anyway, she was almost certain no one else was there.

She swept back her wet hair as she crossed the quiet assembly hall. Reassuringly quiet. *Oh my God!* Her rapidly beating heart stopped with a jolt.

A figure was waiting, in the shadows. It seemed pleased to see her shocked expression and an idiotic smile spread unevenly across its features. It even came towards her: arms extended in a stifling embrace.

Its eyes were hideous blanks. She screamed hysterically,

but it made no difference to the welcome she got. The arms of death rapturously enfolded her.

Ten people died that day. According to the coroner, they all expired from either natural causes or acts of God, apart from Powis Roberts, who was adjudged to have despatched himself.

But the coroner aside, no one doubted that something fearful was loose in the community and their only question was, who would it strike next?

Twenty

Casson switched off the radio-telephone and sighed. 'They're trying to contact the base adjutant.'

Hannah turned away, plucking nervously at her linen dress. 'You must think I'm awfully foolish.'

He shrugged. 'It's not for me to say. Dreams affect people in different ways. I just think you're taking this one a little too far.'

She shivered and rubbed her arms. 'I hope so. I can't even be sure it was Dewi. It looked like him, and yet it didn't. He was listening for the plane. Willing it towards him through the fog and smiling horribly, as if he knew what was going to happen. Then there was a terrible impact and I woke up.'

He pulled her head gently against his chest. 'I'm not surprised you're imagining things, considering what you've been through. Why don't you lie down? Will you do that for me? I can feel your heart beating, just like a drum. I'll wake you as soon as J.J. rings.'

She nodded gratefully and trailed back to his quarters.

Casson felt a quiver of unease when he was alone in the control room again. The circumstances she had related were so vivid: a cartwheeling warplane with its wings snapping off among the unwelcoming rocks. She even read an identification number on the fuselage. If something had happened . . .

Casson drew a deep breath. It was foolish even to think that way. The chances of a dream coming true were a million to one. He ran uncertain fingers through his tousled hair.

Manchester came through nearly an hour later when the power station was quite still. The duty engineer sounded subdued. 'Sorry, old chap. That American officer you asked about had an accident. His base wants to know how you found out. There's a security hold on the details, but apparently his plane came down in bad weather. Killed instantly.'

Casson got up, knocking his chair over. He felt clammy as he walked back to the room where Hannah was lying under a thin coverlet, and her eyes half-opened as he sat on the edge of the bed.

'Hello,' she said drowsily. 'Did they come through?'

He nodded and took her hand; and she regarded him in silence for a long time. 'What did they say?'

'You were right,' he gulped. 'Poor man.'

Hannah looked at him with widening eyes and then rolled away to face the wall. She cried into the pillow, but the only outward signs were occasional little movements of her shoulders.

Later he made her sit up and take a cup of tea in her trembling hands. 'I just don't know what to do,' she said, shaking her head distractedly.

'I do.' Casson looked both ways over his shoulders. 'We've got to get out of here.'

'It's my fault he's dead.'

'That's a ridiculous thing to say.'

'It's a judgement on me for coming here.'

'What are you talking about?' he said dismissively.

'Whatever it is . . . knows I'm a catalyst, a disruptive influence,' she stuttered. 'It's punished me for coming here, and now I've got a terrible feeling it's playing with us.'

A door slammed somewhere far off in the building. Casson swallowed hard and turned back to her.

'I think we ought to leave here as soon as possible.'

I won't let you.

Casson glanced quickly at her. 'What did you say?' But her puzzled look answered for her. He was conscious of how quiet and inquisitive the building had become.

I won't let you go. The hoarse whisper drifted through his mind.

He handed her two sleeping-tablets, each of which she took with a swallow of water.

'Thanks.' She settled, pale as cemetery marble. 'You won't leave me alone, will you?'

He shook his head reassuringly, although he knew well enough that if they were both to get away from this place, as he intended, he must first go to Tan-y-grisiau and borrow Elliyn's pony and trap. His car would be next to useless with so many roads under water; if he relied on any sort of engine they could be stranded within sight of the mountains when night fell. And that would be catastrophic.

'No, I won't leave you,' he lied, soothing the back of her hand. Least, not for long. Her eyes drooped and within three or four minutes she was heavily asleep. Although it was only mid-afternoon, he drew the curtains, left her in soft shadows and tiptoed out. At the most, he would be away half an hour.

He almost did not go at all.

Casson stopped suddenly in the middle of the lofty turbine hall: aware of a sharp rattling noise approaching the reception area. The noise came in brisk bursts with a pause of several seconds in between. There it was again: a metallic rat-tat-tatting.

He pulled swiftly back behind the protection of the big domed turbine covers only to see Hetty loping into the far end of the elongated hall gripping a stick between her teeth. One end reverberated noisily against the wall radiator with its corrugated surface. She bounded up to Casson, squirming with delight.

He released his breath and tickled her pouchy cheeks. 'Not much wrong with you, is there?' he asked rhetorically. Hetty loved being fussed over and stood with her back legs spreadeagled like a show-dog, luxuriating in it. 'You're a gorgeous lady, aren't you? Now stay here.' He extended his fingers. 'Stay, and look after Hannah for me.'

Outside the rain had gone away, leaving a sharp grey day.

He walked to the car, which would at least get him to the village, and turned the ignition key. The engine coughed unhealthily several times. Damp plugs? Damn! There was no time to tinker under the bonnet. Casson slammed the car door and set off for Tan-y-grisiau on foot; it was not far. But, for as long as he could, he cast anxious glances back at the long low building. She would be all right, if he hurried.

Far above him three men watched guardedly from the shelter of rocks until he was lost to sight. Then, one by one, they slithered down the treacherous slope towards Ffestiniog power station.

All three were pinched with hunger and numb from a night spent in the freezing drizzle. Two were little weasel-sharp Londoners, serving ten years for grievous bodily harm and armed robbery, who had formed a tenuous alliance with the granitic third man, Arnold Webb.

Even the solitary double-killer recognized in Dibson and Kitchener two prisoners with an acute sense of survival. Dibson slipped quietly in through the main doors, and crouched against a wall, listening. But Arnold Webb, who followed lumpishly, stood unthinking in the middle of the small reception area and in plain view.

Dibson, resting on one knee, hissed, 'For Christ's sake, get your nut down. We didn't come here to ask the way.'

He was interrupted by Hetty's excited barks as the boxer arrived to investigate. The noise she made echoed shatteringly through the turbine hall.

'God help us. What a racket,' said Kitchener, grabbing a chair and jabbing it at the dog. But before he could do any damage, Arnold Webb plucked it from his grasp.

'What are you up to, pal?' snorted the Londoner.

Webb lowered himself heavily to his knees, drawing Hetty to him, and the boxer responded by licking his face ecstatically.

The two Londoners exchanged glances, and Kitchener said, 'Would somebody tell me what's going on?'

'I think Androcles just met the lion.'

'Who?'

'I've got a feeling they've met before.'

The three men split up to scour the ground floor and it was Dibson who discovered Hannah snoring lightly in the duty engineer's room. Not without humour, he raised his eyebrows quizzically and pulled the door quietly shut on her, locking it from the outside. Even if she woke, she would not bother them.

Kitchener had in the meantime come across the storeroom and made a hog of himself, sinking his teeth into an enormous slab of cheese and emptying a pint of milk mainly down his throat. Arnold Webb wrenched a loaf of bread in half. Partly for himself, and the rest for an ever-hungry Hetty. Dibson, who was marginally more civilized, took the time to open a tin of sardines and make a sandwich the size of a doorstep. While he worked his bulging cheeks, he winked at Kitchener. 'All right?'

'So far, yeah. But we'll need to be in that car and on our way before dark. I wanna be back in East Ham by morning.' His eagerness was tempered by a glance at the lumpish shape of Arnold Webb, still engrossed in Hetty. 'What about him?'

Dibson made sure the double-killer was paying them no heed before shaking his head almost imperceptibly. 'You know what they say about two's company . . . We'd better pack some grub and take a look at the motor. That other geezer might come back.'

They returned to the reception area, Hetty frolicking about and making Arnold Webb grunt with pleasure whenever she snuffled his platelike hands. The lift indicator winked as they passed it, and Dibson did a double-take.

'Watch it! There's somebody else here!' The light showed

the shaky lift to have halted in the inky depths of the lower basement.

Kitchener picked up the fallen chair and held it like a club. 'I thought you said this place was empty!' he said indignantly. 'It's more like a bloody main road.'

Dibson positioned them around the lift. 'Don't take any chances. Whoever's in there, belt him as soon as he shows his face. We can't have anything go wrong at this stage. Agreed?'

The two men looked at Arnold Webb for heavy backing. He grunted and nodded intently, kneading his hands in anticipation.

When the lift slowly emerged from the gloom, they were ready to rush it from three different angles. The door rattled open, and they found themselves looking into the idiotically smiling face of the Demon.

Its appearance stunned them. Dibson dropped his hands and his mouth fell open. 'Jeeesus Christ.'

The smile widened and became quite lopsided as the great cowled shape blocked the opening and prevented the door sliding shut. Its imbecilic smile and ghoulish eyes were so shocking that the men were rooted to the spot.

Only Hetty moved. She barked hysterically and made a series of furious dashes and retreats, recognizing immediately the apparition which had caused her so much distress. The Demon extended its shrouded arms to welcome the yelping bitch.

That was enough to galvanize Arnold Webb. He had been an accomplice of death too often to mistake the Demon's intentions towards his vulnerable friend. He gave a protective bellow, lowered his battering-ram of a head and charged into the inhuman shape.

Both figures disappeared back into the claustrophobic lift which shook violently on its steel hawsers. Hetty scrambled clear, but Arnold Webb was trapped in the restricted space of the vertical coffin with the Demon and the door slid shut on them.

The two Londoners stared horrified as the lift jerked

into motion and descended, according to the overhead indicator, back into the shadowy depths of the building.

'What was that?' croaked Kitchener.

Dibson looked at his hands, which were trembling uncontrollably. He could barely pick up the bag containing their food, and dropped it as he made his way shakily outside towards the car.

Kitchener followed him out, backwards. The car would not start and Dibson swore at it hysterically and went on swearing. Gradually the battery ran down, and the starter motor made increasingly feeble noises. They were both acutely aware that their time was running out.

The doors of the power station splintered open. One with such force that it was torn from its top hinges. On the threshold of the building stood the ghoulish, obscenely smiling figure. It did not seem to want them to go; even stretched out its arms.

'Chriiiii . . .' Kitchener wailed as he fumbled for the passenger door and stumbled out, intent on putting as much distance as humanly possible between himself and the apparition. Meanwhile, Dibson twisted the ignition key desperately and held it there until the remaining power drained from the battery and the key itself bent out of shape.

The running man did not get far. He sprawled on his hands and knees in the middle of a shallow lake of floodwater which covered most of the tarred parking area. He remained there, talking childishly and distractedly to himself. After a while he glanced furtively back and watched how his companion fared.

Kitchener was transfixed. Even in daylight, it was difficult to make out any features in the hideous face, but the grotesque look of mirth seemed to indicate that there was no escape for either of them.

For some inexplicable reason Dibson remained in the car: either he was pinned there, or fear had robbed him of his co-ordination. He jerked his head round. 'For God's sake help me!' But his companion could only sob and lower his head even farther in the water until it lipped his mouth.

Kitchener prayed that Dibson would stop shouting. What could he do? He would be lucky to escape the maniac's attention himself. Perhaps if he edged backwards, digging his soggy toecaps into the tarmac surface and working inch by inch on his hands and knees.

The Demon's dreadful blind eyes turned up to the rock-strewn slopes above the power station, which climbed to meet the abrupt face of the mountain. At first nothing much happened. Then some loose stones and detritus trickled and slid as if they found IT's gaze uncomfortable. One or two small rocks shifted, and skittered down the incline. Their increasing movement was reminiscent of the circumstances in which the Rev. Lionel Pryce-Jones died.

Dibson thrust his head awkwardly out of the car window and stared up, horrified. Then he looked across at the Demon as if unable to believe that anybody could do such a thing.

One by one bigger stones were dislodged and, in turn, a ponderous rock slipped massively. Dibson's head was coming and going through the window like a jack-rabbit.

A twenty-ton section of ancient metamorphic rock rumbled as it picked up speed. The faster it moved the more animated it became until a final ponderous bounce off a ledge carried it directly down towards the car roof. Dibson stared upwards, wide-eyed with horror, as the metal chassis concertinaed: squashing him and it into a screeching layer only a few inches thick.

The weather-worn boulder rolled on across the road under its own spent momentum carrying the car half wrapped round it down into a gully. As the grinding crash of debris and disturbed undergrowth died away, an intense silence settled over the scene.

Roy Kitchener gulped and lay spread-eagled in the middle of the shallow floodwater. He sensed a paralysing presence alongside. But all he could do was shudder as his head was taken in a firm grip and forced down under six inches of gritty water, and the life bubbled out of him.

The Demon turned its chilling smile on the power station. IT had to make one more example. And, if IT waited, the man already marked for sacrifice would return there.

Twenty-One

Casson burst into the front room of the chapel house and found Elliyn sitting there, secretly smiling, as if waiting for him to arrive.

She rocked back and forth without haste, in an elm chair polished by several generations of seated Pryce-Joneses. 'You were quick.'

'Quick? I didn't know I was coming myself until fifteen minutes ago.'

'Didn't you?'

Casson kneaded his hands and explained about the pony and trap, while she glanced from the window at conspiring clouds. 'Take them if you want . . . but it won't make any difference.'

'It will to me. I intend to get as far away from here as I possibly can before dark.'

She shrugged as if it was not worth arguing. 'Say goodbye to Dewi first.'

Casson grimaced. 'I've got nothing to say to him. The dangerous bugger ought to be locked up!'

'He's upstairs.'

'Look, I'll only get angry and start shouting . . . and I don't have time to waste on that sort of thing.'

'He's in the bedroom,' she insisted. 'It'll only take you a minute.'

Casson sighed. 'All right.' He made his way up the steep stairs, avoiding a low overhanging landing, and discovered Dewi lying rigidly on the bed. He looked as cold as a Calvinist prayer book, and his angular face had a faint green tinge.

Casson ventured farther into the room, curious as to why the Welshman was wearing dark glasses: only to find that he wasn't. There was a penny on each eye to hold the lids down.

He returned downstairs, stunned. 'What happened?'

Little tears formed in Elliyn's soulful eyes. 'Died last night in his sleep,' she whispered. 'Had a lovely smile on his face when I tried to wake him; as if he didn't mind.'

Casson was genuinely shocked. 'Was he ill?'

'No. He was never bothered by anything like that.'

'Well, how did he die?'

She looked away awkwardly as if it was none of her business. 'Suffocated, I think.'

'Suffocated?'

'I found a pillow over his face.'

Casson felt a dreadful sense of unease. 'Whose pillow?'

'Mine.'

He backed slowly away. 'Err . . . Look, it's none of my business.'

'That's all right,' she smiled. 'See, he didn't understand. And it was up to me to put it right. Didn't know what he'd got involved in. Not bright enough, I suppose. But don't worry about it. You just help yourself to your pony and trap.'

He took her masculine hand and squeezed it gratefully and left. But while he manoeuvred the lively animal back between the shafts and harnessed them together, she appeared in the doorway.

'I'm the one IT answers to now.' She spoke so quietly that he almost missed it.

Casson turned slowly. 'What?'

There was an odd look on her face. 'IT's started coming to me now; in my dreams. It needs direction. I've felt its terrible throbbing power with my own bare hands. I know it's evil, but I think I can turn it into a sword of righteousness: and bring it down on the profane. I can use it to dismember and rebuild.' Her voice gradually faded. 'IT answers me,' she whispered. 'Does as I say. See?'

He wanted desperately to clamber up, take the reins and drive away without inquiring into the dreadful implications of what she was saying. He made do with climbing shakily up and, even when settled, was reluctant to look her in the eye for fear of detecting an obsession that would show beyond doubt that she had slept with the Demon.

She rambled on. 'At least, most of the time IT listens to me. But I'll tell you one thing: if I hadn't stopped it, IT would have come for you by now . . .' She lapsed into Welsh. '. . . because you are a diethryn (outsider), a ymyrrwr (interloper).'

He looked up sharply. 'Me?'

She returned his gaze steadfastly. 'You'd better go. After dark, I have no say here.'

Casson gulped and gathered the reins. As the trap jerked forward he nodded to her.

'Da boch chwi,' (May you be well) she responded almost inaudibly.

The ground, having gorged itself for weeks on unlimited water, lay bloated on either side of the bumpy slate track. His path was only a few inches wider than the wheels of his tipping and tilting open carriage, but he urged the pony on and put up with the reckless swaying and bouncing in order to close the distance to the power station as rapidly as possible.

IT? Dreadful possibilities seeped into his mind and filled him with queasy uncertainty. Any potent force for evil would use her as wantonly as it had occupied Dewi's dulled razor of a mind. IT needed her eyes, and it would use her zeal to pose as a righteous sword and smite transgressors just as long as it could feed on the victims' terror.

He had an hour or two at most: to collect Hannah and slip away out of range of the Moelwyns and keep going until the mist, which lay wrapped around the necks of the mountains like an insidious chiffon scarf, could no longer reach out and throttle them.

As the track dipped towards Ffestiniog power station in the hazy grey distance, he fancied there was something in his path. Small and motionless. But, even from a long way off, it had a familiar air.

Hetty sat shivering slightly and gazing dolefully at the

rattling contraption that approached. She recognized Casson before the trap squeaked to a halt directly in front of her. But she did not budge; just huddled there shivering.

Casson lifted her onto the open seat and tucked his jacket around her. 'Something wrong, old girl?' he said. She licked his hand and continued trembling.

'What's bothering you?' He quietly nuzzled her soft ears and, while his eyes sought out the low elongated building, stirred the pony back into motion. 'That's okay.'

The power station was silent as the pony and trap approached at no more than a cautious walk. Ripples preceded them across floodwater, stretched thinly over the car-parking area. When they halted in the middle of the shallow lake, it contained nothing more than their distorted reflection.

Casson noticed one of the main doors hanging askew. It was the first real indication of trouble during his absence. His pulse quickened at the thought of Hannah, left alone inside. Nevertheless, he got carefully down from the tilting carriage and indicated for Hetty to follow. The boxer refused: perhaps sensing what awaited them inside. Casson swallowed hard. He edged into the building and then made his way carefully along the corridor and through the deathly stillness of the turbine house.

The bedroom door was locked and he had to turn the key to enter. Bedclothes had been thrown back and there was no sign of Hannah. He kept quite still. Through a mirror he observed a cupboard door fractionally open across the other side of the room. From inside, he sensed a subdued breathing and, at that moment, he was paralysed with indecision. If whatever-it-was burst out, he had little chance of reaching the corridor. It might wrench his arms off. But, at that very moment when he needed most to survive, he acted irrationally.

What made him stretch out and touch the cupboard door he would never know. Common-sense and self-preservation screamed at him not to do it. Nevertheless, he jerked the cupboard open.

Inside was Hannah, standing on terrified tiptoes and

holding her breath. At first only her eyes moved, then after what seemed a long time she sank down flat-footed and expelled the air from her lungs.

He enclosed her in his arms and held her limp body tightly against his.

'I thought you were . . .' Her voice trailed off weakly.

'Me too,' he gulped. 'What happened here?'

'I don't know.'

They stood close together in the sepulchral silence. 'I want you to pack a bag with as little as possible,' he whispered. She nodded.

'Fine,' he breathed, and they looked at each other with a new awareness.

The lift whirred into motion in the distance.

She stuffed a hand into her mouth, and Casson swung around. 'You stay here!'

'Why?' she mouthed in alarm. 'You're not leaving me alone again?'

'Not for long. I'd better take a look.' He squeezed her hand. But she snatched it away, not wanting to be party to any such ridiculous idea.

'Why?' she pleaded.

He bit his lip. He was much less enthusiastic about leaving the safety of the room than she imagined. 'Could be anybody,' he said. 'Just a visitor or somebody quite harmless. On the other hand, it could be an escaped prisoner.'

'All the more reason for you to stay here,' she said hoarsely.

He lifted her clutching hands off him. 'Look, I won't take any chances. But I have to check. I work here. We can't hide like field-mice. It's probably nothing at all.' He forced a smile, but it was not easy.

Outside, he pulled the door quietly shut and hissed through the crack 'Lock it!' When he heard a click, he set off alone past the mummified turbines. Daylight accompanied him from overhead windows, but it did little to alleviate his rapid heart-beats.

As he neared the entrance hall he felt sick with apprehension. He was almost at the lift now but, the moment before it came into sight, he heard the door whirring shut.

Whoever was inside was trying to get away! Someone afraid of him! Someone who had heard him coming!

A great feeling of relief spread through Casson as he ran to the lift; whoever was inside was just as scared of him as he was of them.

His fingers gripped the edge of the door where it fitted into a rubber recess, trying to force it back open before the lift could descend. But it was too late. The little glazed window sank slowly from view, even though he banged the aluminium exterior. 'Come out! You're trespassing! This is Electricity Board property.'

He stood back, breathing hard, and watched the overhead indicator. Only one floor down, the red light came on. It had stopped. Right, you bastard, he thought. I've got you!

He raced for the stairs, through a narrow door, and clattered down two flights of concrete steps to the next ill-lit level.

The lift was there, empty, its door open. He had only a moment to take in the situation before a movement from the ranks of gloomy machinery along the floor behind him drew his attention. Somebody was hiding there!

A good deal of his courage evaporated. Just enough remained for him to shout 'Hey!' and walk hesitantly along the narrow walkway between static shadows. Twenty, thirty, forty feet in and he still could see nothing unusual. Not a thing, until a hollow thud reverberated from not too far ahead. He stood absolutely still.

At first there was nothing to be seen. He felt unbelievably jumpy and was beginning to tell himself how ridiculously he was behaving when a deep shadow loomed from the darkness . . . and groped towards him.

John Casson froze with terror. His back and neck muscles seized up as the Demon smiled a horrific welcome. Half-hidden features. No nose or chin: simply a hideous smile and grotesquely sightless eyes.

IT wanted to kill him, even though Elliyn had cajoled

and pleaded for this man's life. It was not easy to compromise with its own voracious appetite for death.

The Demon offered the man the choice of sacrificing his own life by extending its macabre arms to let him walk into them.

Casson's eardrums were blocked by distorted silence. His feet moved forward mechanically even though he screamed silently at his legs not to comply.

His thoughts were mutilated by razored impressions of Hannah and Hetty: of the freedom of the open hillside outside, which was beyond price, and of the strong uncompromising chapel leader who was now his only hope.

'Elliyn,' he gasped. 'Elliyn, you promised. You said you'd protect me!'

There was a moment of strained confusion, during which his stomach felt like a dish-cloth being wrung out by hand. But he was aware of having stopped; he was no longer moving towards the nightmarish figure. Half a chance was all he asked.

Casson turned on numbed legs and ran. And ran. As fast as he could: blundering into the painful edges of metal machine-casings and clanging over grills.

He could not tell whether the Demon was behind him. For all he knew, he was being chased maniacally. Urged on by blind fear, he stumbled into the shadowy lift. Somehow, by the mercy of God, it had waited for him.

For a moment or two he was completely bewildered. There was little light and barely any air, and he had collided with something soft and resilient which was transfixed to the wall facing him. The door sighed shut behind him and the lift jerked slowly downwards: towards the sub-basement in the grim, dark pit of the building.

A minimum-wattage bulb flickered weakly: enough to reveal to his shocked eyes that he had as a partner, in the perspiring atmosphere, the body of Arnold Webb. It was spreadeagled in a motionless dance against the opposite wall, held there by God-knows-what.

Casson jerked violently back the few inches available to him, almost unable to breathe. Winded by shock and fear.

Oh, God, don't let it move! The lift jogged to a stop on the lowest level, refusing either to ascend or open its doors. Then the light went out.

He was trapped in the choking darkness, terrified to move in case it brought him into contact with the mad, upright body, and quite unable to get out.

Hannah Frost nibbled a finger nail and glanced at her wrist for confirmation that he had been gone only ten minutes. It seemed at least an hour.

She listened at the door, all the time fingering the ring J.J. had given her. She felt desolate. He had such a confident view of the future. Not that she had ever really seen herself as part of it; but a fine man just the same.

She decided at that moment with a gulp of sadness that, even if she married someone else, she would always keep J.J.'s ring: twin garnets set in a coiled gold band. The stones were a handsome black tinged with red. He had picked garnets both because they were her birthstone and because they were reputed to have mystical qualities which warded off accidents.

She smiled wistfully at the memory of her rather curious Italian-American airforce officer and brushed her lips against the ring.

Again she listened intently at the door, but still there was not a sound to be heard within the immense building. Not a whisper of machinery, nor echo of any unnatural intrusion. Where could John have got to? Perhaps something unexpected had happened.

'Whatever you do, don't leave this room.' She recalled his words but was too agitated to pay them further heed. She slid back the bolt and glanced nervously outside.

It was late afternoon. No need yet for lights on the ground floor. She pulled on a loose yellow jacket and walked cautiously through the turbine hall.

There was no sign of John Casson. She swallowed and opened her mouth once or twice in silent practice before calling tentatively. 'Hello. Are you there, John?' Her voice echoed weakly into the distance, apparently without being intercepted.

When she tried the lift it did not respond to the button and, wherever it was, no lights showed overhead.

She ventured outside the building and spotted the pony and trap waiting patiently where Casson had left them, with Hetty sitting dejectedly on the open crossbench. The boxer got up and wagged her stumpy brown tail, balancing precariously on the seat.

Hannah was relieved to see a familiar face. 'Come on, gal. Come over here, my lovely.' At last, Hetty advanced from the vehicle and cavorted delightedly around the tall young woman she now associated with her master. But she refused to go inside the power station, no matter how much she was entreated.

'Pleeease,' Hannah begged. 'You need the company as much as I do.' But the brindle crept under the trap.

Hannah returned indoors and stood, undecidedly, by the lift. There was only one direction: and that was down. She did not like the idea of descending flight after flight of echoing steps to a dark, reverberating basement. But where else could he be?

She called ahead in a wavering voice, 'Anybody there?' Then ventured down to the first turn in the stairs. Hannah made tight little fists, and told herself it was ludicrous to be in such a mortal funk. But she felt she possessed no more courage than a jellyfish.

She stood within sight of the ground floor for some time, reluctant to lose sight of it. Yet indecision gets you nowhere, and she knew it.

Hannah moved down to the next level, where she called apprehensively along a dismally lit gangway between huddled machinery. 'John, where are you? Answer, if you can hear me! Knock the rail or something! John?'

She proceeded to go deeper; slowly but inevitably making her way down to the lowest level, and the further she went the more agitated she became. The air felt heavy and seldom used.

At the bottom was a single permanent forty-watt bulb.

She tried a row of switches, none of which produced any more illumination. 'Shiii . . .' It was rare for her to swear and she was surprised how much of a relief-valve it provided.

She peered along the gangway, past writhing static pipes a metre thick and enormous pump casings. It was much colder down here and the air had a repellent feel to it.

But her attention was taken by a glimmer of light along the gangway: so far off it could have been the other end of the building. Perhaps John had trudged out of earshot, and was thoughtlessly checking innumerable pieces of equipment. Just like a man.

She shivered and hurried along the narrow walkway, conscious of her echoing footsteps. If there was anything fearful down here, it would hear her coming. She still had time to falter and turn back, but that seemed like a typically feminine reaction and she was not going to be intimidated.

Hannah paused by a short flight of metal inspection steps spiralling off to one side, beside a master pump. She slipped off her shoes. The concrete floor immediately seized and froze the stockinged soles of her feet, but at least her progress would no longer disturb the tomblike silence.

She peered towards what was now distinguishable as a lone inspection light; stretching her neck the better to see while the tips of her fingers toyed nervously.

Without warning the light went out, leaving her in absolute darkness.

She was gripped by panic and her hands flew up to her face like frantic birds, the only protection she had. She strained to hear, but her own muffled heartbeats drowned everything else.

Incarcerated in blackness, she retreated several steps, found the metal inspection steps and sank down to feel for her shoes. Where were they? Her fingers extended across one hundred and eighty degrees.

The shoes had gone.

Her throat was choked with pain, and even that took

second place to a new growing awareness. An odd noise. She straightened up slowly, almost too terrified to comprehend. It was somebody breathing loudly: a hoarse, wheezing sound and there was no question of it being John Casson or any normal person.

Fear rose to hysterical proportions and she tightened her blind grip on the metal hand-rail. She trembled from her finely chiselled cheekbones down to the bitterly cold soles of her feet.

Suddenly the dim light came on again and, outlined by it, she saw for the first time the indistinct proportions of the Demon.

She screamed chillingly and, in the eternity of a split-second, recognized the stark lopsided smile of the Welshman who had claimed to be a disciple of the Druids. Except that it wasn't him; this was something horrific, unearthly. The face from her dreams!

She also knew that it was maliciously aware of her presence. IT had lured her there and was now gloating at her shocked reaction.

Abruptly, the light went out again.

She remained frozen with horror in the malevolent darkness, knowing that IT was creeping gleefully towards her. Her line of sight was gone, but she could sense the hideously stupid smile drawing inexorably closer.

Oh, God. Run! She told herself. Run, it's your only chance! She turned blindly, stumbling over the guard rail and then the unseen gangway, and almost immediately was jerked back. Fear caught her by the throat until she realized that a pocket of her loose yellow jacket had snagged a knob on the guard rail.

Frantically she struggled to free it, ripping half of the pocket away before falling clear. Blood dribbled from both knees as she panted back to her feet.

She staggered on and somehow managed to reach the modest reassurance of the next dim light at the foot of the stairs. There was no help from the lift. She stumbled up the first flight of concrete steps . . . horrendously aware of the wheezing, bronchial inhalations of the Demon as it followed her.

Twenty-Two

The evening sky had been painted by Rembrandt. It was unbelievably glorious. A subtle canvas of orange clouds fringed with gold and, on the skyline, the Moelwyns were transformed to breath-taking beauty by the majesty of the setting sun.

The spectacle briefly revealed a tracery of glistening mountain watercourses which were normally invisible to the human eye.

As the wild countryside began changing its appearance for the night, a grouse threshed through soggy grass and took off long-bodied and low across the reservoir. Kok-kok-kok, echoing into the distance.

Dusk stole down the mountainside, disguising the land's virtues and giving it a new identity. Changing from Jekyll to Hyde.

Casson stood on tiptoe and strained to prise open a narrow lid in the lift's roof. Its stiff hinges were determined not to give in easily, and his efforts were made all the harder by Arnold Webb's praying-mantis figure only inches from him: its eyes rolled upwards like milky marbles.

He thrust up his right arm, making solid contact with the heel of his palm, and this time the maintenance flap crashed open. For just a moment he was able to gulp with relief and gaze thankfully at the fading daylight which permeated down the shaft.

But how the dickens could he climb high enough to squeeze through the eighteen-inch gap? There was a hand rail along the two opposite sides of the lift, and he hoisted one foot up and wedged it there. The two rails were nearly five feet apart. He took a deep breath and lunged with his other leg across the gulf. It made desperate, crashing contact with the far wall and he was left doing the splits in mid-air.

After struggling painfully for a minute or two, without making any progress, he thudded frustratedly back down to the floor and reassessed. There was nothing else for it: he would have to rest one foot on Arnold Webb's sagging shoulder and wriggle up through the hatch from there. Either that, or stay in the lift with a corpse all night.

He shuddered with distaste but steadied himself and balanced one-legged on the rail. Grunting with effort he swung his other foot up on to the dead man's shoulder. It seemed firm enough. God knows how it was pinned there; he suspected it was skewered through the chest, but he had no wish to open Webb's baggy jacket and find out.

Casson gingerly transferred most of his weight to the dead man before thrusting himself upright and grabbing the edges of the hole. Arnold Webb shifted; lolled heavily forward as Casson heaved his own shoulders up through the ridiculously small access hole.

God! For a moment something seemed to clutch his ankle. He lashed out with his foot, dislodging the body, so that it thumped to the floor.

Casson struggled frantically up through the gap, gasping as he painfully skinned his arm from wrist to elbow. Heaving with relief he knelt on the dusty, cluttered roof before dragging himself upright by a thick metal cable which swayed and snapped lazily in the half-light high above.

Looking down between his feet momentarily, he could not detect anything trying to reach up after him. Thank God for that, he thought. He spent a moment or two trying to calm himself, but it was difficult. His forearm stung where the skin had peeled back and his hands shook.

He had to climb to escape. There was no other way: not unless he wanted to face the grinning fiend again.

Hannah was alone somewhere up there . . . Hetty was trembling outside . . . and both were relying on him. Yet he could not stop shivering. He felt ill.

After a while, he hooked one shoe around the heavy cable and stood his other foot on top of it; then grasped the snaking line above his head and hoisted his knees about eighteen inches. He straightened up, his feet still locked together with the cable between them. Arduously he repeated the process. Grunting and straining he jacked himself up the echoing shaft.

He was grimacing with effort by the time he drew level with the access door to the next floor. It was closed but he manoeuvred across the gap, swaying precariously, on to a parsimonious ledge which lipped the bottom of the door.

Balanced there, he pressed his perspiring face against the little frosted glass window. He could not see much, only the usual dim emergency light in a corridor on the other side. He said half a prayer about how devout he would become if only God would save him, then jabbed the window hard with his elbow. It cracked and he began to pick out the shards with trembling fingers.

Aaah! He almost severed his thumb on a stubborn triangular remnant of glass but, after sucking it reproachfully, got enough of a grip in the opening to begin forcing back the safety-door.

He kept one hand on the cable and the other jammed in the window panel. There was a great danger he would fall backwards. The air around him was dark and draughty and he was conscious of the almost bottomless drop. He grunted as he levered the door open: four, five, six inches. There was enough of a gap now for him to slide his foot through the wedge and open the door.

But no sooner had he earned a moment's respite, than he was shocked speechless by the hideously smiling face which abruptly confronted him from the landing. An insane grin and dreadful blanks for eyes: the same nightmare as before. Waiting for him.

A dead hand reached in through the gap and would have grasped him, had not Casson jerked back with a strangled sob. He fell and his full weight was now borne on the cable by one arm, almost wrenching it from its socket. Pain speared his spine but he held on while his feet swung about in a desperate attempt to regain their grip on the cable. He made it with no more than a moment to spare. Had his feet not clamped together around the hawser, he would have plunged down to the jagged projections of the stationary lift some distance below.

The Demon put pressure on the far side of the safety-door, which had slid shut. It buckled horribly. Casson pumped his weak legs and reached frantically overhead, climbing up again with numbed hands. Metre by straining metre, he jacked himself higher and higher. The Demon struck a crushing blow which knocked in the bottom of the door. A second blow battered it into the shaft, from whence it cartwheeled down on to the stationary lift.

The screech of metal almost deafened Casson but he could still hear himself whimpering as he urged his hands and feet higher. Almost level now with the next rim of half-bricks.

At that moment he looked down. He found himself staring into the malevolent grimace of the Demon, framed in the missing doorway of the floor below.

Sobbing and panting, Casson swung his legs up to the narrow rim of bricks marking the next floor, only to be dragged away by the cable. It was being shaken from below.

Casson clung on grimly, closing his mind. He dared not look down again. To gaze into the drooling face of the Demon would have finished him.

The cable stretched tight, stiffening with strain. The apparition was coming up after him.

There was now an enormous combined weight suspended from the cable and an overhead cross-girder, supporting the entire structure, groaned ominously. Casson clung to the hawser like a leech.

The girder sagged a sickening five metres, bringing a shower of grit and cobwebs down on his head, before jamming. His feet lost their grip and he dangled helplessly while his strength ebbed. Casson knew he could not remain suspended there much longer. Already all sense of feeling had gone.

Elliyn Pryce-Jones let herself into the darkening chapel and walked purposefully towards the high overhang of the pulpit. She did not need any light. Every flagstone was familiar; every creak and squeak that emanated from the building in which she and her brother had worked to bring the narrow, disciplined principles of Celtic religion back to the people of North West Wales was known to her.

The only illumination was from a candle. A single white sentinel by the altar rail. It flickered for Dewi, who lay in an open coffin: pale as a stoat in death and with just the trace of a deranged smile to welcome the night. His once incessantly twitching fingers were now interlocked for ever on his chest.

She was moved to sadness looking down at him. Poor sly Dewi, who had never had the chance of a normal life. Few saw the innocent side of him, but it was there none the less. She could almost hear his sing-song voice, 'No one really knows me. I've never had a friend and never wanted one. But when I was a boy I was known as Dafydd and I think I liked those times better than now.' She kissed his forehead and whispered, 'Find your way safely, Dafydd.'

Elliyn crossed to a narrow window, opening it wide. The night breeze moved her long hair and searched her long outmoded dress with cold deliberate hands.

She lifted her chin and breathed deeply. It was a time to concentrate; to focus her attention on wherever the Demon's twisted and knotted mind happened to be at this moment.

'I know you can hear me,' she said in Welsh.

The wind breathed through the chapel, carrying her words back and at first seeking an answer in all the wrong places.

'Answer if you hear me. You must not defy me.'

There was no response, but the wind bustled distractedly up the dark slope, bending small trees and searching sparse patches of grass.

She closed her eyes, set her mouth obstinately towards the invisible Moelwyns, and sensed Casson's awful dilemma. 'Leave him be! Leave the interloper alone for now. You have chastised enough. I know what you're doing, and I won't have it! There will be plenty of other times.' She paused. 'Do you hear me? Answer to your faith through me. Or remain forever in darkness with no one to help you feel the way.'

Two miles away in the murky lift-shaft at Ffestiniog power station, the Demon was staring sightlessly up at Casson's barely gripping hands. Now the quirky smile disappeared. Doubt and suspicion clouded its narrow mind.

Elliyn walked back to the coffin and dipped her arms inside. She pulled Dewi up into a limp sitting position. His head flopped and his mouth fell dumbly open under the pull of gravitation.

'Judge for yourself,' she called in a voice which reverberated around the candle-flickering shadows on the high chapel walls. 'This man was your disciple, your white stick. You snapped it yourself by taking his life. So now you need me to feel the way. But I won't. You might as well kill me too, unless you do as I say.'

Her words were not lost on the eerie gloom of the chapel. She sensed a gathering awareness; a build-up of malevolent evil made it difficult for her to breathe. Now even the wind kept its own counsel, contenting itself with moving little eddies of dry leaves in secret corners.

'I alone,' she panted, facing first one way and then the other, 'Elliyn Pryce-Jones, am the meistres of your existence. Together we will lay bare the sins of the wicked and condemn all who dishonour the ways of our fathers. Our hand will stretch across the land like Jehovah's. There will be no mercy for transgressors and no hope of salvation save for the pious and righteous. We must serve one another without question. I shall be your shepherd. Leading and guiding. And you will listen. But if not . . . I shall turn my back on you, and no more will Druids walk this land.'

Casson felt his fingers sliding down the brutal, uncaring

cable. He hung on as long as he could, gave a despairing groan, and fell.

Fifteen or twenty feet is a long way to drop through blurred darkness on to the roof of a lift straddled by metal attachments. But the fact that he was limp with exhaustion saved him.

There was no terrifying figure waiting below. Nothing but a sheaf of wires and protruding bars, which winded him and jarred his knee. His chin cracked against the open lid but he was alive and, for the moment, the nighmarish satyr was nowhere in sight. Even the huddled shape of Arnold Webb inside the lift worried him not at all.

Casson manoeuvred himself down through the opening. Tumbled across the inert body and felt along the walls for the control panel. Astonishingly, a dim interior light came on and the lift door slid open, as if nothing had ever been wrong. Whether it was an outside influence, or whether the jarring it had gone through had caused the electrics to work again, he neither knew nor cared.

John Casson climbed the concrete steps to ground level. He arrived dishevelled in the main reception area and tried the central light switches, which responded immediately. Overcome, he turned on every light he could find. Soon the entire building was illuminated. Blissful, glaring, protective light.

Apart from himself only one thing moved: a shape which appeared hesitantly from the turbine hall. Ashen-faced, Hannah Frost put out a shaky hand.

'Is it you? Is it really you?' she asked. 'Thank God.'

Twenty-Three

They sat huddled together on the side of the bed for the rest of the night, a blanket around their shoulders. Even when dawn came dawdling to the rescue, they did not dare leave his quarters. He noticed that no birds sang, but refrained from mentioning it.

They had talked in whispers about anything apart from the Demon during the anxious hours of the night; but their nerves were screwed up to the knowledge that IT was still there, walking the lower levels.

Once she said, 'When you told me J.J. was dead, all I could think about was, now I shall never be Mrs Andretti.' Her voice was barely audible. 'I wasn't thinking about him; just myself. Isn't that awful?' He kissed her with gentle understanding.

'I'm sorry I got you into this.'

'I'm not.'

He held her pale, fragile face in his fingertips. 'What would you say if I told you I loved you?'

She simply looked at him for a while and shrugged sadly. He didn't know quite how to take that, but did not press the point.

They held on to each other as the sky grew lighter and the electric lights gradually lost their brilliance. But it was still too soon to risk moving.

The telephone rang. Echoing stridently from the reception area.

They listened in silence. 'Don't answer,' she implored. 'IT might be waiting out there.' He nodded and pulled the all-too-thin blanket more tightly around her shoulders. But the intermittent ringing persisted.

He stirred. 'I have to.'

'Not without me.'

'No, you stay here. It's safer.'

Her eyes were defiantly steady. He sighed and together they moved quietly into the corridor, carefully through the turbine hall and skirted the phlegmatic lift door, which was closed and looked quite respectable in the strengthening daylight.

Casson picked up the phone as if it was wired to explode. 'Hello,' he ventured.

A strong Welsh voice responded: unmistakably Elliyn's. 'Why are you trying to leave? You mustn't, you know.'

'Leave here? What makes you think that?' He was shocked that she could so easily read his mind.

'John, IT knows what you're thinking. IT hates you. I don't know why. It's probably something to do with me. A sort of twisted jealousy.'

'Have you got *any* influence over this thing?'

'I'm not sure. I think so.'

'Well, we are going to leave here in an hour or so. I don't care what you, or anybody, says. Just keep it away from us. Please.'

'Us?' There was a subtle change in her attitude. A drop in temperature. 'Is that lady who dreams still with you?'

'Yes, and we're going to leave here just as soon as it gets light.'

'IT won't let you. IT's fighting me, and I don't know how much sway I have. You'd best stay there, John. Let her go on alone and I'll hold IT back.'

Casson hesitated, and put his hand over the mouthpiece. 'She says you'll be safe if you go alone. But I'm to stay.'

Hannah clung to his arm and scrunched up her face with pleading. 'I won't go without you.'

Casson found himself breathing hard. He uncovered the mouthpiece. 'How do I know you're not making all this up?'

Elliyn did not answer for a while: hurt by his suspicious tone. 'IT could have slaughtered you both last night. Almost did. But I summoned IT back to the chapel for your sake . . . John.'

'My sake?'

'The love-spoon,' she said and her voice trailed away. 'No one ever gave me anything remotely as lovely before. I know I'm nothing special. I know well enough why people don't bother with me first off. So I have to be strong in other ways. Stands to reason, doesn't it? But that doesn't mean I don't have natural yearnings.'

'I think you're very special, Elliyn.'

'Don't butter me up, boyoh,' she chided, 'or I might change my mind. Look, all I'm trying to do for you is a token of my . . . of my . . .'

Elliyn did not finish her faltering sentence. Instead she said determinedly, 'So for God-in-Heaven's sake, take it.' The line was disconnected.

A minute or two later Casson let himself gingerly out of the power station into the sharp morning air and, when he returned, felt considerably relieved. 'The pony's still there. We'll take a couple of blankets, and some food and water, and go. Once we leave the mountains behind I think we'll be safe.'

Hannah nodded vigorously. Her face was grubby and her hair in disarray but she looked superb, he thought. He ran his fingers lightly down the side of her jaw for the last time. 'You're really rather brave.'

'No I'm not,' she insisted.

They hurried back to collect whatever food they could find in his rooms. 'I don't think I could have handled this situation if you hadn't been here,' he admitted.

'Yes you could,' she said firmly.

He paused and made her stop also. 'No, I couldn't,' he said adamantly.

She matched his gaze. 'No, you couldn't,' she said briskly. And they both laughed for the first time that day.

Elliyn sat on the edge of the front pew, bowed forward with her hands spread like half-open pages and her face buried in them. Praying. All around her, the silence of the new day. Then quite suddenly she sat bolt upright.

The Demon could reach into her mind, just as she could now look directly into its.

Casson was leaving the power station . . . and IT was waiting outside.

She extended her long fingers: fanned them open like the spokes of an umbrella, and then shut them. Open and shut. Her back teeth pressed together until they ached as she strained to make contact with the Demon.

'I want you back here now. Back in the chapel!'

She had a distorted picture in her mind of the vengeful apparition looking over its shoulder with the hideous grin that it copied from Dewi. But there was no obedience in the expression, only derision as it moved on.

Elliyn pressed her fingers tightly against her forehead, uncertain what to do next. Then snatched up her homespun cloak and ran out of the chapel, heading with long inelegant strides towards the narrow valley surrounding Llyn Cwmorthin.

The closer she drew, the more she became aware of a musty, unventilated atmosphere which seemed to be seeping out of the past and settling over the remote mountainside. Death was in the air.

Casson gathered up the reins and said firmly to Hannah, 'Hold on to me. Tight as you can, around my waist. That's it.' Then let out an urgent shout of encouragement and they jerked on their way. Leaving the power station behind.

He had no thought of conserving the horse's strength; only to get clear of this terrible place as swiftly as possible.

The road twisted and dipped as he flicked the pony's straining flanks with his lunge whip. Water hissed from under the trap's two wheels and Hannah gasped, 'You'll have to slow down.' But Casson had seen the twisted smile on the face of the Demon and he knew its intention.

They made good time at first. The air seemed full of the noise of drumming hooves and squeaking trap. But gradually it faded and Casson sensed a familiar clammy silence descending around them. He could see nothing amiss either ahead or behind them, but his ears were blocked by increasing pressure which came from God-knows-where.

Hannah was no better off. She buried her face in his lap and Casson now had little choice. If he was to escape the shrivelling silence that would soon bring the Demon upon them, he had to change direction.

There was a steep path of loose sliding stones off to his left, winding up a gully. Straining with all his might, he dragged the pony in that direction. It whinnied with distress as hooves slipped and wheels juddered, but then the carriage bumped violently up and over the rise that led into the old slate-quarrying valley of Cwmorthin.

Casson's flesh crept in ridges of fear up his tense neck. He no longer had control, and he knew it. What if the fiend was playing with them: funnelling them towards a place of its own choosing?

They swayed recklessly along the splendidly isolated valley, which contains a lake three quarters of a mile long and is flanked in perpetual silence. The ruins of slate homes and dead quarry buildings stood in numb groups like quarrymen thrown out of work.

The pony was snorting condensed air from its nostrils as they rattled around the top edge of the lake and clattered across a heap of discarded slate. But now they were overtaken by Nature's outriders: fat drops of rain that fell heavily, darkening the slate and agitating the surface of the high lake.

The rain became a brisk downpour. Within a minute they were soaked and the pony had lost its sense of direction. Casson groaned in despair and reined in by the entrance of an abandoned mine. From there they ran for cover into what was left of an office with dusty windows, half of them broken. Hetty emerged from under the seat and scurried after them.

There were odd signs of recent occupation: probably by someone making random checks for flooded workings and keeping a general eye on equipment which might one day be needed elsewhere. An enamel mug half-filled with cold coffee was anchored by a delicate cobweb. There was also an old-fashioned upright wall telephone. Casson lifted the earpiece and got the clicking noise that indicated it was working, although no one answered. He jiggled the receiver-hook. 'Operator . . . operator.' He eventually hung up, frustrated.

Hannah tugged nervously at his sleeve. 'What happened back there?'

'I don't know,' he confessed. 'It didn't feel right. I think we ought to stay here until the rain eases off.'

She smiled wanly and nodded. A few seconds later the phone rang of its own accord. They both jumped.

'Yes?' he said tentatively.

It was Elliyn Pryce-Jones. Her snatched breathing indicated the strain she was under. How she had found them he could not begin to guess.

'It's no good hiding there,' she warned in a low voice, as if someone might overhear. 'IT knows and it's coming for you.'

'What can we do?' he pleaded.

'Get out of there.'

'For Christ's sake! There's nowhere else to go! Anyway, I'm sure nothing followed us here.' He bent forward as he spoke, trying to get a clear view through the unwashed windows and down the ominously silent valley.

'IT knows where you are. What I know, IT knows.'

'Then keep away from us,' he said vehemently. 'Both of you!'

'No, John, I'm coming over. I'll do what I can. You won't stand a chance alone.'

'Go back, Elliyn!' he implored. 'You'll lead it to us!' But the phone was already dead.

A dust-encrusted cage was waiting at the pithead. Steel wires stretched up to a winch-drum under an enormous corrugated iron roof. Casson investigated an adjoining control booth with a desk, which had a tattered ledger on a sloping lid, and a switch panel on the wall. He fingered the biggest lever, marked 'Power On-Off,' and released it. Next to it was a switch which carried the words 'Stop. Start. Override.'

He stuck his head out of the booth's rickety window. 'Keep well back, Hannah.' Then flicked the starter switch. It worked. The cage vibrated and inched down a fraction or two, then dropped like a stone. The big overhead drum spun rapidly and the wire snaked out with such speed it was almost invisible to the eye.

After nearly thirty seconds there was a change in pitch and the wire unravelled at a much slower pace. The echo of a bump filtered up the shaft, then there was silence.

Casson listened for a while until satisfied the lift had reached the bottom, and brought it up again.

Hannah stood watching and shivering in the background. 'What are you doing?' she called.

Casson looked at her remotely. 'Eh?' She began to repeat the question but he waved her into silence. 'Listen!'

It was happening again. Sounds became distorted. The hum of the machinery and even their breathing were encompassed in the invisible, echoing vault.

Casson ran back to the mine entrance from which he could see the length of the valley; there was no one in sight. Only the clouds moved, but nothing could assuage his feeling of inevitability.

'IT's here,' he said quietly. 'We've got to go underground. There's nowhere else to hide.' He gripped her urgently by the forearm and led her to the flimsy cage that awaited another stomach-snatching descent.

'I don't want to,' she pleaded. 'We'll be trapped down there.'

'We'll probably be better off than up here. I can't stop IT. All we can do is buy time. For God's sake, Hannah, don't fight me now.'

They clambered into the cage and he lowered a crossbar which was wet and dirty. There was a start button which Casson pressed. 'Here we go,' he gulped. 'Hang on to me like grim death. I love you.'

She clung, gasping with fright, as the lift fell. It did not simply accelerate; it dropped. Casson's stomach lifted abruptly into his mouth and the air was sucked from his lungs.

Pressure blocked their ears, and their feet seemed to dance on the shuddering floor. A rush of air up the shaft made them cling together, while the walls blurred.

Even fear of the Demon was wiped from Casson's mind by a conviction that they were plunging out of control, any moment to be shattered at the bottom of the shaft. But their vertical fall was abruptly checked, and slowed to no more than a gentle descent. A bump, and they had arrived in complete silence.

Casson lifted the bar unsteadily and helped Hannah out. He could hardly believe they were unhurt. To one side was the dim outline of another control booth. He felt his way inside and swept down a set of six light switches; and was relieved at the illumination of a stretch of tunnel curving away into the distance.

Hannah indicated an upright telephone, sticky with cobwebs. 'They don't encourage personal calls,' she said apprehensively.

He gave her a half-amused glance.

The lift mechanism started. It caught Casson unawares and, by the time he flung himself at the cage to try and stop it, he was too late: it was already inching back up. In a moment it jerked swiftly towards the surface. He spluttered through a cloud of descending grit, and was left staring up into the void.

The desk phone rang, and Hannah almost fell off the stool trying to get away from it. Casson swore. He desperately needed time to work out why the cage had ascended. Was it governed by an automatic return-to-surface mechanism? Or was somebody waiting at the pithead?

He lifted the phone, and cleared clinging strands of cobwebs from the mouthpiece. At first he did not say anything, just listened.

'Hello.' It was Elliyn's unmistakable voice. 'Hello?'

'Where are you?' he grated, 'and how did you find us?'

'I'm on the surface. But it's all right, I'm alone.'

'Are you absolutely sure?'

'Absolutely . . . wait a minute. Something's coming,' she gulped. 'Perhaps it's help.'

Hundreds of feet above Casson, the outer office and a partition wall of reinforced corrugated iron were smashed flat.

He shouted into the phone, 'What's going on?' But the surface receiver was by then dangling unattended.

Elliyn Pryce-Jones had been knocked to her knees as debris pancaked around her. She struggled through a cloud of dust to the waiting cage, got inside and set it in motion. First inching, and then plunging down through the darkness almost without control.

Dull grey shadows moved across the cage, quite remote from the hurtling walls beyond. Elliyn's eyes widened with shock. She was not alone. Filling the opposite side of the cage was the grinning, baleful figure of the Demon.

Casson ran to the foot of the shaft. He could hear the cage dropping towards him: rattling and banging like an old train at more than sixty miles an hour. He had no idea what to do next.

'Can't you stop it?' Hannah was beside him, gripping his arm in a tourniquet.

'God knows! I don't!' He flung himself back into the booth and jabbed the button marked 'stop-start'. Nothing happened. The cage continued its plunge unabated. He swore, and rushed over to the screened lift machinery. There were two pick-axes and a long-handled crowbar. He grabbed the latter and tore off the winch-drum cover. It bore a metal plate marked in red letters 'Danger: Do not remove while cage is in motion'.

The noise was overwhelming. Whether it came from the descending cage, the screeching wire or the oncoming fiend, he could not tell. But it drowned the warning he shouted at Hannah. Instead of running clear she ducked forward to hear what he was saying. He had no option but to push her violently away. As she fell back, he thrust the heavy metal pole into the whirring mechanism.

There was an incredible squeal of protest from grinding cogs and gears. The crowbar snapped halfway up and part of it lashed back, missing Casson's face by a few inches and hurling him back past the flimsy booth. Sparks scissored in all directions while he lay stunned.

High above them, the frail metal cage shuddered to a halt.

It was no more than a temporary respite, but Casson got painfully to his feet and pressed the Up button. Steel wire tightened, winding itself around the pithead drum a few desultory times before snapping with the crack of a dead branch.

Down came the cage. Like a stone, but this time with no control whatsoever. Scraping the sides of the shaft, its screeching descent brought slate cascading down. Then it arrived with a shattering roar; flattened itself and burst into flames.

Casson shielded his eyes and was vaguely aware of Hannah pulling him back.

Clearly silhouetted against the fierce and outraged blaze, they saw the great hunched shape of the Demon. Blind eyes and demoniacally grinning mouth encompassing all that is evil.

IT gloated at their fear and, in doing so, allowed itself to be more closely observed. He saw with frozen fascination that ITs features shifted vaporously: dissolving and reforming as he watched.

Casson was too hurt to move either backwards or forwards, and Hannah leaned down to kiss him. The kiss had a dreadful air of finality to it.

'What are you doing?'

'It's my turn now,' she mouthed. Then, unbelievably, she stood in front of Casson and blocked him from sight so as to draw attention to herself, and moved forward to confront the semi-transparent figure. Deliberately provoking.

Casson got up, hobbled a step or two. 'Hannah!' he screamed. 'Come back. You don't know what you're doing.'

But she took no notice and Casson bit his mouth in apprehension, praying she had inherited her mother's wisdom.

The Demon had a slack, welcoming smile on its face. Willing sacrifices were a curiosity. Especially when they talked as they gave themselves up.

Casson listened, dazed, as she raised her voice over the confusion. A strong, clear voice.

'In the name of barbaric justice, I summon the essence of Druidical truth to avenge the death of its last surviving daughter, Elliyn of Tan-y-grisiau. In her name I seek the destruction of your selfish rancour.'

Nothing happened. Hannah looked calmly and without haste up through the mountains that had, centuries before, nourished the first Celts.

'Where there are no eyes to put out, and no tongue to cut away, then shall the body be scorched.'

Nobody moved for several seconds. Then a finger of heat reached almost lazily from the burning cage and sparked the hem of the Demon's fungus-dry cloak. In a moment the cowl was alight with a rush of flames.

The castrating fire that Druids had once used to purify their victims, before casting them into a chasm of the Moelwyns, began to consume the Demon. A natural element against an unnatural spirit.

Casson pulled Hannah back and held her head against his chest. He was unable to take his horrified eyes from the spectacle. The wheezing, bronchial apparition became distraught with pain, and the lopsided grin distended as it groped and blundered through the watery darkness.

Eventually it withered out of sight down a crevice leading to the cavernous belly of the mountains. Drawn-out moans reverberated and faded. IT was gone; perhaps for ever. Who could tell?

Casson and Hannah went on along the tunnel, at times confused by a honeycomb of passages which seemed to wander aimlessly under the mountains, but choosing whichever led them upwards.

Once their path led across a cathedral-like cavern quarried in lofty and awesome proportions by generations of Welsh miners. They waded up to their waists through swirling water and trudged on towards dimly perceived light until emerging at the foot of the sodden valley.

They sat for some time, numb with relief on the corrupt green grass, before returning together to the town of Blaenau Ffestiniog to await the anaesthetic of an approaching winter to heal their wounds.

Aftermath

A year later Casson jerked awake in the middle of the night after coming abruptly face to face with the Demon. He sat listening, rigid with fright, but in the utter silence of the bedroom he and the slumbering Hannah were quite alone.

He shivered and sipped a glass of water, grateful there was no substance in the dream, and yet he was drenched in perspiration and the imbecilic smile cut deeply into his consciousness.

Thereafter, every month or so without warning, it returned. He was aware of IT feeling blindly through distant shadows of his sleeping mind: trying in vain to get back into the daylight world.

In time Casson came to terms with it.

He pushed to the back of his mind the nagging thought that one night, inevitably, IT would manage to reach the foot of the Moelwyns and grope its malignant way towards whoever lay sleeping.

ITs charred fingers would eventually find him *or anybody else who knew of ITs existence.* And there was nothing they could do to prevent it.